SLEDDING HILL

Withdrawn

THE IRVING SCHOOL

ENTER HERE TO BE AND FIND A FRIEND

THE TRAGEDY PAPER

THE TRAGEDY PAPER

ELIZABETH LABAN

ALFRED A. KNOPF
NEW YORK

Text copyright © 2013 by Elizabeth LaBan
Jacket art copyright © 2013 by Lee Avison/Trevillion Images

All rights reserved. Published in the United States by Alfred A. Knopf, an imprint of Random House Children's Books, a division of Random House, Inc., New York.

Knopf, Borzoi Books, and the colophon are registered trademarks of Random House, Inc.
Map art copyright © 2013 by Fred Van Deelen

Visit us on the Web! randomhouse.com/teens

Educators and librarians, for a variety of teaching tools, visit us at
RHTeachersLibrarians.com

Library of Congress Cataloging-in-Publication Data
LaBan, Elizabeth.
The Tragedy Paper / Elizabeth LaBan. — 1st ed.
p. cm.
Summary: While preparing for the most dreaded assignment at the prestigious Irving School, the Tragedy Paper, Duncan gets wrapped up in the tragic tale of Tim Macbeth, a former student who had a clandestine relationship with the wrong girl, and his own ill-fated romance with Daisy.
ISBN 978-0-375-87040-8 (trade) — ISBN 978-0-375-97040-5 (lib. bdg.) —
ISBN 978-0-375-98912-4 (ebook)
[1. Interpersonal relations—Fiction. 2. Dating (Social customs)—Fiction. 3. Boarding schools—Fiction. 4. High schools—Fiction. 5. Schools—Fiction. 6. Albinos and albinism—Fiction.] I. Title.
PZ7.L1114Tr 2013
[Fic]—dc23
2012011294

The text of this book is set in 12-point Adobe Caslon.

Printed in the United States of America

January 2013

10 9 8 7 6 5 4 3 2

First Edition

Random House Children's Books supports the First Amendment and celebrates the right to read.

TO ALICE AND ARTHUR

THE TRAGEDY PAPER

CHAPTER ONE

DUNCAN
ENTER HERE TO BE AND FIND A FRIEND

As Duncan walked through the stone archway leading into the senior dorm, he had two things on his mind: what "treasure" had been left behind for him and his Tragedy Paper. Well, maybe three things: he was also worried about which room he was going to get.

If it wasn't for the middle item, though, he tried to convince himself, he would be almost one hundred percent happy. Almost. But that paper—the Irving School's equivalent of a thesis project—was sucking at least thirty percent of his happiness away, which was a shame on such an important day. Basically, he was going to spend a good portion of the next nine months trying to define a tragedy in the literary sense, like what made *King Lear* a tragedy? Who cared? He could do that right now—a tragedy was when something bad happened. Bad things happened all the time. But the senior English teacher, Mr. Simon—who just happened to be the adult overseer of his hall this year—cared. He cared a lot, and he loved to throw around words like *magnitude* and *hubris*. Duncan would much rather work with numbers than words, and he had heard of the occasional Irving senior getting by without doing too much. Maybe all he had to do, really, was get a C on the paper. He would not let this ruin his senior year. Not after the mistakes he made last year. But when he thought about it, he realized it might be good to have a distraction; it was certainly better than dwelling on the past.

Duncan forced himself to walk smoothly under the arch—the pull to stop and read the message etched in the stone was strong. But he had been going to this school for three years already—he certainly knew what it said. He would look silly if he paused and read it, so instead he said it to himself, under his breath: "Enter here to be and find a friend." He had walked under this pronouncement many times; he had to when he went to the dining hall or the headmaster's office. And he had never paid much attention before. But now, well, now he hoped there was actually something to it, that these people were really his true friends, whatever that meant. After what he had been through, he was going to need their support more than ever.

Seniors got to live right on the quad—the beautiful courtyard that was surrounded by the school's main buildings. And the rooms that were the equivalent of the doubles he had lived in the last three years with Tad were all cut in half so seniors could live alone. It would be his first time ever at school not sharing a room with another person. Of course, the rooms were tiny. But he would have happily lived in a closet to be on the quad and alone.

He walked into the building, taking in the familiar smell of food from the dining hall and, he always thought, paper, ink, and brains thinking hard, and walked toward the stairs. He hesitated, knowing that his entire summer's worth of wondering and hoping for the room he wanted was now going to be answered—for better or worse. He knew what would make him happy: one of the rooms facing the quad, in the middle of the hall, next to Tad if he could have everything his way.

A hand touched his shoulder and he flipped around.

"Come on, man, what are you waiting for?" Tad asked, a huge grin on his face.

Duncan leaned in to shake his hand, but Tad pulled back at the last minute, challenging Duncan to chase him, and ran two steps at a time up the stairs. Duncan made a move to follow him but stopped. This was it and he almost didn't want to know. The only people who were told which senior would get which room were last year's seniors, and they were sworn—literally, they took an oath that involved dropping a few notches in their grade point averages (with the promise of their colleges being notified) if they broke it—to never tell. The last day of school, they each wrote the incoming senior's name and posted it on the door, leaving behind a "treasure" for that student to find on the first day of school the next year. After that the halls were sealed until the following August. Many a new senior had tried to wend his or her way onto that floor, even trying to bribe the cleaning crew that came in the week before school started to take the musk and dust out of the air. As far as he knew, nobody had ever succeeded.

And the treasure awaiting him could be anything.

"Hey, Dunc," Tad called down. "If you don't come up here, I'm going to steal your treasure."

Duncan had the urge to yell up to ask which room he got, but he couldn't. What was wrong with him? This wasn't that big a deal. No matter which room he lived in or what was left for him, how much of a difference could it really make in his life? But he would love to have a good story to tell at dinner tonight. At the very least that would help him steer the conversation away from what he worried everyone would really want to talk about.

Treasures in the past had ranged from an almost three-month-old rotting pizza to a check for five hundred dollars. There was a rumor that different lucky seniors were left two tickets to a Yankees game, a share in some famous company, and a gift certificate to one of the fanciest restaurants in Westchester County. And once, legend had it, years ago a senior was left an English bulldog puppy (the school's mascot). Apparently, the administration wanted him to find a new home for it, but ended up letting the dog stay and they named him Irving. There's a picture of him in the library, but every time Duncan asked a teacher if it was really true, he or she refused to tell. There were also plenty of stories of lame treasures: bags of M&M's and random books. Duncan slowly made it up the stairs. Other seniors flew by him, slapping him on the back. This was the staircase used for both boys and girls, but the senior girls went around the corner to their long hallway, which looked out over the wooded area behind the school. He heard a girl squeal that there was a bunny in her room—could that even be possible? Someone must have gotten through to the cleaning crew and they agreed to bring it in recently, which is what must have happened with the mysterious bulldog. He hoped he didn't get an animal. That was the last thing he wanted.

He was almost to the top. If he looked, he would be able to see the doors that were still closed; he might be able to begin to guess which was his. But it was a long hall. Most of the doors at this end were open, so their occupants had already found them. He could see doors at the other end of the hallway pulled shut—some with construction paper taped to the front, others with the letters of people's names cut out and arranged across the door. His name did not pop out at him. He was halfway down the hall when he got the sinking feeling. Tad ran out of a door just then.

"I have Hopkins's old room from last year," he said. "And guess what he left me."

"What?" Duncan asked, not really caring. He wanted to snap out of this funk. Tad was acting normal enough; maybe nobody was even thinking about what happened last year. Whatever room Duncan lived in, whatever treasure he got, it would all be forgotten in a day or two anyway. Only the really great treasures were talked about any longer than that. And as for his room, he'd get used to anything. There was really only one room that nobody wanted. "Come in," Tad said, bringing Duncan back to the moment.

Reluctantly, Duncan walked into Tad's room and looked around. It wasn't as small as he expected it to be. In fact, it seemed pretty big. There was a bed—smaller than a twin, if that was possible—and a tiny desk, though nobody really worked in their rooms, they all went to the Hall to study. Tad pulled open the closet door and gestured inside. Duncan could see a bottle—it looked like some sort of liquor—with a huge gold bow, pushed to the back of one of the shelves. Tad reached for it.

"Bourbon," Tad said proudly. "The good stuff. It says it's from a family reserve. It's twenty years old!"

"Huh," Duncan said.

"Want to have some?"

"No, not now. I want to find my room," he said. But then he added, "Maybe later."

6

"You haven't found your room yet?" Tad asked incredulously. "Go, man, find it."

Duncan walked back into the hallway. There were people everywhere, running back and forth from room to room, throwing balls, playing music. Tomorrow everything would be quiet, but today almost anything was allowed, though probably not the bourbon. This time Duncan walked right to the end of the hall. He knew what had been bothering him: he had a feeling he was going to get the corner room, the one that nobody wanted. And he was right. Scrawled on a piece of white lined paper was his name. He opened the door and immediately remembered why nobody wanted this room—there was barely any light, just the tiniest circle of a window that looked cool from down below but not from up here. And it was so much smaller than Tad's room. Duncan sank down onto his unmade tiny bed. All of his things were neatly stacked in the corner, sent ahead and brought up earlier in the day. He was so disappointed that he almost forgot about the treasure. If it was possible, as soon as he spotted it, he started to feel even worse. On the small desk was a pile of CDs. Great. Music—that was almost worse than the rotting pizza, because it wasn't even interesting. And who listened to CDs anymore anyway? He knew who lived here last semester: it was that albino kid. Duncan could not believe his bad luck.

He leaned toward the desk—the room was so small, you could reach anything from any point without getting up or moving. The CDs sat neatly stacked with a folded note. He unfolded the paper slowly—it was typed, and signed in that scrawled handwriting,

Dear Duncan,

I know what you are probably thinking right now. Well, I bet you're thinking a lot of things, but at the top of your list is probably that this room sucks. It doesn't. There's a secret compartment in the closet that nobody else has where you can hide anything: third shelf, just push the wood plank evenly and it will move. It's hard to see in through the window, or under your door for that matter, so you can pretty much get away with keeping your light on later than anyone else. And Mr. Simon will feel sorry for you for having such a bad room, so he'll bring you extra food.

Having said all that, overall I would say my time in this room did suck, and I think you know why, but I want to explain. When I was told you'd be living here, I have to be honest, I couldn't believe it. Maybe you can guess what I'm about to say, but I'm going to tell you anyway. It is important that you know why and exactly how everything happened. Someone has to—someone might be able to use the information and not make the same mistakes I made. Maybe. I don't know. Listen to my story. You might think CDs are a dumb gift, but, considering my reaction to you in the dining hall last year and how I can only imagine you feel, I hope you will appreciate them. It's easy enough to play them on your laptop.

I don't know how well you actually knew Vanessa, but she's the only other person in the world who has a copy of these, and I have no way of knowing if she will listen to them or has listened. I hope so. Or maybe I hope not. But let me say one important thing I would bet money you didn't expect and then I will leave you to your senior year: what you are about to hear—the words, the music, my downfall, as well as your perceived or actual role in it—will serve you better than you ever could have imagined. Basically, I am giving you the best gift, the best treasure, you could ask for. I am giving you the meat of your Tragedy Paper.

Yours truly,

Tim

Duncan could hear everyone in the hall. He wanted to be out there with them, but he had to admit he was curious and, if he was being really truthful, a little scared. He pulled his laptop out of its bag, put it on the desk, and slipped in the first CD. Then he put on the headphones and pressed Play.

CHAPTER TWO

TIM

. . . *IT WAS FINALLY TIME TO GO*

First, let me say thank you for deciding to listen. I've thought so many times about our last encounter, and how I wish I'd made a different choice. In the end, it wouldn't have changed most of what happened—that was already done. But it might have made a difference for you—assuming any of this had an effect on you. I can only guess that it did.

I picture you at my desk, your desk now, fiddling with the CD cases, and the idea of you there listening to my story gives me comfort. In reality, it's the only comfort I can find, short of figuring out a way to go back and do it all over, which will never be possible. So here it is—my best attempt at making sense of everything. I will try to re-create what happened, but you have to understand what led up to it first—that is important too. The conversations you'll hear are pretty close to the truth, but one thing is for sure: I remember every word Vanessa ever said to me and every word I ever said to her.

I have spent a lot of time trying to decide where to start my story to you. I can see now that in many ways the place where this begins is really the end of so many other things.

The day I went to Irving, I was the last one to leave my house, and I don't mean for the day. I mean forever. My parents—my father died when I was a baby, so I am referring here to my mother and my relatively new stepfather—had already moved to New York. Their things had moved there anyway; they were in Italy for six months starting a branch of their travel business. So I slept two nights alone in the house. I didn't mind, really; I like being alone. I had my laptop and microphone and kept busy recording the familiar house sounds, since I knew I would never hear those exact noises again. At night, I burned them onto CDs so I could take them with me. I slept in a sleeping bag on my bedroom floor. Then it was finally time to go. I tried not to look back after I locked the door and walked toward the cab. I'll admit it, I looked back once.

The cab driver didn't say much, and I spent the whole drive watching heavy gray clouds cover the sky. I liked the ride to the airport: it was a relief to be out of the house, and I always preferred to be tucked in somewhere—not out in the open. I just had to make it through the airport to my seat on the plane before I could tuck in again.

I guessed, when I really thought about it, being tucked

in to me meant being as out of sight as I could possibly be. As you know, I'm pretty hard to miss, and when people first see me, they stare—almost always. I have tried many things to blend in over the years: makeup, which just made me look like a goth wannabe; dyeing my hair and eyebrows black, which made me look like a vampire. My mother hated all that, and by the time I turned fifteen, I hated it too, so I decided not to try anymore.

What did you think when you first saw me? Had you seen many other albino kids before? Did you rush back to your room, the way I imagine people doing, to look it up and see what caused it and if it was contagious? If not, I'll help you out: it is not contagious, and it simply means that I have no pigment in my skin or hair; that's why my hair is shockingly white and my skin is even whiter. Sometimes I feel like I have a spotlight shining on me as I walk in a crowd—that's how washed-out I think I look. Even in the airport, with tons of people all around, you still can't miss me.

The drive to the airport went way too fast. When the cab driver asked which airline I was flying and then pulled up to the curb, I didn't move. To be perfectly honest, I wanted my mother. As grown-up and normal as we all pretended I was, as I assured my mother and Sid I was, I was about to travel halfway across the country to a school I had never been to. Maybe I should have started the story here to let you know why I was going to Irving in the first place.

My mother met Sid about three years ago, and all I can say is I wish she had met him sooner. Before that we were okay, but something was always missing. I was seven months old when my father died, so I don't even remember what it was like to have him around, but my mother always did. When she met Sid, she was so happy, right from the start. She wanted to take it slow, but we both couldn't resist him, and, I'm happy to say, he couldn't resist us. It wasn't too long before he got my mom interested in his travel business, and he moved in. I was just slogging through high school. I liked lots of the classes, but, how can I say this nicely? The kids just weren't my cup of tea. Or maybe I wasn't theirs. So I went to school each morning, came home, and waited for it to be over.

I talked to Sid about this a lot, and he was a good listener. But I think Sid didn't want to come into our lives and take over too much, I get that. He had loved high school. Guess where he went? You guessed it: Irving. So at some point, he later confessed, he couldn't stand by and watch me suffer, knowing that he had something that could make me happy. My mom was all for it. They knew they had to make a change when I came home the first week of my senior year with a calendar I had drawn up during lunch counting down the days to graduation. Sid talked to Mr. Bowersox and arranged everything. For my birthday in October, they gave me the gift of a last chance at enjoying high school—I would spend the second semester of my senior year at the Irving School. In the end, it made sense for all of us, and freed Sid and my mom to be able to move sooner. And really, I had nothing to lose. Or so I thought.

Don't misunderstand me, I was excited. But to get there, I was going to have to navigate the airport, walk off the plane on the other end, find my way to another cab, and, once there, I worried there wouldn't be too many places to tuck in. I got out of the cab, grabbed my humongous backpack—everything else had been sent ahead—ducked my head as close to my chin as I could, and let the automatic door welcome me in.

The airport was packed. I had checked in electronically with my boarding pass on my phone, so I walked right to the gate, stopping in the bathroom to gather myself for a minute. Luckily, they were boarding when I reached the gate. In a minute I'd be on the plane. There might be someone sitting next to me, but that would be okay—it's the initial shock I hate reliving over and over. Once someone gets used to me, it isn't usually so bad.

I saw Vanessa before she saw me. I know this for a fact, and it isn't something I am usually able to claim. The reason I know is because she had her eyes closed. She was sitting in the first seat on my left in first class as I stepped onto the plane. There was a bit of a line, some holdup or other as someone far into coach was trying to jam a carry-on into the overhead bin. I noticed her immediately, not for all the reasons that came later, but for the very reason that she wasn't looking. Who doesn't look to see who else is getting on the plane with them? I mean, in this day and age, aren't we told to look out for suspicious activity? And there she was, eyes closed, iPod buds in her ears. Then I noticed everything else. Her long blond hair (pretty blond, not, most definitely, albino blond) was in two braids fastened with green rubber bands. From what I could see, her earbuds were also green, the green wire leading from her jeans pocket, across her tight yellow sweater, to her tiny ears. Her big backpack was at her feet. She had spread out her caramel-colored shearling coat face-up behind her, and she was sitting on that.

I am usually careful not to stare. It is one of my rules of life. I don't turn my head to see which baby is crying so loud in a restaurant; I never let my eyes wander to someone on crutches who is missing a leg or someone wearing an eye patch. In the airport, for example, just a few minutes before, a woman walked toward me whose face was disfigured, but it was subtle. Had she been burned? Was there something wrong with the muscles in her face? I could see, or actually I should say I could feel, everyone around me looking at her, trying to figure out what was wrong. But I didn't. I looked straight ahead and kept walking. It didn't matter how she got that way, really; it wouldn't change my life in any way, and I knew too well what it was like to be stared at.

So I was shocked when Vanessa opened her eyes and caught me looking at her. She pursed her lips slightly and widened her eyes before I forced mine to drop to the thinly carpeted floor. I felt a shove from behind as the line heaved forward, and then I was out of her sight.

I kept my eyes down as I slipped into my seat at the back of the plane, then looked out at the darkening sky. The plane revved up a bit, and we pushed away from the gate.

"Are you okay?" I heard someone screech behind me. Heads turned, but I looked straight ahead.

"Robert? Robert?" the voice yelled, panicking. "You're scaring me!"

"Is there a doctor?" someone else yelled. "We need a doctor!"

I concentrated on not turning around. I didn't want to break my no-staring rule for the second time in less than twenty minutes. By then everyone was turned to face the back of the plane. In a lot of ways, it was more interesting to look at them. I could get the story there, I was pretty sure. Some people looked pale, others looked excited. Funny how some people hate a crisis but others love it, welcome it, and try to rise to the occasion, as they say. Although I don't think that was what actually went through my head at that moment. I had not yet had that revelation.

Things did not go well. I won't bore you with the grisly details, but the man had to be taken off the plane by paramedics. I remember feeling vaguely sick while we waited for that to happen. I have never been good in an emergency. I heard words—*headache, seemed okay, unconscious*—but I tried not to listen either. My eyes focused on the curtain between coach and first class, which had been neatly tied back in anticipation of takeoff. And that was when I saw her again. When I thought about it, she was the only one sitting in first class when I walked by; maybe she was lonely. Vanessa stood on her side of the curtain looking at the back of the plane, her eyes wide.

With all the commotion, I felt freer than usual. I wasn't the freak show here. There was a scarier show going on behind me. The plane moved back to the gate. We had gone only a few feet, I realized, but that first push away from the airport always seems so huge to me—like there is no going back. But apparently sometimes there is.

I wanted out. I have a tendency toward claustrophobia. It's funny, really, because there is nothing I like more than being in a small place hidden from view, but it has to be on my terms. I don't like being held hostage, and that was how I felt. I thought we'd just get started again, but by that time it was snowing, so we were all asked to deplane. We were told that even though it wasn't awful in Chicago yet, airports were closing up and down the East Coast. I had to, once again, untuck myself, and get off the plane and wait in the terminal.

I found a seat in the corner facing a wall and started to read a comic book I had stuffed in the front pocket of my backpack. I had the fleeting thought that I could catch a cab back to my house—spend one last night there. But then I remembered the weather, and the fact that as of the next morning, the house no longer belonged to me and my family. I realized at that moment that I had literally no place to tuck in—I was, at least for the moment, homeless.

Duncan sat for a minute, waiting, but it seemed that Tim had stopped talking. He looked around, almost startled to find himself where he was. It was quieter in the hall now, but he decided to stop listening, to go see his friends. He took the CD out and put it back in its case, glancing at the next one. Slowly he slipped it in, telling himself he would listen for only a minute.

CHAPTER THREE

TIM
THE UNIVERSE WAS OUT OF WHACK

It's hard not to wonder what would have happened if things had gone differently. If the flight had left on time, or if I hadn't dared leave the gate area for a few minutes. But I did. I craved getting out of view. So I lifted my huge backpack onto my seat and walked through the crowd with my head down, toward the bathroom across the extremely busy hall. The bathroom was more crowded than usual too, and I felt lucky that the stall at the end—the one meant for a wheelchair—was open. I locked the door and sat on the toilet seat, just breathing and trying not to think about the line growing outside. When I felt better, I washed my hands and, with my head down, rushed out the door and back toward my seat.

Considering how often I walk around with my head down, I am surprised this doesn't happen more often, but it doesn't. I was two steps across the hall when I felt the impact, a strong but petite body crashing into my left side followed by cold, icy liquid on my shirt and neck. I think some also hit me in the back of the head. It wasn't that I minded being knocked into or spilled on, but I hated the idea of having to stop and talk to a stranger who, once he or she got over the shock of what had happened, would then look at me with that question: *What is wrong with that guy?*

"Sorry, sorry, sorry," the girl said. Right away I could tell she wasn't really sorry. She was annoyed. Keeping my head down and my eyes to the ground all the time has definitely strengthened my other senses, and one of the many things I've learned is that tone tells you a lot more about what a person means than the actual words.

"It's okay," I said, still facing in the direction I'd been heading. I could see my seat ahead—at least I thought it was my seat—and it looked like there was someone sitting in it. I should never have left my backpack there.

"Let me help you," she said, coming around to face me with a bunch of napkins that had been scrunched in her hand. I could see her pulling earbuds out of her ears, and the green flashed in front of me, then the braids, then the yellow sweater. It was *her.*

"I'm fine, really," I said, not meeting her eyes.

"You have Diet Coke all over you," she said. "It's going to get sticky."

"Does Diet Coke even get sticky?" I asked. "There's no sugar in it."

She looked exasperated and handed me a bunch of napkins. I halfheartedly ran one over my neck and shirt.

"Thanks," I said. "I have to get back. I think someone moved my backpack when I went to the bathroom."

"You left it?" she asked. I turned to look at her. By now she must have noticed I was different, so I was just wasting my time pretending and trying not to be seen.

"Yeah, it was so crowded and I didn't want to lose my seat," I said.

"But it's the airport," she said. "You can't leave things unattended in the airport. Someone will think it's a bomb."

"Oh, I hadn't even thought about the bomb thing." It occurred to me to question why she had her eyes closed while the plane was boarding if she was so interested in airport safety, but I decided not to.

A voice began to talk into the microphone, and we both turned to look, moving toward the gate at the same time. I walked to my seat, which was now occupied by an old man, and she walked right toward the gate. I nodded as we parted ways.

"Was there a backpack here when you sat down?" I asked the man. He had greasy white hair and must have been at least eighty.

"Shhhhh," he said, putting his finger to his lips. With

his other hand, he pointed to my backpack, which was propped up against a wall. Then he pointed at the gate agent. "She's going to tell us something."

What she told us was that all flights were canceled. Every single one of them. The relief at finding my backpack was quickly replaced with panic. A night with absolutely no place to go—a night of being in a huge, crowded room with nothing to hide behind—was one of my nightmare scenarios that had not even occurred to me as a possibility. Why did I think I could do this? It was turning out to be more than I could handle. I did what anybody would do. I called my mother.

She didn't pick up, so I left a voice mail telling her about the weather and asking if she could get me a room at the hotel that was connected to the airport—which happened to be affiliated with her travel business—since I doubted I could get one myself. I also mentioned that I had sent the bunch of CDs I promised her with the noises from our house and neighborhood. I was actually pretty excited about them because there was a bird that drove us crazy, and I was able to record it the afternoon before I left.

I quickly calculated that they were seven hours ahead, so it was almost midnight for them. It could go either way if she'd get the message today or tomorrow.

Next I called the hotel. I was right: no luck, all sold out.

I hung up and closed my eyes. When I opened them, I

looked across the room and saw the girl, her shearling coat spread out behind her in the same way it had been on the airplane. Maybe it was her weapon against the germs and dirt of the airport. She was listening to her iPod again, but her eyes were open this time. And, without giving it too much thought, I let my eyes meet hers. She smiled quickly—almost tersely, I would say—shifting her eyes to the window. My phone vibrated in my hand.

"Hey, Mom," I said. "Or should I say *ciao*?"

"Hey, sweetie," she said. I missed her already. "I just happened to check my phone one last time before we hit the hay. You're all set—there's a room waiting for you. Just give them our last name—it's paid for. Go check in, order room service, and watch a fun movie. Call me in the morning and let me know what the status of your flight is."

"Thanks, Mom," I said, not wanting to hang up yet. "How are you guys?"

"We miss you, but it's beautiful here," she said. "We can't wait until you visit in March. We keep talking about all the things we can do together."

At that moment I wished I could go right then, that I could forget about getting myself to the East Coast and just go straight to Europe.

"That sounds great, Mom," I said.

"Bye, sweetie. Don't forget to call me in the morning,"

she said. "Oh, I almost forgot. Sid wanted me to say 'Go, Bulldogs!'"

Usually I would say *Go, Bulldogs* back—we'd been saying it back and forth since October. But I didn't feel like it.

"Tell him I miss him" was all I said.

Slowly I put my book into my backpack and slipped on my coat. I could have avoided walking by the girl, but I would have had to squeeze between two tight rows of seats—it would have been so obvious. Besides, I had nothing to lose, so I walked toward her and turned left just before her seat. She looked vaguely annoyed.

"Where are you going?" she called out, surprising me.

I stopped. She still had her earbuds in. I didn't know if she had turned the music down or off, or maybe it was still blaring in her ears.

"To the airport hotel," I said.

"Don't bother," she said. "I called and they're all booked up. I also called a cab company and apparently the streets are almost impassable. So I think we're stuck here."

"I got a room," I said.

"That's impossible," she said. "I called even before the final announcement about tonight's flight."

"Huh," I said. "Well, I have a reservation."

"That's impossible," she said again.

"My mom's travel company works with the hotel," I heard myself explaining. "She called and apparently they had at least one room left because she booked it. It's waiting for me. I'm just heading over there now."

"Wow," she said. I could see her eyes light up. She seemed so much friendlier suddenly. "Do you think it has two beds?"

"Maybe," I said. For some reason I was not at all surprised by her question. I had the distinct feeling that the universe was out of whack and normal rules didn't apply. I sort of liked it.

"You could come along and we'll see. And if not . . ." I let the words hang in the air. She frowned and rolled her eyes, but responded by gathering her things. For a second I thought she was going to hand me her coat to carry, but she didn't. I was glad because the truth was, if she had, I would have.

CHAPTER FOUR

TIM

I FELT LIKE NONE OF THE NORMAL RULES APPLIED

Neither of us talked at first. I could have asked *Where are you from? Where are you going?* But I didn't want her to think that I was going to talk all night. Later, when we talked about this moment, she told me she wished she could have just kept listening to her iPod, but she knew that would be rude. Maybe she should have.

We were almost there before either of us spoke.

"I'm Vanessa, by the way," she said, reaching out her hand. It was one of those memorable moments because, as strange as it may sound, even when people are nice to me, they don't usually volunteer to touch me—unless they know me, of course. I looked at her for a minute before I took her hand and shook. And then I smiled.

"I'm Tim," I said. "It's nice to meet you."

"Maybe if we're going to spend the night together, we

should know each other's last names too," she added. Was she flirting with me?

"Okay," I said, trying to sound casual when really my heart was beating so fast and hard I was surprised she couldn't hear it. "I'm Tim Macbeth." As soon as I said it, I wished I had said something cooler, like "It's Macbeth" or just "Macbeth." But I couldn't go back.

"I'm Vanessa Sheller," she said, smiling a smile that I didn't quite trust but that I liked anyway.

We pushed through two sets of heavy doors and went down one escalator before we reached the entrance to the hotel. I love hotels—they make me feel calm and hopeful, in a weird way. I think also that they make me feel like I'm escaping something. Are you starting to sense a theme here? But that was not what I felt when I entered this lobby. It smelled like hot, sweaty, anxious people with some wet dog mixed in. Almost every single possible surface had someone sitting on it—chairs, sofas, even the coffee tables. Some people were eating, others were sleeping. A bunch of little kids were playing ring-around-the-rosy.

I had never checked into a hotel alone before. There had never been a need. But I didn't want Vanessa to know that. And adding to my anxiety was the fear that these people were going to mob me when they saw me get a room key. I glanced around for the front desk and was happy to see it off to one side. I could feel the eyes on me as I walked toward the exhausted-looking teenage girl behind the desk, but as I moved, I realized that not *all* the eyes were on me—a fair amount were on Vanessa.

"I'm sorry, we have no rooms left for the night," the girl said before I even opened my mouth.

"Oh, I know," I said, stopping short of saying my mother called. "I have a reservation under Macbeth." I waited. I might not have ever checked into a hotel alone before, but I had stood next to my mother or Sid many times and I know how it's done. She click, click, clicked at the computer with a skeptical look on her face.

"Huh," she finally said, her eyes showing her surprise. "And it's a nice one. You'll be in room 956 with two double beds."

"Thanks," I said. I didn't add *I told you so.*

Vanessa stood next to me like she belonged there.

"Two keys?" the girl asked.

"Yes," Vanessa said before I could.

We waited while the girl activated the keys, put them into a small white envelope, and slid it across the marble counter.

"Enjoy your stay," she said like a robot.

Again, I felt like none of the normal rules applied. I was seventeen years old; I had no idea how old Vanessa was, but she had to be in that ballpark. Nobody asked to see ID, or if we had luggage. We simply turned in unison, avoiding the eyes of the room-hungry crowd.

"So foul and fair a day I have not seen," Vanessa said when we got on the elevator.

"What?" I said, not sure I had heard her right.

"Come on, you have to know that play, don't you?" she said, smiling. "Shakespeare's *Macbeth*? I studied it last se-mester. With your name, how could you have avoided it? I've always loved that quote because it's like one bad thing and one great thing at the same time. You know? Like the weather is awful, but we got this room. Something bad and something good."

Of course I had read *Macbeth*, but I didn't know any of it by heart. Still, I felt I owed her something.

"In brightest day, in blackest night, no evil shall escape my sight," I offered.

"Green Lantern?" she asked.

I had to admit, I was impressed.

"How did you know?" I asked. I was so curious.

"I have brothers," she said. Then she tilted her head and looked me right in the eyes. "Let me guess: it's the only thing you have memorized?"

"Pretty much," I said.

By then we were out of the elevator and walking down a hall that smelled like new carpet, following the signs to 956. Just as we found the room, my phone rang. While I reached for it, Vanessa grabbed the small envelope, opened the door, and squeezed in front of me to go inside. I stayed in the hall to take the call. It was my mom, wanting to see how it went at the hotel. I felt a little annoyed. I didn't miss her like I had an hour before. And, besides, wasn't it the middle of the night where she was? As always, she wanted details, but I wanted to get into the room. She knew I was rushing her, but I didn't care.

As soon as I hung up, though, I wanted her back. I wanted the comfort of sharing a room with my mother and Sid, not some strange girl—no matter how cute she was. I stood in the hallway for a moment longer than I had to, thinking about how I would get through the night ahead.

"Tim?" Vanessa called from the other side of the door. "Are you coming?"

Again, Duncan waited for more, but Tim had stopped talking. He was starting to understand that he wasn't going to be alerted to the end of a thought or CD. Just as he was about to press Stop, Tim's voice started up again. Duncan wondered if he had just paused to collect his thoughts, or if he had recorded the next part at another time and the dead air was an accident. He hoped he hadn't missed anything on the last CD, but he didn't think so; there didn't seem to be any holes in the story so far. He tried to imagine Tim sitting somewhere, talking into a microphone, but he couldn't. All he could conjure up was the image of the last time he saw him. Or, worse, the time before that.

Duncan knew he should go to dinner. By now everyone had probably had a chance to talk about their treasures. He didn't want to miss that entirely. But Tim and Vanessa were actually in the hotel room. Alone. That was surprising, and seriously hard to imagine. He was dying to know what happened there. He'd listen just a little longer, he decided. Maybe just ten more minutes.

CHAPTER FIVE

TIM

IF YOU GIVE A GIRL A PANCAKE . . .

Something changed between the time she called out to me in the hall and the time I came into the room. She had been pretty nice getting there. Maybe it was part of her plan, but I actually don't think so. Maybe she suddenly felt as uncomfortable as I did. Who knows? We never really talked about that later; it wasn't one of the things that came up.

Vanessa had already claimed the bed closest to the window, and was unrolling the wire of her iPod and placing an earbud in each ear. I walked by her to the window and looked out. The view of incoming planes would have been amazing if the snow wasn't so heavy and if there were any incoming planes. The wind had died down. A flag across the way was barely blowing anymore, but the snow looked pretty deep—probably five or six inches already, and it was still coming down.

"Are you hungry?" I asked, turning back toward the room. How was I going to make it through the night so close to her? I would never be able to relax, let alone sleep. I should have stayed in the hall.

She didn't respond. I tapped her foot and she jumped a bit. She reluctantly lowered the volume on her iPod and looked at me expectantly—I had the distinct feeling I was bothering her.

"Are you hungry? We could order room service."

"Okay," she said, turning off her iPod but leaving the earbuds in. "Is there a menu?"

I found one on the desk and handed it to her. She smelled like lemon mixed with Tide. I wasn't really that hungry, but I felt the urge to keep busy.

"How about a club sandwich and fries?" she asked.

"Okay," I said. "Do they have steak—filet mignon, maybe? That seems like a good room service thing to order."

She looked. "Yep."

I picked up the phone and dialed the operator. She went back to her music.

"Hey, no," she called before anyone answered, pulling out her earbuds. "I have a better idea."

"Hello? Room service," someone said in my ear. I felt like a deer trapped in a car's headlights. What should I do? Hang up? Stick to our original plan?

"Hi, we're in room 956, and we wanted to order room service, please," I somehow said. "Can you hold on one minute?"

33

I put my hand over the mouthpiece of the heavy phone. "What's your idea?"

"Let's order breakfast for dinner, I love doing that," she said. "Pancakes, bacon, sausage—all of it. Oh, and do they have any cinnamon buns?"

I smiled to myself because it fit in with the fantasy that was quickly developing in my mind: the normal rules didn't apply—checking into a hotel with a beautiful girl, breakfast for dinner. What else could it mean?

I cleared my throat and ordered everything from the breakfast menu.

"Would you like a pot of coffee with that, sir?" the voice asked me.

"Sure, why not," I said.

"Give us about half an hour, then, sir," the voice said.

"Okay, thanks."

I turned on the TV and waited. When the knock finally came, I almost jumped three feet into the air.

"What is it?" Vanessa asked, looking up.

"Just room service," I said, embarrassed.

Once everything was inside the room, Vanessa got up and pulled off all the silver domes. There was a large stack of steaming pancakes dripping with butter and white pow- dered sugar, bacon and sausage and a loaflike meat I couldn't identify, an omelet with miniwaffles, and a small plate of cinnamon buns.

"What do you want?" she asked. I took a few steps toward

the movable table. I could smell all the food, but I tried to catch her scent over it. I pretended to look at the choices, but I imagined I could feel energy coming off her arm, like she was electric or something. I took it in for a minute and then moved back.

"You choose," I said, trying to breathe normally.

"How about we share?" she said, smiling at me.

She took the plate with the pancakes and cut the stack in half. With her perfect hands, she made two perfect plates with a little bit of everything. What would it feel like to be touched by one of those hands? When she thrust a plate at me, I was sure I was blushing, which, as you might imagine, looks a little like a brush fire on my face.

"Yum!" she called out as she sat on the edge of her bed and ate hungrily, dripping syrup on the blanket and her shirt. I was in awe of her lack of self-consciousness.

I sat at the desk. Everything was delicious, and once I started eating, I couldn't stop.

"So, what do you like to do? I mean, what are your hobbies?" she asked. I couldn't help but laugh. She was trying to make dinner conversation.

"I like to read," I said, realizing immediately that it sounded dorky. "And I like to run. Cross-country." I didn't tell her how running was one of the best ways for me to escape and be alone. But I did tell her it made me happy.

"Me too! I'm on the track team at school," she said, looking up. She dripped some maple syrup on her leg. She saw me watching and used her finger to wipe it off, then stuck her finger in her mouth.

"Oh, sorry, I am such a pig. I love this stuff," she said. "At school they do this once a week—have breakfast for dinner. Waffles, omelets, frittatas, quiche, cinnamon buns. Some people hate it, but I love it."

"Where do you—" I started to say, realizing I had no idea where she was traveling to, but she cut me off.

"You know what this makes me want to do?" she said, looking the happiest I'd seen her. "This makes me want to play in the snow!"

"You're kidding me, right?" I said. "I book the last hotel room within twenty miles and all you want to do is go outside?"

"Well, yes, actually," she said, smiling. "But I'll be happy to come back in after."

"That's a relief," I said. "For a minute I thought I did all this for nothing. And can I mention how nasty it is out there?"

She jumped up and went to the window.

"It doesn't look so bad," she said. "There's a parking lot right down there that looks empty. We could build a snowman!"

I joined her at the window and looked down. Our hands were dangling next to each other. Again, the energy.

"Maybe we could make a snow statue of that man who got sick on the plane," I suggested.

She looked at me like I was crazy.

"Like a voodoo snowman," I explained. "Maybe we could make him better that way."

We laughed for a minute, and it felt really good.

"I wonder what was wrong with him," I said.

"Brain aneurysm is what I was thinking," she said matter-of-factly.

"Oh, I was hoping he was just dehydrated or something," I said seriously.

Again, she laughed. I hadn't meant that to be funny, but I would take her laughter any way I could get it. I stood there trying to think of what else she might find funny.

"So, what is it about eating pancakes that makes you want to play in the snow?" I finally asked, desperate to break the silence.

"Every winter when I'm home, my mother makes us pancakes on a snowy morning—just like this with bacon and syrup—and then my brothers and I spend the rest of the day in the yard playing. It's usually one of my favorite days of break."

"How many brothers do you have?" I asked, stalling. I wasn't sure I wanted to go out there.

"Stop stalling," she said, reading my mind. "And I have three brothers. Are you ready?"

"Yes," I said.

We started pulling stuff out of our backpacks. I decided to keep on my jeans and put my sweats on when I got back inside. Did they have holes? Please, don't let them have holes!

She was already wrapping a green scarf around her neck and pulling on her coat. When I didn't move, she stopped and looked at me.

"I'm not going to give up," she said. "If you don't come, I guess I'll just go alone. You know that book *If You Give a Moose a Muffin*? Well, in this case, *If You Give a Girl a Pancake in a Snowstorm* . . . I am unstoppable."

Vanessa tossed me my jacket and I put it on, watching as she continued to twist her green scarf around her neck so that her braids were stuck underneath it. I had an urge to walk over and free them from their captivity—but I didn't.

We stood for a minute and then walked to the door at the same time, almost knocking each other down like a comedy routine, and she giggled. I stepped back, letting her get to the door first, and followed her through.

"So, what do you think, snowman or snowball fight?" she asked as we stood in the elevator. For a second I had almost forgotten where we were going, I was so focused on her. "If you choose snowball fight, we have to agree on an amount of time each of us is allowed to build a fort and compile ammunition. I always think seven or eight minutes are enough; my brothers usually fight for ten."

"Wow, you're really serious about this," I said. "But I have a better idea."

"What?" she asked just as the doors opened and we saw

the crowded lobby. For a minute the spell was broken. I was quiet as I followed Vanessa out of the elevator. All the faces turned toward us, and it didn't seem like they were looking at my strangeness or Vanessa's beauty. Their looks were calculating and a bit desperate.

"Why do I feel like someone is going to jump us for our room key?" I whispered to Vanessa as we walked quickly toward the door. It whooshed open and we both breathed a sigh of relief.

"So, what's your idea?" she asked again.

"How about we build an igloo?" I offered. Even now I don't know where that came from. I was never allowed to build them when I was a kid because my mother thought they were dangerous (and sand tunnels too, for that matter). I never understood that. You could always push your way out, right? Besides, at that moment, the idea of being buried in the snow with Vanessa sounded pretty good.

Vanessa surveyed the snow, judging how deep it was, and then leaned over to pick up a handful and consider its texture.

"Good packing snow," she concluded. "I've never made an igloo. How do you do it?"

I really had no idea, but there was no turning back now.

"Allow me to demonstrate the fine art of igloo assembly, Vanessa Sheller," I said confidently. "Let's push the snow into a big pile, maybe over there, and hollow it out. Then we can pack down the back and it should hold."

"Sounds like a good plan," she said, but didn't make a move to start building. "Wow, it's beautiful out here." I watched as she lifted her head to the sky and then caught a few snowflakes on her tongue. But for some reason what I was really mesmerized by was the way the snow collected at the top of her boots. I wondered if it dropped down at all to her ankles, making them cold. And then I imagined her socks. I hadn't noticed them up in the room, but now I wished I had. Were they striped? Maybe they were green and yellow—that seemed to be her color combination. And what about her toenails—were they painted? And then I realized that standing out there in all the snow made me feel, amazingly, like I blended in instead of sticking out.

"What are you waiting for?" I asked, starting to kick snow over to one corner of the empty parking lot just off to the side of the hotel. Vanessa joined in, picking up armfuls of the wet snow and adding to my pile. We worked like that for a long time, and eventually I gave up trying to stay dry. My jeans got soaking wet and my jacket was snow-covered. I didn't have a hat with me so my hair was wet, but I liked it because I knew when my hair was wet, it could, especially in the dark, look almost brown.

A snowball hit me from the side and I looked up to see Vanessa smiling at me.

"Very funny," I said, trying to act normal, not wanting to let on that I could barely breathe and that I knew I would remember that smile, and the feel of that snowball, for a long time.

"Hey, you didn't finish your side of the igloo," I said.

"You're a real taskmaster," she said, but she said it nicely.

"You're the one who wanted to come out and play in the snow," I said. She had gone to the other side of the structure we were making and couldn't see me, so I had time to make six snowballs.

"The operative word there would be *play*," she said.

I put the snowballs inside my jacket and walked around the front of the igloo, pretending to survey our progress. And then I whacked her with one snowball after another. By the time I threw the sixth one at her, she was laughing so hard she had to sit down in the snow. That laughter . . . it was like a drug. The more I got, the more I wanted.

By then our pile had grown into a minimountain, so I got down on my stomach in the snow and started scooping out the inside. My hands were frozen, but I kept scooping anyway. Before I knew it, I had a little room carved out. I backed into the space.

"Hey," I called from inside. "It worked."

Vanessa came around and peered in skeptically. Then she turned and shimmied in beside me. It was a tiny space, so she was practically on top of me. The left half of her body was right up against the right half of mine. Her wet hair gave off a lavender or rosemary scent that I hadn't smelled before. I closed my eyes and breathed in.

Dare I kiss her?

Five hours before, it was the last place in the world I thought I would be—like if, when I had walked into the airport, someone had said to me that in five hours I would be on a sandy pink beach in the Bahamas swinging on a hammock with a piña colada, it was that unbelievable. I moved my hand on top of her mitten.

"Is your hand warm?" I asked.

"Yeah, these are great mittens," she said, looking down at her hands and, I guess, my bare hand. "They're my brother Joey's, actually. I stuck them in my bag at the last minute—he is going to be so mad."

"Can you take one off?" I heard myself saying. "My hand is frozen."

"Oh—sure," she said, pulling it off. "Here, put it on for a minute." She handed me her mitten, but I shook my head.

"No, I just meant, if I could put my cold hand next to your warm hand, it would warm me up," I said, smiling. "Isn't that what you're supposed to do if you're freezing, body-to-body contact?"

She rolled her eyes, but there was the trace of a smile there too. She held out her hand, and I grabbed it. Those must have been amazing mittens, because that was the warmest hand I've ever felt. We sat like that for a while; it could have been two minutes, maybe three. When I started to squeeze a little harder, I felt her pulling away and moving out of the igloo. I stayed put for a second longer and then I followed her.

"We should go back to the room," she said. "But thanks for doing this with me. It was really fun."

"Do we have to?" I said.

She stopped. "You're the one who didn't want to come out in the first place," she said nicely. "But I'm ready to go in. My feet are freezing."

I didn't want her feet to be freezing.

"Okay, let's go back in, then," I said. "For the record, and I don't usually admit being wrong to people I have known for less than half a day, you were right. This was really fun." What I didn't say was that I worried it might possibly be the most fun I was ever going to have.

CHAPTER SIX

DUNCAN
THAT WAS THEN AND THIS WAS NOW

Duncan looked around his tiny room and was shocked to see it was beginning to get dark out. He checked his watch and it was just after six p.m. Dinner had been going on for half an hour already. He wanted to kick himself for being so drawn into the albino's story. He wanted to be done with all that and not even think about last year's senior class. He had promised himself that he wouldn't let any of that affect this year. This year was going to be better. Great, even. It had to be. He thought of how Tim said his going to Irving was his last chance to have a good time in high school. He didn't want to compare himself to Tim, but he realized this was *his* last chance at doing high school right too. He wasn't going to let anything get in the way of that.

But Duncan couldn't help himself, and he was struck by how just minutes before first coming into the room, he'd been thinking about that stupid Tragedy Paper, and then it ended up being tied in to the treasure Tim left behind for him. That was freaky, and just way too intriguing. It was like Tim was reading his mind. For another minute he let himself think about that last time he saw Tim, then he tried to will away the image. Duncan always thought he was odd, and, in addition to everything else, he did remember hearing about goings-on with that cute girl Vanessa, things that were never confirmed but were speculated about after what happened. There was something Duncan couldn't quite remember, about some fooling around, or a crush. No, that wasn't it—but there were rumors going around that involved a competition or something between the albino kid and Vanessa's boyfriend, Patrick, who happened to be one of the most popular kids at the school. He was the one who left Tad the bourbon. That was a coincidence, too, that Tad had Patrick's old room. Still, he told himself, he didn't want to care, he didn't need to know. That was then and this was now.

Duncan stopped the CD, took off his headphones, checked his face and hair in the hazy mirror over his dresser, and opened the door. It was still nuts out there. Duncan felt like he had been inside a soundproof box, he was that engrossed in Tim's CDs. He had to shake it off. But as he walked down the hall, he kept thinking about Tim and Vanessa in the snow and about how this past spring, on the last day of classes, he and Daisy Pickett had ended up being the only two people at the lunch table and how they had sat there for hours because neither of them had a class to go to, talking and laughing, and, by the end of the afternoon, giving each other back rubs while the kitchen staff started getting ready for dinner.

He thought that was going to be the turning point for him, the moment during his high school years when he finally got everything he wanted, especially after he came so close to losing it all. He had considered, after that amazing afternoon, asking Daisy to take a walk, or to go out to breakfast with him the next morning. Second-semester juniors were allowed to do that sort of thing with permission, and he had always wanted to take advantage of it. But then he started to think too much, wondering why she was being nice to him suddenly. Did she feel sorry for him? Or was it his new position in the class that made her like him? Or, worse, was she just curious, trying to get close to him so he would tell her about it?

By the time he saw her again that weekend, things had shifted—he couldn't quite figure out how or why—and then on Tuesday everyone moved out and Daisy went back to Connecticut and he went home to Michigan and that had been that.

Duncan peeked in Tad's open door as he went by and was relieved to see he was still there.

"Hey," he called.

"Where have you been, my man?" Tad asked. "I knocked on your door but there was no answer."

"You did?" Duncan asked, confused. "I was in there."

"I don't know, bro, you seem a little zoned-out to me," Tad said, patting him on the back. Duncan had to try to relax. The last thing he wanted was for people to start asking if he was okay.

"No, man, I'm fine," Duncan said as casually as he could. "But I *am* hungry. Have you had dinner?"

"No, I think it's breakfast for dinner. I hate that. Who wants to eat pancakes at night? I came by before to see if you wanted to order a pizza from Sal's. I've been thinking about their onion and pepper pie all summer," Tad said, sitting on his neatly made bed with his cell phone in his hand.

Again, another crazy coincidence: breakfast for dinner. That was the last thing Duncan wanted. He felt like he had just lived it. But he wanted to see Daisy, and he knew the dining hall was his best bet for running into her.

"If I start ordering pizza the first night, I'm going to be in trouble," Duncan said. "Plus, I want to see everyone."

"You know what? You're right," Tad said, stuffing his phone into the front pocket of his jeans and standing up. "That wouldn't be very social of us."

He put his hand on Duncan's shoulder and guided him out of the room.

"Hey, later I'm throwing a poker game here. I'm going to

pull my bed away from the wall and we can use it as a table. Are you in? And don't forget I have bourbon."

"Yeah, that sounds great," Duncan said.

They walked down the stairs and through a round room with stained-glass windows and into the busy dining hall. They both stopped for a second. After a long summer of eating in their own quiet kitchens with their own families, it was a bit of a shock. But then they each took a deep breath and moved into the bustling room. Duncan had a routine last year—first check the entrée being offered, and then, if that wasn't good, the soups and the salad bar, and, as a last resort, he would make a peanut butter and jelly sandwich. The thing was, the food was pretty good at the Irving School. They made a big deal about using fresh local ingredients, and since they were close to New York City and the Hudson Valley, there was a lot to choose from. One night a week there would be fresh pasta from Arthur Avenue in the Bronx. Another night lamb chops from a farm up the road. The salad was supposed to be grown in the area too. But Tad was right about dinner: it was breakfast, which wasn't Duncan's favorite either. Tonight there were pancakes—blueberry or plain—just as Tad had predicted. They were being served with maple syrup; a chalkboard sign nearby said it came from a farm in Poughkeepsie.

Duncan wandered over to the soup and salad bar, absently looking at the choices, which included tomato bisque and corn chowder, when he saw Daisy across the room. He was surprised by the physical reaction he had, completely losing his appetite and feeling an intense need to sit down because his legs threatened to give out from under him. At the same time, he couldn't take his eyes off her. She was in line for the pancakes, wearing a light purple bulldog T-shirt and a pair of tight gray sweats that showed off the curve of her body. Duncan had never thought of sweats as being elegant before. And the shirt, he remembered it from last year. It was the school T-shirt—a simple bulldog on the front, no words. But every year one color would become popular and everyone would wear it. Last year it was the purple and all the kids had one—boys and girls. He wondered what the color would be this year.

He started to move toward the pancake line. He could eat pancakes tonight. That wouldn't be so bad. He could get the plain and eat them with the Poughkeepsie maple syrup. He could talk to Daisy. He had it all worked out in his mind—he'd say hi, and ask how her summer was, and then they could talk about the T-shirts and what color might take off this year. Orange could be a nice change, he would say. He didn't really care about the color of the T-shirt, but he knew she would. Still, he couldn't do it. She was with her friends—Violet, Sammie, and Justine. They were all wearing their purple shirts and pajama pants, an Irving tradition for seniors when breakfast was served for dinner. He looked around. Most of the senior girls seemed to have some form or other of pajamas on, but the boys didn't. He saw Raymond Twinkle across the room and laughed. He was wearing red plaid flannel pajamas. But the other boys were wearing jeans or khakis.

"Aren't you hungry?" Tad asked, coming up behind him. His tray was piled high with all the offerings—pancakes and bacon, soup, salad, the cinnamon buns that were at the dessert station.

"I thought you hated breakfast for dinner," Duncan said, pointing to Tad's tray.

"A guy's got to eat," Tad said. "Why are you just standing around? Pick something!"

"I'm trying to decide," Duncan said. "I'll meet you at the table."

Duncan quickly ladled the corn chowder into a bowl and grabbed some crackers. When he checked the pancake line again for Daisy, she was gone. He headed toward the table where Tad sat, and he could see the other guys there. A few were waving and smiling at him. But he found himself thinking about Vanessa and Tim. What had Tim's first night in the dining hall been like? He didn't sit with a big group, Duncan knew that; he had sat mostly by himself at one of the smaller round tables in the corner by the big windows. Funny, Duncan had been here the whole time but hadn't paid much attention to him. At least not until the end.

As he sat down, Duncan had the definite feeling that he had interrupted something. He could have sworn he heard

Tad shush Jake. But he told himself not to be paranoid. He worked hard to keep the conversation light at the table, telling what was now—with some perspective—a funny story about a fishing trip he took with his family in northern Michigan in early August. But it was an effort to stay focused, and when he got to the part about what his family now referred to as "the endless hike," he could barely stand to continue. Somehow, even though it hadn't at the time, it reminded him of that terrible night last February.

"So my father was, like, five hundred yards ahead," he said. Everyone's eyes were on him, he couldn't stop now. "And my mother had pretty much given up. She was sitting on a rock with her eyes closed. We had been out there for hours, everyone blaming everyone else for not reading the map right. The fishing poles were heavy. We had no food. And then my father went around a bend. When he came back, he was laughing. He yelled for us to follow him. And right there, down a long hill from where he was standing, was a huge strip mall with a Target and a Burger King! We thought we were lost in the wilderness."

"What'd you do then?" Tad asked.

"We had a Whopper," Duncan said, and everyone laughed. But he felt empty. Not all excursions into the wilderness turn out that way. Everyone sitting at that table knew that, but Duncan had been the only one to actually see it; everyone else had just heard about it. He saw the moment when things went from good to bad. He saw the blood in the snow. He shook his head to try to send the image back into the far reaches of his mind where it wasn't so easily accessible. He had worked hard over the last few months to do that.

When everyone stood up with the plan to meet as subtly as they could in Tad's room in ten minutes, Duncan already knew he wouldn't be joining them. He had to see what happened back in that hotel room in snowy Chicago eight months before. He needed to know what led up to that awful night.

CHAPTER SEVEN

TIM

WHAT'S THE DEAL WITH YOUR BULLDOG SHIRT?

Order to chaos and back to order again. Has Mr. Simon talked about that yet? How a tragedy in literature should do that—move from order to chaos, and then, once the tragic hero has seen his fate, sometimes his death, order is restored. Keep this in mind as you listen: Was there ever really order to begin with? Did chaos ensue? Was order ever restored? I know what I think.

Vanessa and I walked back through that hotel lobby. We were good at it now, eyes down, feet moving, hands clutching the pockets that held the room keys, right into the empty elevator. We were wet and cold, she was limping because her feet hurt, and I had the distinct feeling that we were very much alone. It wasn't a bad feeling—I didn't feel scared. If anything, I felt free. Nobody was watching us. Nobody could get to us, for that matter.

"Next time I'm home, I'm going to build an igloo with my brothers," she said. Her cheeks were bright red—they reminded me of candy apples. "Funny that we've never done that before."

"Now you're an expert," I said. "But I doubt you will ever build one quite as perfect as ours. Hey, do you want to order hot chocolate?"

"Sure," she said. "My feet are killing me."

By then we were at the door, so I pulled out my key, my hand so red, discolored, really, from the cold, but I did my best to hide it below my sleeve. I pushed the key card into the slot and it didn't take. I did it again, but this time my hand was shaking. Gently, she put her warm, beautifully colored hand over mine, moving it out of the way. Her key card was in her hand; I hadn't even seen her take it out. She skillfully slipped it into the door slot, and the red light turned green. She let me push the handle down, thereby letting me be the official door opener. "Allow me, mademoiselle."

Vanessa immediately started to take off her wet clothes. I walked right to the phone and dialed room service. It rang and rang. I dialed the front desk.

"We're in room 956," I said, confidently, I think. "Is there anyplace in the hotel we can get a hot beverage?"

"Housekeeping can bring up coffee or tea," the man said cheerfully. "The restaurant is closed and room service won't pick up again until five."

"How about hot cocoa?" I asked.

"I think so," the man said. "I'll give a call down to housekeeping."

"Great," I said. "Thanks."

Vanessa disappeared into the bathroom wearing only a tank top and wet jeans.

"Wait," I called, and then briefly regretted it. What would she think? That I wanted to join her?

She poked her head around the side of the door and raised her eyebrows.

"I just wanted to say, don't get into a hot shower with your frozen feet; that could hurt. You have to warm them up slowly. Soak them in warm water first, okay? Not even warm; tepid would be better."

"Tepid?" she asked, a smile spreading across her face.

"Yes, you know, tepid. Lukewarm."

"I know what *tepid* means," she said, still smiling.

"Oh, good," I said, hoping I hadn't made a fool out of myself. And then . . .

"You're not at all how I thought you would be," she said, and closed the bathroom door.

I never asked her what she meant by that. Was I better or worse than she thought I would be? But really, I guess I didn't have to. I saw the look on her face when she said it. I heard the tone of her voice. I wish you could have too.

I heard the water run in the tub, then she was quiet while she must have been soaking her feet, and finally the shower started. I got the strangest feeling in my stomach, which I did my best to ignore.

I was still wet, but I had no idea how to deal with it. I didn't dare start to change. What if she was about to get out of the shower? I finally heard the squeak of the faucet at the same time there was a knock at the door. I walked past the bathroom, where she was barely feet away from me toweling herself off, and opened the door. An older woman pushed a tray at me and turned to go. I immediately knew it was coffee—I could smell it. I wanted Vanessa to have hot chocolate; I wanted her to have everything she wanted, really. I remembered I had two Hershey bars in my bag, so I found them and crumbled one into each steaming mug.

As Vanessa emerged from the bathroom, I handed a mug to her. She took it, sniffed, and smiled. Her hair was brushed and wet. She was wearing a lavender T-shirt and flowered pajama bottoms. The image on her shirt was so familiar—I couldn't place it. A lone bulldog—where had I seen that before? And then it came to me. The bulldog was the mascot of the Irving School.

Maybe there were other schools that had the same mascot. A bulldog was pretty common, right? It was probably the mascot for a slew of schools on the East Coast. Or maybe she had a friend at the school. That was likely, even. It was a nice shirt. If I visited someone who went to a school with that shirt, I would buy it for a souvenir. I have no idea how long I stood there trying to mentally explain away the coincidence of the bulldog.

"Is something wrong?" Vanessa asked, hesitating at the bathroom door.

"No," I said. My mind was telling me to just ask her, maybe I was overreacting. But I couldn't. I guess I didn't want to know. "Actually, I have a confession to make. This isn't hot chocolate. It's coffee with a Hershey bar melted in."

"Mocha! Perfect!" she said, taking a sip.

I watched as she put her mug next to the bed, dug around in her bag, and pulled out a tiny stuffed monkey. Then she sat straight-backed and cross-legged with her head against the pillow, which she had propped up on the headboard.

"Nice lovey," I said. My cousin had a little gray elephant that she took everywhere with her that we all referred to as her lovey.

"Thanks," Vanessa said sleepily. "You know, I was wondering what time we should go back to the airport tomorrow. I meant to call the airline. Do you wake up early?"

"Usually," I said.

"Well, don't leave without me," she said.

"Believe me, I won't," I said, smiling to myself. That was the funniest thing I had heard all night.

"Thanks," she said, yawning. "I am so tired." She looked really drowsy. It was so surprising to me that she could be that comfortable. But it was also a relief. This wasn't going to be so hard. She would fall asleep, and then I could shower and read. I could take my time getting to sleep. It would be almost like being alone, I thought.

"Hey," I said quietly, just in case she was already asleep. I didn't want to wake her; I could always ask her in the morning.

"What?" she asked. Her eyes were closed. She looked so peaceful. She was hugging the tiny monkey. I had the urge to tell her to lie down so I could tuck her in.

"What's the deal with your bulldog shirt?" I asked.

"Oh—it's from my school. It's where I'm going. I'm a senior," she said. Her eyes were still closed. "I'm sort of dreading it and also dying to get there at the same time. I had a big fight with my boyfriend, and I really want things to be okay between us when I get back. Things have been complicated. He hasn't really been himself lately. He's there already. He got there today. We were supposed to see each other tonight. I texted him to tell him about the storm and everything, but he didn't text back. Ugh. I can't even stand to think about it."

She hesitated and then confessed: "I got him something."

She leaned over and browsed through her backpack. Then, proudly, maybe reluctantly, she showed me a bracelet. It was some braided yarn thing.

"It's nice," I said. In my head, though, I was having a whole different conversation. Of course she had a boyfriend. People like her always had boyfriends. And those boyfriends were never people like me.

"What's the name of your school?" I croaked out.

"The Irving School," she said casually, taking another sip from her mug.

So our time together wasn't over. And I had said and done all those stupid things; I felt like an idiot. And she had a boyfriend. Well, what would that matter? It wasn't like *I* was going to be her boyfriend or anything. Suddenly the smell coming from the mug was starting to get to me.

"Where are *you* going?" she asked. This time she turned out the light on her side, leaving mine on, and settled into bed. She pulled the cover up high and closed her eyes.

When I didn't answer, she opened her eyes.

"Do you go to school?" she tried again.

"For now, I'm just heading to New York. I have a few things I have to sort out," I said. I couldn't tell her.

"Where in New York?"

Her phone beeped then, alerting her to a text. She grabbed it and looked, then groaned. It must not have been the text she was hoping for.

"Hey, give me your phone," she said.

"Why?"

"So I can give you my number," she said, sitting up a little.

I got up slowly and walked to my backpack, found my phone, and handed it to her. She clicked the keys for a while and then handed it back to me. I could see she had written her name on my contact list in all caps—VANESSA—like she was really important or something. I thought about deleting it. I knew she wouldn't want to be in my phone when we got to school. How was she going to explain being friends with me? But I left it. I turned and put it back in my bag, and when I faced her again, her eyes were closed. Unbelievable.

I stood up, gathered my small pile of dry clothes, and went into the bathroom. It was still a little steamy from her shower, and I could smell the soap and shampoo she used. A few minutes before, I would have let myself enjoy the fact that I was stepping into the shower she had just stepped out of, and that I would be using the same soap that had just touched her body. But I didn't let myself think about that. I locked the door, took off my wet clothes, and got into the shower. I didn't even end up turning it on. Instead, I stepped out and put on my dry clothes. I pulled a dry towel from the rack and dried out the tub. Then I climbed in and stayed there for the rest of the night.

CHAPTER EIGHT

TIM

I'M THINKING THE CHEDDAR BURGER, A COKE, AND THE TRUFFLE FRIES

The first thing I felt was my stiff back. And then I heard the knocking. *Knock knock knock,* quiet, *knock knock knock,* quiet. I could not figure out where I was—it was pitch-black except for the tiny line of light coming through the door, where I guessed the knock was coming from. Was I in the closet back home hiding from the new owners? Had I been knocked out while going to the bathroom on the plane? Bathroom . . . Right, of course, I was in the hotel bathroom, and the person knocking on the other side of the door was Vanessa. That stunning girl who was nice to me for five minutes, who had a boyfriend, and who I would now have to see every day because, as luck would have it, I was going to be her classmate.

I stood up too fast and had to sit back down on the edge of the tub for a second. *Knock knock knock,* quiet, *knock knock knock.*

"One second," I called.

"Oh, good," she answered through the door, and I was struck by how familiar she sounded—like I had known her for much longer than a day. Come to think of it, the day before at that time I hadn't even met her, had no idea she existed in the world. "I was worried you weren't in there. Or that you had passed out or something."

I tried standing again and this time turned on the light, blinking at the awful brightness. Once my eyes adjusted, I stepped out of the tub and took a look. In the unforgiving light, I was startling, even to myself. And to make matters worse, my clothes were completely wrinkled, and my hair, which had been wet from the snow when I fell asleep, was as messy as I had ever seen it. And my breath. Ugh.

Knock knock knock, quiet.

"I'm coming," I said, wishing that there was some alternative, some escape hatch in the bathroom—a window, even. But of course a window wouldn't do me any good on the ninth floor anyway.

"It's late," Vanessa called through the door. "It's almost nine. I phoned the airline, and they definitely think we can get out today. Come see. It isn't snowing anymore. It's beautiful outside."

I had to pee so badly, but I didn't know how to do it with her standing right outside the door listening. So I turned on the shower, hot. I quickly did what I had to do, rinsed off, and put my wrinkly clothes back on. I used the mouthwash from the tiny bottle by the sink. It had been opened and about a quarter of the blue liquid was missing. Vanessa must have used some. I liked that idea as I took a swig. Now my only problem was a hairbrush. I ran my hands through my hair—not so bad—took a deep breath, and opened the door.

Vanessa was right there, still wearing her bulldog shirt and pajama bottoms. Her hair was messy but in a good way, a really beautiful way.

"What were you doing in there?" she asked.

"What do you think I was doing? I took a shower."

"No, I mean before that. Did you sleep in there?"

"Oh, um, yes," I said sheepishly. "It just seemed easier."

"You didn't have to do that," she said. We were quiet for a minute, and then she pointed to the window. "I can still see our igloo, but it's covered with more snow. Hey, do you want to order breakfast or go find something in the airport? I could use a pick-me-up now, even though I slept surprisingly well."

It was so bright, I knew I should be wearing my sunglasses. I'm sure you never saw them because I spent the entire semester avoiding ever putting them on, but I'm supposed to wear them to protect my eyes from the sun. Another perk of being an albino. Needless to say, I didn't.

Why was she still being so nice to me? But then again, as far as she knew, we would spend the morning together, get on the plane, and go our separate ways once we landed in New York. She had no idea that she was going to be stuck with me. That she'd have to run into me and face me and, worse, face the wrath of her friends, who I was sure would never, ever understand why she might want to be friends with a freak like me. Believe me, I knew. I'd been through it more times than I liked to admit.

So here's what I did: I decided I wouldn't tell her. I decided I would enjoy the little time we had left together. I marched out of the bathroom and right over to the window. It took me a full minute before I could really look outside. I pretended to, but I had my head turned away from her and my eyes closed. Every few seconds I would open them and then shut them and then open them again. And every time it got a little easier. I could hear the doctor's words in my head, telling me how important the glasses were, that it wouldn't take long to damage my eyes beyond repair. But I also heard Vanessa's voice in my head, and it was louder than the doctor's voice, telling me to look at the igloo we made together last night. I remembered how she backed in beside me and we sat like that, so close to each other. It wasn't just that I had never been so close to a beautiful girl; that's true, but it was also the closest I had ever been to a nonalbino girl. My mother would wring my neck for implying that an albino can't be beautiful. And just to be really clear—and I don't know why I feel I must confess this—there had been only one albino girl. It wasn't like I knew a ton of other albinos.

Once my eyes had adjusted, I turned back toward her, and I think she was looking at me suspiciously. Maybe I hadn't been as subtle as I thought. But she didn't say anything about it.

"So what do you think?" she asked.

"It's a masterpiece!" I said, forcing myself to appear as casual as I could while I looked out the window and down toward the lot where we had been the night before. "I think we are expert igloo builders. You know what they say: 'Those who build igloos together—'"

"No, I mean about breakfast," she said.

"Oh," I said, feeling silly. "I don't know, why don't we go and grab something at the airport," I said, worrying that if we stayed put, I might blab my secret, and I was determined to do my best to not ruin the moment. "I wouldn't mind taking a walk."

"Okay, I think I'll skip a shower since I took one last night," she said. "Just give me a few minutes to get dressed."

She took a step toward the bathroom and then came back and stood just inches away from me.

"What *do* they say about people who build igloos together?" she asked.

She was almost standing on her tippy-toes. She was totally flirting with me. I loved it. I pushed all the bad stuff out of my mind. I was not going to let this moment go by. And then she turned again and disappeared into the bathroom. I heard the water running and a toothbrush being used and then, in what seemed like just seconds, she emerged looking as fresh as she had the day before. She was wearing jeans and a bright blue sweater. Her hair was braided and secured with a bright blue rubber band. She wasn't a green and yellow girl. She changed colors each day. I liked that.

"Okay, I'm ready," she said, checking her bed one more time and hoisting her bag over her shoulder.

"Do you have blue iPod buds?" I asked. I couldn't resist.

"I do," she said, smiling. "Are *you* going to make fun of me too?"

"Who else makes fun of you?" I asked, truly curious. She didn't seem like the sort of girl who was made fun of.

"My friends," she said.

"Oh," I said.

"So, are you?"

"No, of course not," I said. "Well, maybe a little."

"Go ahead, you won't bother me," she said. "Actually, this started out as a bet—a friend at school challenged me to color-coordinate my outfits every day for a week, and I had fun. So now it's sort of become my thing."

I looked down at her toes. Yep, blue socks.

"You're good at it," I said.

She swatted my arm, but then her fingers wrapped around

my wrist gently and we stood like that for a minute. I was the first one to move, grabbing my clothes and stuffing them into my backpack.

"Okay," I said. "I'm ready."

I turned and looked at the room one last time. Something on the floor caught my eye and I walked toward it. It was her tiny monkey. I bent down and scooped it up in one hand. It was soft, and I could tell it was old: one of its legs was almost completely worn.

"Hey, you forgot this guy," I said, holding it out to her. She smiled and reached for it. She held it to her chest for a second before stuffing it into her bag.

"Thanks," she said. "That could have been a disaster."

I think I heard the ding of her phone before she did. We were already outside the room. The door had closed behind us. She pulled her phone out of her pocket and fiddled with the buttons, pulling up a text message, probably from the boyfriend she mentioned the night before.

"What did he say?" I asked. I had nothing to lose. She was going to hate me in a few hours anyway.

She looked up, surprised. Then she looked at the floor and kicked one shoe with the other.

"That he misses me," she said. "That he can't wait to see me."

"Oh, good," I said, trying not to sound sarcastic. "You guys made up. Now, what kind of food do you want to get?"

"I was thinking that since we had breakfast for dinner,

maybe we could have lunch for breakfast," she said. "I could eat a burger, or some pasta. What do you think?"

"I think it's a great idea," I said. Actually, I was thinking it continued the tradition of the rules not applying, but I didn't want to say that.

She smiled, then took my arm and led me down the hall like we were off to see the wizard. I hated how much I liked it because I knew I couldn't keep it.

The elevator came, we got in. Vanessa let her heavy bag drop to the floor. I watched the floors count down. Nine—then eight—then seven. She was looking right at me, expectantly, even. What did I have? An hour left, ninety minutes tops, before this would all go away. I dropped my bag to the floor next to hers. I took a step toward her and kissed her on the lips. Her lips were full and, I was surprised to feel, welcoming. For a few seconds it seemed like just the right thing. And then the elevator stopped, the doors opened. We both hurried to get our bags, but before we stepped out into the real world, Vanessa turned to me. I felt the claustrophobic urgency to get out, the doors might close again. But they didn't. I forced myself to stand there.

"You have really nice eyes," she said. And then that was that. She stepped out and I followed.

Down in the lobby, things seemed to be restored to normal. The couches and chairs were occupied by a few people here and there, but there were no crowds, no sense of desperation.

"Can I help pay for the room?" Vanessa asked as we walked back into the airport, retracing our steps from the day before. "You saved me last night."

"No, it is my pleasure," I said, having a hard time answering. Had my lips really just been touching hers? "Actually, my mom paid for it. So don't worry."

I knew I should call my mom. In fact, I was surprised she hadn't called to check in on me. But I didn't want to lie, and I certainly didn't want to tell her I had spent the night in the hotel room she rented for me with a girl I had just met.

The airport, it seemed, was even more crowded than the day before. We quickly found a restaurant and settled in.

"This is my treat," Vanessa said, smiling. "I owe you one. Actually, I owe you two since you found my monkey. Or should I say my lovey?" She looked around. "We're the only people here. Do you think the food is really bad?"

"Hey—if it's half as good as those pancakes last night, I'll be happy," I said, realizing with some surprise that I was hungry. "But it's really expensive. Maybe you want to take back your offer, or maybe we should go to a different place."

"No, I like it here," Vanessa said. "I have an emergency credit card. I would say this is an emergency. Order whatever you want. I'm thinking the cheddar burger, a Coke, and the truffle fries. What about you?"

I was distracted for a minute. I wanted to tell her about Irving—by then I felt like I was actually lying to her—but I was being unusually selfish. Once I told her, I was pretty sure our connection, which at the time I would have gone so far as to describe as miraculous, would evaporate. She reached across the table to get my attention, touching my hand. The energy that I had felt yesterday had grown. She might as well have shocked me with a defibrillator.

Just then the server came back to take our order. He smelled like cigarette smoke.

"What can I get you kids?" he asked. His teeth were yellow.

"I'll have the cheddar burger, medium rare, and the truffle fries. No, make that regular fries, please," Vanessa said. "The truffle might be a little too much for breakfast. Oh, and a Coke."

"How about you?"

"I'll have the steak," I said. "Well done."

The server nodded and then we were alone again.

I couldn't waste any time. I got up and joined her on her side of the booth. She moved over a little to make room for me. And that was how we ate our lunch for breakfast. It was the best steak I ever had.

"Hey, I had an idea," she said after we shared a huge piece of chocolate fudge cake. "I have extra points and I imagine the planes are going to be packed—I know they will be—so do you want me to see if you can sit with me in first class?"

Suddenly I wished I hadn't eaten so much. The steak was heavy in my stomach. The cake was lying on top of that. I had not thought through to the plane and where we would sit and, most important, what we would do on the other end. But now I was starting to think, hope, that the crowds would work in my favor, that we would be forced to split up.

"No, I couldn't, you should save your points," I said.

She hesitated, leaning into me for a brief minute, but then I got up and moved back to the empty bench across the table.

"Are you sure?" she asked.

"I'm sure," I said. My mood was changing. I was starting to feel trapped. Maybe it was for the best, I told myself. This had to end at some point.

She signaled to the server for the check, and he was there with it in an instant. Her phone started to ring, but she ignored it. Then it was quiet. She pulled out what I guessed was her emergency credit card and handed that and the bill back to him. Her phone jingled, and she jumped.

"Voice mail," she said, typing in her code. I could see her face change as she listened.

"Patrick," she said quietly, her eyes on the phone. "The guy I was telling you about. This is what I was afraid of."

"What?" I asked.

"He's been drinking. I can tell," she said. "I mean, it's, like, ten in the morning and I know classes haven't started yet, but he is going to get into trouble. I just know it."

"Is that usual?" I asked, alarmed. That was not the bucolic image I had in my mind of the Irving School.

"No. Well, I mean, kids drink. Especially at the beginning of a semester, people sneak alcohol from home. But Patrick doesn't usually. He just hasn't been himself since his mother died last year."

"Oh," I said.

We sat quietly for a minute.

"Are you going to call him back?" I asked.

"Maybe," she said, sliding out of the booth. "But let's go check on the flights first."

"Thanks for that," I said, gesturing toward the table.

"You're welcome," she said.

We walked back into the crowded airport and found our way to the main gate at the entrance to the terminal. There was a place for first-class passengers, a much shorter line, and then a line for the rest of us. She joined me in my line, but I was starting to act weird, I know I was. I was nervous, and more than anything I wanted to tuck in somewhere. I didn't smile or nod; I paced in my tiny space. After a few minutes, my cell phone rang. It was my mom. I could have not answered it. I could have called her back later, or even in a little while. But I didn't.

"Hi, Mom," I said into the phone. I could see Vanessa looking at me. I pretended I didn't.

"Timmy," my mother said. "How was your night?"

That was a loaded question.

"Hey, Mom?" I said. "I'm back at the airport about to check in, can I call—"

Vanessa was waving at me. I guessed she wanted me to tell my mom she said thank you. But that would have raised so many other questions I couldn't answer.

After a second or two, Vanessa gave up. I can still remember the look on her face, a mixture of confusion and sadness. Maybe a little anger thrown in. She picked up her bag, threw it over her shoulder, and left the long line, joining the one for first-class passengers. She was agitated: she kept tapping her foot and making huge sighing sounds. I was pretty sure she wasn't used to being treated that way. A minute later she came back to me. I still had the phone to my ear, even though I wasn't talking. She leaned in.

"Thanks for the last eighteen hours," she said. I could have told her then, I should have. But I didn't. And then she turned her back toward me and walked away, and I knew she wasn't going to come back.

"Tim, are you there?" my mother called into the phone.

"Yeah, I'm here," I said.

"Do you want to call me back?" she asked. "I just wanted to make sure you were all right."

"Okay, I'll call you back when I figure things out," I said. "Bye, Mom."

Eighteen hours. Eighteen hours. That was almost a whole day. But more than that—and this is a question I still ask myself—when and why had she bothered to count the hours we had spent together?

CHAPTER NINE

TIM
"GOOD" WAS ALL SHE WROTE

The familiar notes of a guitar were suddenly playing in Duncan's ears, and he was momentarily snapped back to his own time and place. What was that? Was it . . . John Denver? And then he heard the beginning words to "Leaving on a Jet Plane." What the heck? Maybe Tim was crazy. He hated that song. He wasn't going to waste his time listening to it when he could be playing cards with the guys. But then, before he had a chance to turn it off, Tim was back. And he was laughing.

I thought we could both use a little comic relief. My mother actually loves that song. She's into corny folk music. Me? Not so much. You? I'm guessing not so much either. Sorry about that. It won't happen again, though I promise I'll leave you with some of my favorite music of all time. But that's a long way away.

In the end, we weren't on the same flight, though I wouldn't realize that for a while. She checked in at the first-class counter and then headed onto a short escalator and disappeared. By the time I wound my way to the beginning of my own line, almost two hours had passed. The first flight out that day was overbooked, so I wasn't scheduled to leave until four that afternoon. As I walked to my gate, I hoped she would be there. I wasn't sure what I would say, but I hoped. The gate was crowded, and after I saw that she was nowhere in sight, I found a chair facing a window and pulled out a graphic novel I was reading. That was when I started convincing myself that we were both better off for having cut our time together short.

I didn't want to call my mother. I knew I should have and she ended up being pretty mad at me, but I just couldn't pretend that I was the same person I had been the day before. If anyone would pick up on that, it would be my mom. But I did call Mr. Bowersox. He was my only contact at the school—anywhere in New York, really—and I suddenly worried he would wonder where I was.

He and my stepfather, Sid, had been at Irving together and then gone on to the same college. They stayed pretty close over the years. If Mr. Bowersox had not become the headmaster of Irving, then I would probably be telling a whole different story, but he did and so there I was. I had his cell phone number. I wasn't sure how acceptable it was to use it to call a headmaster, but I almost didn't care at that point.

He answered on the first ring.

"Mr. Bowersox? This is Tim Macbeth, Sid's—" I started to say.

"Yes, of course. I'm so glad to hear from you," he said. He was so kind and sounded so truly happy to hear from me that for a minute I felt close to tears.

"How have your travels been, young Tim?" he asked when I was quiet for a minute too long.

We talked briefly about the weather and the delays at the airport and at school. He said classes would not start on time. I'm sure you remember that. I told him I would take a cab from the airport, but he insisted on coming to get me.

When I hung up, I realized how relieved I was to have someone waiting for me on the other end. But I also started losing my resolve about Vanessa. Where was she anyway? The gate agent had said we should be boarding in about forty minutes, and she was still nowhere in sight. As the time ticked by, I considered asking someone to help me find her, or searching those lounges myself. I wasn't sure if you could get in without proof that you were a first-class passenger, but I was willing to try. Then I decided I was just being stupid. She probably hadn't given me a second thought since she headed up that escalator away from me. I was sure that she had spent those last few hours texting her boyfriend, counting down the hours until they could be together again.

When the gate agent announced that she was going to begin preboarding the plane, I realized for sure that Vanessa had made another flight. It felt for a minute like I had been hit in the gut. Why had I not accepted her invitation to try to go with her to first class? I missed her and wondered what it would be like the next time I saw her. Suddenly I would have given anything to be sitting next to her on that plane.

I looked through the contact list on my phone: Mom; Sid; Steve, who was my one good friend from my old neighborhood; a few other random kids; and then VANESSA. Without giving it too much thought, I pushed the buttons to get to a blank text screen and proceeded to write one of the longest texts ever. This is what I wrote:

> I have another confession 2 make. I didn't want
> 2 tell u because I didn't know how u would take
> it. But here it is. U deserve 2 know so u won't
> be surprised. I'm going 2 Irving 2. I'm also a
> senior. U haven't seen the last of me.

And then I pressed Send.

At the entrance to the plane, there was a minor incident going on. A small child was literally holding on to the open door, refusing to move into the plane, begging to not go on. The mother was pulling as hard as she could. As soon as I rounded the corner and saw what was happening, I lowered my eyes and kept moving forward. I did not stare—certainly she didn't need that on top of everything else. People were huddled just outside the plane, watching. It seemed to me like they were waiting to see if the child would agree to board before they did—like maybe the child knew something no one else did. There was plenty of room to move around them, so I kept going. And then I broke my no-staring rule. As I walked through first class, I did stare—at every single passenger sitting in each of the big, fancy seats. That was when I knew without a doubt that Vanessa was not there with me. Every seat was taken, and Vanessa wasn't sitting in any of them. She was long gone.

Just as I sat down, my phone beeped. I didn't get many text messages, so I fumbled a bit and then saw her word on my screen clear as day.

"Good" was all she wrote.

I put my head back against the seat, feeling suddenly like I had been drugged. The next thing I knew, the captain was announcing our descent into New York's LaGuardia Airport. The weather was finally clear, though a bit windy, and we were going to land right on time.

"Right on time, sure," the man next to me said. "The right time maybe, just not the right day."

CHAPTER TEN

DUNCAN
"THE SORROWS OF YOUNG TIM"

There was a light knock at the door, and Duncan was startled awake, the earphones digging into the side of his face. He pulled them off and dragged himself out of bed, rumpled but still dressed from the night before, and answered the door. Before he could even see who it was, he smelled cinnamon.

"Hey there, Duncan," Mr. Simon said. "I'm making the rounds, first morning of classes and everything, but I wanted to start with you and bring you this sticky bun. I was trying a new recipe and wanted to share. Hey, I'm glad to see you're dressed. It's never easy to get back into the routine. I'll see you in my classroom in about thirty minutes. Oh, and do you like coffee? I just bought a few pounds from Guatemala that I grind and brew myself. Here."

He thrust a full mug of steaming coffee at Duncan,

smiled, and then turned and walked down the hall. He stopped and came back.

"You know," he said, "the last guy who lived in this room was named Macbeth."

Duncan sucked in his breath. Did Mr. Simon somehow know what he was going through? That Tim had left the recordings for him? Had Mr. Simon snuck in and listened to them? No, Duncan couldn't imagine that he had. He just stood there, not knowing what to say.

"You guys don't get along so well historically," he said. "Rumor has it that he wants to kill you."

When Duncan still didn't say anything, Mr. Simon sighed softly.

"Sorry. I couldn't help myself," he said. "That was just a little Shakespearean humor. But given the circumstances, perhaps that was in bad taste. Please forgive me."

Mr. Simon bowed and offered a weak smile. Duncan watched him walk to the end of the hall and then down the stairs. Why did *he* get the bun and the coffee? And then he remembered. It was just like Tim said it would be: Mr. Simon would bring him food because he felt sorry for him that he had this lame room.

He closed his door and sat down at his desk. He sipped the coffee and ate the bun. Both were delicious. He didn't usually drink coffee in the morning—it seemed so adult—but he really liked it. Soon enough he'd be like his father, having to have coffee at various intervals during the day or he'd get a headache. Starting a vacation by saying he would not, under any circumstances, drink Starbucks coffee that week. He would drink only locally brewed coffee. And then, after a few cups of watery coffee, they would be driving miles out of their way following the signs to Starbucks, Duncan and his sister groaning in the backseat. He liked the idea of that too. It reminded him of their recent trip to northern Michigan. It made him miss his family, especially after listening to Tim's seemingly endless journey to the Irving School.

After he downed about half the cup and started to feel a bit of a caffeine buzz, he placed the mug on his desk, pulled a clean shirt out of his suitcase, and changed into it, leaving on the same jeans he had slept in. He knew he would have to unpack and get his room organized—the fact that it was so tiny made it even more important that he find a place for everything—but every time he was about to do it, he was drawn back to the CDs, Tim's voice, and his story.

He grabbed the bucket that held his soap and toothbrush and went to get cleaned up. When he walked into the crowded bathroom—bright but a little dingy with white tiles, three sinks, and four stalls, each with a swinging wooden door painted white—he had that same feeling he had when he walked into the cafeteria for the first time, that it was going to be hard to get used to this after being home all summer.

He waited patiently for his turn at the sink, and as soon

as he got it, he realized he had left his towel in his room. He thought about running back, but he would lose his place in line. Instead, he grabbed some toilet paper and tried to dry off a bit, but it was so thin, it just stuck to his face.

There were two places that connected the boys' hall to the girls' hall. One was tucked behind the rooms, just beyond the last doors, and led to a fire exit and outside steps toward the back of the senior dorms. The other allowed everyone to reach the main stairs that led down to the first floor. Duncan's room was the last one on the hall, so the rear connecting hallway was just past his door. He was about to enter his room when he just happened to look to his right, and there, in the hallway, was Daisy. She shouldn't have been there. Unlike the hall in the front, where you could run into someone at any time, this one was almost never used, mostly just for fire drills and emergencies. Otherwise, it was strictly off-limits. A sign on the door leading to the outside stairs said not to open it, that an alarm would sound. But Daisy had her hand out the door, as if she was trying to feel the temperature, and there was no alarm going off.

Duncan couldn't be sure if Daisy saw him. It was so quiet right there, she must have heard his footsteps or his bucket rattling, but he moved by fast and went into his room, which luckily he had left wide open. He pulled the door shut and was about to grab his notebooks for class when there was another light knock on the door. He thought to look in his mirror quickly and saw he had smudges of toilet paper on his chin and below his left eye. He furiously used his fingernail to work them off. By now they had dried there, and he made bright red marks where he scraped the paper off with his fingernail. Another knock.

He pulled open the door. Unbelievably, Daisy was standing there. So many things ran through his mind: that she could get detention or worse; that he wished he had saved some of his sticky bun; that he wished he hadn't scratched his face, but better that than bits of toilet paper; that she looked beautiful.

"You shouldn't be here," he said.

"Can I come in?"

"I don't know," he said. He was generally not a rule breaker.

"You know what, you're right," she said. "I shouldn't have knocked."

She turned and started to walk quickly back through the hall to the girls' side.

"Daisy!" he called in a loud whisper. What was he thinking? He wanted to talk to her. And now he was making more of a spectacle than if he had simply let her in and closed the door. She didn't even hesitate: she kept walking and then she was gone. He wanted to curse himself. Why had he done that? What had she wanted? He saw Mr. Simon leave the hall to go to his classroom. Why hadn't he thought of that a second ago? And why was he so scared of getting in trouble anyway?

He didn't have the nerve to walk over to her side of the dorm. Somehow a girl on the boys' side didn't seem quite as bad as a boy on the girls' side. And, besides, how did she know which one was his room?

He glanced at his watch. He couldn't believe it but he ran the risk of being late, and he didn't even have to go to the dining hall, thanks to Mr. Simon, who thought he was ready for class a long time ago. He would have no excuse.

Part of him wanted to give up, just stay in his room and listen to the next installment of what he was now calling "The Sorrows of Young Tim." He was dying to know how Mr. Bowersox treated Tim. He was usually so distant and uninvolved with the students. He was pleasant enough— he smiled and waved whenever he passed a student—but he never seemed to actually engage anyone. It seemed so out of character to offer to pick up a student at the airport. And of course Duncan knew that at some point Tim and Vanessa would run into each other. He wanted to know when and how. But he didn't have the time. He knew Mr. Simon was going to start talking about the Tragedy Paper today—he always did on the first day, even though they didn't have much actually due before second semester. And sometimes he would drop an important detail—the paper has to be exactly fifteen pages long; or I want you to number the pages on the bottom right; or if you highlight the title of your paper in neon green, I'll give you ten extra points—the minute the bell rang, telling everyone who was there that if they revealed the secret to any latecomers, they would not benefit from it themselves. Sometimes he would even lock the door for a few minutes when the bell rang, briefly excluding everyone who wasn't already there while he finished telling the students who were on time some important tidbit.

Duncan grabbed his notebook and ran, all the time on the lookout for Daisy. He had no idea who would be in his class—this class that loomed so large throughout all of high school: senior English. His graduating class was made up of about forty-five people, so he guessed there would be three sections of the class, since there were never more than fifteen students in a class—one of the school's claims to fame. But maybe he was wrong—he really didn't know exactly how many people actually came back after the summer, so there could be more or less. What he did know was that there would be two sections at the very least, so Daisy might or might not be in his class. His odds were fifty-fifty or more likely a thirty-three percent chance. Wow, he liked numbers so much more than words. He wondered why there wasn't as much fanfare around his math class—calculus for him, not senior math. Of course he knew the answer whether he liked it or not. Everyone was at a different level of math—but all seniors, no matter what, went through the same English class. This year that meant reading *Moby-Dick* and participating in "the" *Moby-Dick* project. They loved that because it was so much less rigid than the Tragedy Paper. You could do anything, really, as long as it had to do with a whale. In years past, people had made cakes, painted pictures, put on plays, written and performed rap songs. He had no idea what he was going to do. He dreaded it. After that came Shakespeare and the reading of various plays, ending with *Hamlet* and the all-embarrassing performance of the "To be or not to be" soliloquy in front of the entire senior class. And then, of course, the Tragedy Paper.

Duncan ran down the stairs, and then turned in the opposite direction from the dining hall, walking quickly through the long, narrow hall that housed teachers' offices and the office of the guidance counselor, who would attempt, however lamely, to help Duncan decide where he would spend his next four years. He turned then to his left, past the Hall, where everyone came to write a weekly composition and spent many evenings doing homework. And then into the long main corridor, which was a little too empty. Before classes, usually, people were sitting on the floor everywhere. But now the hall was mostly clear, and there were only a few stragglers. He couldn't believe it—he was going to be late.

He ran past the main office and then slowed, catching his breath as he neared the classroom. He could see the door closing. Mr. Simon must have been pushing it shut, but Duncan eased his arm in between the door and the frame and it opened wide for him. Mr. Simon smiled at him, bowed slightly, and let him pass, then shut the door hard and turned the lock.

"Nice of you to join us, Mr. Meade," Mr. Simon said. Duncan quickly scanned the room. It was big, with desks pulled into a semicircle facing the blackboard. The first thing Duncan noticed was that Daisy was not there. The second thing he noticed was that there must have been at least four or five students still missing—depending on how many were actually in this class—because there were so many empty desks. Mr. Simon waited while Duncan chose his desk. He decided on the one to the far right next to Tad. Duncan gently tossed his books down on the desk and smiled at Tad, who grinned back and then nodded his head toward the door. In the window of the door were three scared faces peeking in with wide eyes. They were the late-comers. They had already lost something, though no one was sure what yet. And those people might never know. Mr. Simon had a reputation for remembering everything. He knew who was here and who wasn't, no question.

"Okay, now that everyone is settled," Mr. Simon said calmly, his back turned to the door and the panicked faces with the pleading eyes, "I want to welcome all of you bull-dogs to the most thrilling, the most exhilarating, the most magical classroom experience you might ever have. Welcome to senior English." He paused for dramatic effect, and there was a frantic *knock knock knock* on the door. Mr. Simon didn't even flinch. Duncan looked up, and there was Daisy's face pressed against the glass. She must have pushed everyone else out of the way. Duncan wanted more than anything to stand up and let her in. Why did Mr. Simon have to be so unbending? Couldn't he have started this craziness on the second day of classes?

"Don't worry, I don't plan to keep those disrespectful poky students out in the hallway forever," he said. "But let me tell you this . . . and I suggest you write this down. . . . If you manage to work the word *magnitude*—and I hope you all begin to think about that word and how important it is—into your Tragedy Paper exactly seven times, using it correctly, of course, I will add ten points onto your grade. That means, young students, that if you write a paper deserving of an A, you will get extra credit. Now, you know the rules: if any of you utter this to any of them," he said, for the first time turning slightly toward the window in the door, "then you will all lose those extra points. Understood?"

Mr. Simon meandered over to the door, slowly released the dead bolt, and opened the door. By now the faces out there were no longer panicked, but defeated. They knew they had missed something important—something that could never be gotten back. Daisy was in the room first.

"I have an excuse, if you'll let me tell you about it," she said kindly to Mr. Simon as she chose a seat across the room from Duncan.

"I'm sorry, Miss Pickett, but you know the rules," Mr. Simon said, also kindly.

The other students took their seats, and it turned out the class was full—fifteen students in all.

"And so we begin," Mr. Simon said, launching into *Moby-Dick* without a moment's pause. There would have been a time when Duncan would have felt good about being in on the secret. To mention the word *magnitude* seven times and get ten extra points! That could mean the difference between a D and a C, or a C and a B. He knew that there would be a few more chances to increase his grade this semester, though none as big as this one. But as the minutes ticked away slowly, Duncan felt worse and worse. What was Daisy's excuse? And had he done anything to delay her? If he had let her into his room, would that have made a difference? He tried many times to meet her eyes, but she wouldn't. She was fully engaged in the discussion, taking notes, answering questions, and offering ideas. It became clear to Duncan that she had already read *Moby-Dick,* and yet she was the one playing catch-up here. It didn't seem fair.

"Read at least the first two chapters before our next class meeting," Mr. Simon finally said. And then he paused. Everyone waited, on the edge of their seats.

"Now go forth and spread beauty and light," he said, his regular dismissal from class, but this was the first time he was saying it to them. A few kids smiled; a few leaned back in their seats clearly relishing the moment. And then everyone was off. Daisy was the closest to the door, and Duncan was surprised when she bolted. He had expected her to try to offer her excuse again. He grabbed his books and took off after her. He had a free period and hoped she would too. Maybe they could take a walk or something. But when he got within reach, he turned and started walking back to his room. What did he have to say to her anyway? And, besides, Tim had just landed in New York. He had to know what happened next.

CHAPTER ELEVEN

TIM
RAIN, SNOW, SNOWBALLS

Yes, believe it. Mr. Bowersox picked me up at the airport. He stood at baggage claim holding a sign that said MACBETH, as if he might mistake another albino for me. I still had my phone in my hand hoping to channel Vanessa, and as it had been doing for a few hours now, one word kept running through my mind—the simplest word, and yet I had no idea what it meant: *good.*

In the end, I was glad he had the sign because I spotted him before he saw me. You are probably so used to him by now that you don't even think about it, but he looked just the way I would expect a headmaster to look—jolly, with a round crown of hair surrounding a shiny bald spot, and a red tartan plaid scarf around his neck.

"Mr. Bowersox?" I said a little too eagerly, before I had even reached the bottom of the escalator. I was so happy to see him. Finding a cab and getting to school by myself would have pushed me over the edge, I was sure of it.

"Tim!" he said, offering me his thick hand. I took it without hesitation and shook enthusiastically.

"Welcome to New York, welcome to the Empire State, welcome to your new home," he said, smiling wide. "We are so happy to have you join us at the Irving School this semester."

"Thanks," I said, feeling myself relax for the first time in what seemed like forever. In a weird way, it was such a relief to be in the presence of a grown-up. I could actually feel myself slouch.

"Shall we?" he asked, folding up the sign carefully and putting it in the pocket of his blazer. "Do you have any bags?"

"Just this one," I said, pointing over my shoulder at my big backpack. "Everything else was sent ahead."

Mr. Bowersox took a hat the exact same plaid as his scarf out of his other pocket and pulled it over his head, warning me about the cold. All I could think was that he should try hanging out in an igloo. We were quiet while we settled into the car and he started to drive, navigating the winding, complicated ramps of the airport. And then we were on the highway.

"Let's get some dinner on our way back. I was thinking we could stop in the city for Italian, if you like," Mr. Bowersox said. "Or we could head back to Westchester and have Italian there. There's a good place in Yonkers that I hear makes a mean gnocchi."

"That sounds good," I said, having no idea what or where Yonkers was.

He asked about my old school. I told him about my teachers from my first semester of senior year, how there was only one I would especially miss. That teacher chose a theme every month and everything we did had to do with that theme. He was an English teacher, but he didn't focus only on that—he brought food into it and sometimes science and history. But, I assured Mr. Bowersox, I was happy to try something new.

I think it was possible that thirty or forty minutes had gone by and I hadn't thought of Vanessa, but after I said that about trying something new, I had to stop talking for a minute; I felt like the wind was knocked out of me. I guess I *wasn't* so happy to try something new. I'd tried something new for half a day and a night—or maybe for just about forty-five seconds in that elevator at the hotel. And now I wanted to go back to before I knew what that could be like. Or maybe I wanted to go back to before I knew what I was missing—that was more like it.

Mr. Bowersox seemed so genuinely interested in me, asking about my favorite themes, really listening when I told him. I remember telling him all about the Greek gods we studied, and about how we had a whole month's unit focused on baked goods. And that was when he told me about Mr. Simon.

"In that case, I think you will like the senior English teacher very much," Mr. Bowersox said. "He's the token adult on your dorm floor too, so you will get to know him very well. His name is Clark Simon. He doesn't teach through themes like that—although he might argue that the *Moby-Dick* unit could be looked at that way; he does bring in food and a bit of science and history there—but he believes in becoming fully immersed in whatever you're learning at the time. You will see that there are days he'll come down to breakfast dressed as one Shakespearean character or another, or days he will choose to eat only things that Captain Ahab might have eaten on the *Pequod,* though I'm not sure what that would be. I think he might end up a little hungry on those days."

I nodded, forcing myself to focus and not wonder where Vanessa was at that moment and, worse, what it would be like when we ran into each other. "So, what are they studying now?" I remember asking.

"Well, you missed the section on *Moby-Dick* and the introduction to Shakespeare. They read *King Lear* and *Macbeth* before break. I think you move into Greek tragedies now as he really gets you guys geared up for the Tragedy Paper."

"The Tragedy Paper?"

"Ah, well, you'll learn about this soon enough," Mr. Bowersox said.

(I hope you're getting a kick out of this part, by the way. I worked hard to impersonate Mr. Bowersox's voice. I think I do a pretty good job. Close your eyes and listen. Don't I sound just like him?)

"It is meant to be a culmination of your high school years—your reading comprehension, your writing skills, your method of analyzing material and then formulating and communicating your own thoughts," he told me. "It's great fun, really. And I've taken a look at your transcript. You should have no problem keeping up. But let's not talk about that now. Are you hungry?"

I *was* hungry. When was the last time I had had a good meal? The steak that morning? Maybe if I got a little food in me, I would feel better.

We drove in silence for a long time. On occasion Mr. Bowersox would point out landmarks—this bridge or that tall building off in the distance. The highway looked different, but if I closed my eyes halfway, I could almost convince myself that I was in Chicago and pretend I was on my way home. We ended up having a nice dinner at some small Italian restaurant in what Mr. Bowersox kept saying was Yonkers. What a strange name for a town. I ordered spaghetti with meatballs and worried it would be messy. Mr. Bowersox got the baked ziti and spent most of the meal with strings of melted cheese hanging down his chin. I'm sorry I couldn't get a picture. It would be great to have if you ever need to blackmail him.

After that, everything sped up, and before I knew it, we were getting back in the car and school was our next stop. I actually thought about running, literally running down the sidewalk and away from Mr. Bowersox. I wondered what he would do. Would he run after me? Call the police? Hang around Yonkers until he found me? I knew it was all crazy. I would run around the corner and be alone, in a strange city with a strange name that rhymed with *bonkers*. School had to be the better choice.

We drove for about twenty-five minutes before Mr. Bowersox put on his turn signal and got off the highway. There was a strange merge at the exit. He was getting off, but a car came up behind him that was getting on. For a moment I thought we were going to crash right into it, but we didn't. And then we were on small streets going up a hill.

A big sign said THE IRVING SCHOOL. I could make out an athletic field off to our left, and what I guessed was the gym. We drove up a twisty road, and then I saw the main buildings I had seen on the school's website so many times. He pointed out his house. Finally, he pointed out the senior dorm.

He drove around the small circle and pulled up to a stone arch, then paused, letting me take it all in.

"Enter here to be and find a friend," he said dramatically.

"What?"

"Enter here to be and find a friend," he said again, pointing to the inscription in the stone over the wooden door. "It is one of our driving principles at the Irving School. I just didn't want you to miss it."

The whole time I kept wondering, how close exactly was I to Vanessa? Was she twenty feet away, a hundred, a thousand? She couldn't have been far. Assuming she made it to school, she had to be there somewhere.

It was so quiet. There was a rustling in the trees, but I wondered what would happen if I started screaming her name. I imagined pounding my fists on the door and yelling for her.

I followed Mr. Bowersox inside. I noticed the wood-paneled walls and the big carpeted staircase in front of us. I followed Mr. Bowersox up the stairs. At the top, he turned to the left, pointing out the girls' side to the right as we went by.

"You'll get all the house rules," he told me. "But you can probably guess that hall is off-limits."

Again, I had that crazy urge to do the unexpected. I wanted to run down the girls' hall calling Vanessa's name. And, again, I didn't. I followed Mr. Bowersox, past room after room. It was so quiet and all the lights in all the rooms were out except for one; I looked at the bottom of each door as we walked by. At the farthest end of the hall, I saw a door open and light coming out.

"That's your room, young man," he said, stopping and letting me go ahead of him. I walked into the room. The one you are probably sitting in right now. It was tiny but seemed nice enough with that minuscule round window. I wondered if it got any light during the day. We both know the answer to that. The bed was made, which surprised me, and my bags were neatly stacked in the corner. On the desk was a plate with cookies and a glass of milk set in a bowl of ice.

"I hope this is to your liking," Mr. Bowersox said, stepping inside and looking so huge in my tiny room. "I don't get up here as often as I should. It's good to see."

"Thank you," I said. "It's very nice."

"Well, sleep tight," he said. I didn't want him to leave. I didn't want to be alone. He told me again that classes were not yet on a normal schedule but that there would be some orientation activities the next day. He promised to see me at breakfast. I reached out my hand, thanking him again. And here is what he said:

"I'm glad to have you here, son," he said. "I look forward to a great semester."

Do you think he thought that two months later?

I watched him go down the hall. At one point, he stopped and bent to look under a door. He knocked gently.

"Lights out," he called, and then he was gone.

I slowly closed my door. For the first time in hours—days, even—I was going to be completely alone. My light was still on, which I assumed was okay because Mr. Bowersox didn't mention it. I sat on the bed and let my eyes wander around the room. I debated unpacking but decided it was too late and I worried about not having enough to do the next day. At least I could use the excuse of having to unpack as a reason to stay in my room—though I had no idea who I might have to offer an excuse to.

My eyes caught something green on the floor. It was a strange green, sort of yellowy and kiwi-looking. *Gyellow,* I thought to myself. It was exactly like the green Vanessa had on the day before. It looked like paper rain or confetti leading from under my bed to my closet. I got down on the floor and glanced beneath the bed. The green rain went all the way under to the far dusty corner at the foot of the bed. There was something there. I inched under the bed with my arm out until my hand touched what looked like a crumpled piece of paper. At first I told myself that it must have been left over from the previous student. But to be really honest here, I knew the green was too much of a coincidence. My heart was beating like a jackhammer as I shimmied out from under the bed and sat on the floor with the paper ball in my hand. Slowly I spread it out, and I could see there was writing on it. I didn't let my eyes focus as I smoothed out the paper on the floor, and then I looked.

Rain, snow, snowballs, it read at the top in green marker. Was it some sort of nature poem? I turned it over, and on the back it said:

Dear Tim,

　　It is an Irving School tradition that the senior who lived in your room the previous year leaves you what we around here like to call a "treasure." We get it on move-in day, and there have been some crazy things, let me tell you. This year my friend Madison got a package from Omaha Steaks that she persuaded the people in the dining hall to cook. That was a good one. My other friend Julia got a bottle of wine from the girl who lived there before because her parents own a winery. I bet you wonder what I got. Well, I got a kit to make a snowman. A girl named Suzanne lived in my room before me, and she knew how much I like playing in the snow. The kit included a plastic carrot for the nose, a black top hat, and a red scarf.

　　I didn't want you to get here and miss out on the tradition. Take a look in your closet and see.

　　　　　　　　　　　　　　　　Vanessa

I was careful not to mess up the line of green paper rain-drops leading into my closet. I wanted them to stay the way she'd scattered them. I loved the idea of having something she touched right there with me. I opened the tiny wood door and was faced with a small bar to hang clothes on one side and shelves on the other. At first I didn't see anything else, but when I bent down, I saw a little cooler below the bottom shelf and a small plastic bag. I pulled out the bag first, and in it was the plastic carrot, the top hat, and a scarf—only this one wasn't red, it was green. I dragged the cooler out and opened it. Inside, there were three perfectly formed snowballs.

CHAPTER TWELVE

TIM
EIGHTEEN HOURS

Duncan couldn't get to the next CD fast enough. This wasn't quite how he had imagined the scenario playing out. He was actually touched by Vanessa's kindness, but he couldn't help asking himself, why? He had to pee, he was going to be late for another class, and yet he felt like the need to listen was almost beyond his control, he couldn't resist it. So he quickly took the CD out, dropping it on the floor then scooping it up, and slipped in the next one. Sitting straight up on the edge of his bed to prevent himself from getting too settled in, he closed his eyes and let Tim's voice fill the room.

When I woke up, my bed was wet and I couldn't figure it out. Then I remembered the snowballs and cursed myself for falling asleep with one in my hand. Before I had a chance to process what was going on and locate my second set of sheets, there was a knock.

"Well, you must be Tim," said the person at my door. At first I thought he might be a student, he looked so young and wore those cool black-framed glasses. But then he told me, "I'm Mr. Simon."

"Hi," I said. He had a plate in his hand with what looked like a blueberry muffin on it and a glass of orange juice. He handed them to me, his eyes resting on the uneaten plate of cookies from last night. Shoot, I thought, he must have brought those.

"Wow, thanks," I said, realizing I was starving. "Is this usual? Is there, like, room service or something?"

"Well, I'd like to say yes, but no, you'll have to make your way down to the dining hall most mornings. But I do like to bake and I live alone, so because you are the lucky winner of this room, I will share my confections with you whenever I can. I figured your first morning here was as good a time to start as any," he said. "How was your trip?"

Complicated, I wanted to say, *and I think I fell in love on my way here.* "It was long," I said instead.

"Well, the bathroom is down there, but you've probably figured that out already, and the dining hall is at the bottom of those stairs at the end of the hall," he said. "The schedule today is irregular, but I suggest heading down to breakfast as soon as you get cleaned up because there will be activities you don't want to miss. I think there's a hike planned, and maybe a game of capture the flag."

"That sounds like fun," I said. I wanted to ask if he knew Vanessa—and Patrick, for that matter. But I didn't dare.

"Is this room special or something?" I asked.

"You mean because I said I'd bring you my baked masterpieces?" Mr. Simon asked me. I was starting to like him already. "It is. This, my fine young student, is where an English teacher was hatched! This was my room when I was at Irving. It suited me well." He leaned in and lowered his voice. "The trick is that it's hard to see from outside or under the door if your light is on, so you can get away with reading deep into the night. I did—lots of Shakespeare and Ernest Hemingway. I hope you find it to be at least as grand as I did. I'll see you downstairs. Welcome to the Irving School."

"Happy to be here," I said, surprised to find myself smiling.

The muffin was warm and smelled great. I sat on the edge of my bed and ate the whole thing. Then I did what I was dreading: I opened the cooler to check on the other two snowballs. I had thought about creeping down to the dining hall and trying to find a freezer, but to what end? Someone would find them and throw them away. When I slid the lid to the side, I saw that one had melted completely, and the other was now smaller than a golf ball. I closed the lid, and headed to the bathroom. Don't worry, I am not going to tell you about all my trips to the bathroom, but this one has some significance, so please indulge me.

I didn't see anyone along the way, the hall was so quiet. Maybe people were sleeping in since there were no classes. I was glad. I didn't want to face anyone yet, and I knew I was going to stand out like a polar bear in a grizzly maze. How much had they been told about me? Did they know I was an albino? I didn't want to deal with that. I decided right then and there that I would skip the hike.

I was relieved to see the bathroom was also empty. I was almost ready to head back when the door swung open. I was facing the mirror and had my back to the person who came in, but I could see he was tall with short brown hair and bright blue eyes. His eyes were so blue, in fact, they were like a flash in the mirror. He was wearing green pajamas and was humming to himself. He looked at me and I registered; I could feel it. There was a long pause while he looked me up and down, and I had no choice. I was about to turn to him and introduce myself. He must have wondered, in addition to how white I looked, what a stranger was doing in the bathroom. But before I had a chance to, he was standing in front of me, towering over me, it seemed.

"I hear you spent the night in a hotel room with my girlfriend," he snarled.

This was by far the worst-case scenario. *Please let someone else come in,* I chanted to myself. *Please let someone else come in.*

He moved in even closer. His nose was practically touching mine.

"If you weren't so weird-looking already, I would mess you up," he said. "Maybe I'd break your nose, or give you a black eye. Nobody—and I mean nobody, except for me—gets to be alone in a bedroom with my girl. Is that understood?"

"Don't worry," I said, perhaps a bit too sarcastically. "I can't imagine she'd let that happen again."

"Let what happen?" he asked.

I was scared, I'll admit it. I hadn't meant for it to sound that way, and I knew once you started trying to dig out of a hole, you only made things worse. In my mind I could still hear her voice saying *Thanks for the last eighteen hours.* Eighteen hours. Eighteen hours. I hoped Patrick couldn't read minds. For a second I distracted myself trying to think of which superhero could read minds. Just to let you know, it is Professor X of the X-Men, but I was so frazzled I didn't think of it until I got back to my room.

"Nothing," I said finally. "I mean, she won't ever want to spend a night in a hotel again, with me, that is. . . ."

I didn't seem to be making Patrick feel any better. I thought about telling him there were two beds and I didn't even sleep in one of them, but I was fumbling and knew I would somehow mess it up more than I already had.

"Why's that?" he asked. He could lean over just a bit and bite my nose if he wanted to. It would suck to have to meet new people looking the way I look with a big festering bite

107

on my nose. But he didn't, and I should have realized that nobody would want to get that close to me anyway. Just then the door swung open and a redheaded short guy walked in. He was wearing red-checked boxers and no shirt even though there was a sign reminding us to come to the bathroom in more than just our underwear. He smiled at Patrick, then his eyes rested on me.

"Hey," the kid said, looking from me to Patrick, then back to me.

"Hey," Patrick said. I think I managed a weak smile. We all stood there for a few seconds, and I wondered if he forgot what he came to do. Then he nodded and went into a stall.

"I'm just joking with you, you know that, right?" Patrick asked suddenly, patting me on the back. "I was just kidding around. Hey, Peter, introduce yourself to our new friend."

"I'm Peter," a voice said from inside the stall. We could hear him unrolling the toilet paper.

"I'm Tim," I said.

"I didn't mean to scare you. Did I scare you?" Patrick asked. I remember thinking the guy was crazy, he was all over the place. Before I had a chance to say anything, he kept talking. "So, do you want to come to my room later?" he asked. I just stood there and looked at the floor. I assumed he was talking to Peter.

"Hey, you," he said, nodding in my direction. "We're organizing this semester's big Game, and you should get in on it. It'll be a good way for you to meet people. What do you say?"

I had no idea what he was talking about. The big Game? But I didn't want to stick around for an explanation. My head was spinning, and the smell in the bathroom was getting overwhelming. I had to get out of there.

"I'm thinking a little strip poker might be in order," smelly Pete said from inside the stall.

"No way," Patrick said. "I don't need to play a game to get some action. I have other ideas. What's that game called when you have to off someone and it's a secret and . . ."

"Assassin," I said without thinking.

A slow smile spread over Patrick's face.

"Okay, then," he said. "See you in my room after dinner."

CHAPTER THIRTEEN

DUNCAN

EACH DOOR WAS PAINTED A DIFFERENT COLOR

Duncan turned off the CD. He had to work hard to bring his focus back to this year, and stop reliving last year.

As soon as he got to the bottom of the stairs, he could tell something was up. People were talking about an incident that happened on the senior girls' floor. Nobody seemed to know what it was, but it was *something*. Duncan had a very hard time concentrating on the first classes of the year. He went to math, which was his favorite, but failed to show off in his usual way. He liked to let everyone else know how good he was from the beginning, but the truth was, they already knew. They had been going to school with him for years.

Between math and science—which involved a walk down one hall, then another smaller one leading outside, and finally down a tree-lined path to the science building—Duncan kept his ears open. He heard the words *sick* and *fire* and *mouse* and *ambulance,* but had no idea if any of them pertained to what had happened on Daisy's hall. He also kept his eyes open for Daisy—she had to be somewhere. But she was nowhere. He wished he had talked to her last night at dinner and asked about her class schedule. Even more than that, he wished he had let her in this morning. He would give anything to go back to that moment and make the other choice. He told himself over and over that he would apologize for this the next time he saw her. But the whole morning went by—and there was no sign of her anywhere. Just before lunch, he saw Abigail, a girl who knew Daisy but wasn't deep into the social politics most of her friends were, so he asked if she'd seen her. She hadn't, and she was still trying to figure out what had happened on the hall that morning. Basically, she was no help at all. He thought about asking other people where Daisy might be, but he didn't want everyone talking about him, wondering why he was so interested in her all of a sudden.

When he didn't see Daisy in the dining room—and it was one of his favorite lunches of all, grass-fed beef burgers from the Hudson Valley—he started to get worried. He wrapped up his food in napkins and left. He intended to go up to his room—he had almost an hour until his next class—and listen to more about Tim. But when he got to the top of the stairs, he did something reckless: he veered off toward the girls' side. He couldn't believe he was doing it even as he was actually doing it. He tried to look like he belonged there, which was ridiculous, but somehow it made him feel better. He rounded the corner, prepared for anything, and stopped short. The hall was empty, but what struck him the most was how totally different it looked from the boys' hall.

The carpet was a bright but not tacky blue; the walls were yellow with painted vines and flowers here and there. There was a window seat that they didn't have on their side with a plaid pillow and a small pile of books perched on top. Each door was painted a different color—mint green, bright orange, lavender. It reminded him a little of Dr. Seuss, and while it was so much nicer than their dingy grays and browns, he wasn't entirely sure he would want to live there.

It certainly didn't look like there had been any sort of disaster on the girls' side this morning. He checked the carpet for blood and the walls for fire marks, which he knew was silly. Most of the girls should be at lunch, but one of the privileges of being a senior was that you were allowed to go back to your room at any time if you needed or wanted to as long as you didn't miss class or another important activity. So if you wanted to eat lunch in your room, that was okay. Still, no one seemed to be around.

Duncan walked down the hall slowly and realized he had no idea which door might be Daisy's. There were pictures and stickers and some big bows decorating the different doors, but no names. He wondered how the girls figured out which room they had. Over on the boys' side, the names were still up on most of the doors. Then Daisy's friend Justine came out of her room. It was the one with the purple door—not the lavender door but a real deep purple. She looked so startled that Duncan thought she was going to scream. She opened her mouth but clamped it shut before she said anything. They stood facing each other.

"Hey, I'm looking for Daisy," he finally said, his voice a little too high and squeaky.

"Yeah, I figured," she said.

Duncan had to try hard not to smile. If Justine guessed he was looking for Daisy, then he wasn't crazy thinking there was some sort of connection between them. Other people must see it too.

"She's not here," Justine said.

"Is she at lunch? I didn't see her there."

"No," Justine said. "She's at the hospital."

Duncan took a step back.

"What?! Is she"—he didn't know what to say—"sick?"

"Maybe. Maybe not," Justine said, turning to go. He never really did like Justine.

"No, wait," he said, reaching out and grabbing her wrist. She turned but pulled her wrist out of his grasp. "Please, I need to know."

"Why do you need to know?" she asked. "You haven't talked to her in months."

Justine was right. He *hadn't* talked to Daisy in months, except for their brief exchange this morning when he had practically shut his door in her face.

They stared at each other for a few more seconds.

"What's for lunch?" Justine asked, like they hadn't just been talking about a friend going to the hospital.

Duncan remembered his burger and pointed to the wrapped food in his hand.

"I didn't touch this," he said. "Ketchup, mustard, and pickles."

"Just the way I like it," she said. Duncan noticed that her eyes looked a little red, like she'd been crying or something. Her chestnut-colored hair was perfectly brushed into a high ponytail, and she was wearing a madras shirt and faded jeans. She was pretty, but not nearly as pretty as Daisy.

"Were you offering that to me?" she asked.

"Oh yeah," he said, handing it over. "Sorry."

"Thanks," she said, taking the burger and lifting it to her nose to take a sniff. "I'm starving."

"Can you at least tell me if Daisy is sick? Or hurt?" Duncan pleaded again.

Justine didn't answer. She turned and went back to her purple door. Duncan wondered if the inside was purple too. It was like a different world over here. With her hand on the doorknob, she turned and looked back.

"I'm going to talk to Daisy later," she said. "Do you have a message you'd like me to give her?"

Duncan thought. There were so many things. That he was sorry he'd let so much time go by without really talking to her. That he was sorry he hadn't helped her this morning when she came to his door and hoped that had nothing to do with the hospital. That he hadn't felt this way about any other girl ever. That on many summer nights he would lie in bed and wonder what she was doing and if she ever thought about him.

"Just that I hope she's okay," he said. He didn't wait for Justine to comment; he simply turned and walked to the back of the dorm and to the tiny hall that connected the two sides. He could almost hear her snickering as he turned and disappeared, jogging to his room. As soon as he crossed over to the boys' side, he worried about running into Mr. Simon. But he made it inside and shut the door, sitting on his bed to catch his breath. It took him a minute to realize that he would have nothing to eat until dinner and he still didn't know which door was hers. That was when he remembered the hidden compartment Tim had mentioned in his letter.

Duncan found the letter in his desk drawer and followed the instructions that led him to the hidden space, opening it slowly. He expected it to be empty. He guessed, when he first read that note—it seemed like weeks ago now—that it was just a concession for having this room, which, Duncan had to admit, was growing on him.

But the space wasn't empty. Duncan could see that right

away. He got down on his knees so he could get a better look. It was a tiny opening, about six inches by eight inches, but he could see there was a surprisingly large space beyond that, maybe two feet by two feet, or even bigger. Duncan slowly started to pull the items out and placed them on the floor. There was a bundle of lined papers folded in half. He could see they were written on, but he didn't stop to read the words yet. There was a green scarf. There were strange-looking sunglasses that seemed like they wrapped around your head. Duncan put them on and then pulled them off quickly. They gave him the creeps. He put those on the floor next to the pile he was building. There was a small paperback book—Shakespeare's *Hamlet*, Duncan saw. There was a Post-it on the cover that said in that scrawled hand-writing: *Read this—and don't miss the point.* By now, Duncan was fairly sure the note was meant for him—that all of this stuff was meant for him.

And finally, toward the back of the space, there was a key ring with three keys. Duncan had to reach almost to the wall to get them, and even then it was tricky. The key ring itself looked like a souvenir from Chicago—it said THE WINDY CITY with a picture of a lake being blown by a strong wind. The three keys were each different: one was silver with a complicated design where it fit into the lock; one looked like a skeleton key; and the other was small and copper, turning green at the edges.

Duncan reached into the space and moved his hand

around, touching every surface to make sure he hadn't missed anything. He could guess about the scarf, but he wanted to know about all the other things. Maybe they weren't all left here by Tim. Maybe some had been left by the previous occupants of the room. Maybe that was one of the traditions of the room, though Duncan had never heard of that. He picked up the folded papers, hoping they would offer a clue. But when he looked, he could see they were notes about tragedy, probably for Tim's paper. There were words followed by definitions. Duncan could read the words, but what followed was written and then erased and rewritten so many times he couldn't make it out. He read the words slowly to himself: *monomania, catharsis, irony, error in judgment, tragic flaw, pity, fear.* Duncan turned page after page looking for Tim's draft of his paper, but it wasn't there.

He glanced at his desk, where the CDs were stacked in a pile. He hadn't eaten, he hadn't solved the mystery of what happened on the girls' floor, Daisy was at the hospital for some unknown reason, but all he wanted to do was listen to Tim's voice methodically tell the story. There was so much he needed to find out and actually do here, in his own reality, but it was easier to press Play, lie back on his bed with the red flannel sheets that just last week were on his bed at home, and listen.

CHAPTER FOURTEEN

TIM

SHE SAW ME AND STARTED TO WAVE.

Meeting Patrick in the bathroom was enough to make me never want to go there again, let me tell you. I mean, I even scouted out all the other options—the bathroom near the dining hall, the one in the library—but there were a few problems with them, as you may know. The biggest one being that there wasn't even a shower in any of those.

Already it seemed like things were bordering on unbearable. I was new to the school, and there were two people I completely wanted to avoid—and I mean avoid—never, ever run into or see again. Well, maybe that wasn't entirely true of both of them. But that guy was such a freak. Why had Patrick gone from wanting to pummel me to wanting me to be part of their Game? I didn't trust him for a second, and yet I wasn't quite sure how I would get out of it.

These were the things I was thinking when I heard a

rustling sound. Something was being pushed under my door. I wanted to hide in the tiny closet or pull the covers up over my head and pretend I wasn't there, but my adrenaline was still raging, so without much thought, I yanked open the door. It was a kid I hadn't seen before.

"Uh, hi," he said, standing up with the paper in his hand. "You're Tim, right?"

I assured him I was.

"I'm Kyle," he said, handing me the paper. "Vanessa asked me to give this to you."

"What is it?" I asked, assuming it had to do with the hike or capture the flag.

"I have no idea." Kyle shrugged. "Sorry. But it's nice to meet you."

"Wait! Are you friends with Vanessa?" I thought I might as well try to figure out the social landscape while I had a chance.

"No, not really," he said. "She was waiting at the top of the stairs. I must have been the first boy she saw."

I wanted to ask so many other questions but didn't dare. Also, I was dying to see what the paper said. "Well, thanks," I said. I watched as he waved and walked down the hall.

I closed the door and sat for a minute with the paper on my lap. There was tape keeping it closed, so I broke through that and slowly unfolded it, my heart beating so fast it hurt. It was also hard to breathe.

Dear Tim. I loved that: Dear Tim!

Dear Tim,

How did you like the treasure I left for you? So, I just want to get this out of the way, and then we don't have to talk about it. You should have told me. You could have told me, and it would have been all right. At least it explains your strange reaction at the airport. I still thought you might be on my flight and was truly sorry to see you weren't. I hope your trip was okay. Mine was lonely. Anyway, I wondered if you would meet me for a run at noon today? I know that's lunchtime, but it's the only time I can disappear for a while. And I remember that you said you like to run. Didn't you say it makes you happy? Also, I forgot to say, it's school policy that we not run through the woods alone, so we are supposed to go on the buddy system. I'll meet you just outside the science building: go out the door behind the main office and follow the path, you can't miss it. Don't forget your running shoes.

Fondly,
Vanessa

Fondly, Vanessa. I loved that too. Noon was still hours away. How was I going to get through the morning until then? But, worse, how was I going to go? It was so bright outside, between the winter sun and the intense white snow.

I thought I just might have to actually wear my glasses. But when I put them on and looked at myself in the dingy mirror, I realized that there was no way. I hated them. And Vanessa had said I had nice eyes; I wasn't going to cover them up with those ugly things. I stuffed them back in my bag.

I usually wear my glasses when I run alone—I think they help me hide. There was one time last year, though, when I was fairly sure I would run into a girl from school and I decided not to wear them. One time wouldn't hurt. I had to sneak out because my mother would not go for that sort of reasoning. In the end, it was a disaster. My eyes hurt, and I had to stop constantly to cover them to take the sting out. Just as I got within sight of the girl's house, and I could actually see her in the yard, my mother pulled up behind me and handed me my glasses through the window. I put them on and turned, glad to have something to cover my face, which was burning from embarrassment. I headed home and didn't look back. Still, I'm pretty sure the girl saw me.

I got ready and waited, and when it was time to meet Vanessa, I left my room and followed her good directions to the science building. She wasn't there yet, even though I was about three minutes late, so I opened the door and waited just inside. I finally saw her coming toward me along the same path I had just taken. She was wearing black pants and a gray sweatshirt. Her blond hair was in a high ponytail pulled through the back of a bulldog cap. I was surprised to see her lack of color. As she got closer, I had the urge to leave through the back door, but I willed myself to stay put. I hadn't seen her since she left me in the airport. It hadn't really been that long when I thought about it, but it seemed like weeks—months, even. She saw me and started to wave. I waved back.

I waited inside, expecting her to come get me. But she sort of pointed toward the woods and headed there without stopping. I walked out and jogged to catch up. She did not slow down.

"Hey," I said. "Is there something wrong?"

"What? Why?" she asked, still moving toward the woods.

"Because you aren't very colorful," I said, smiling.

"No, I'm okay," she said, not smiling.

"Good, I'm glad," I said, waiting for her to look at me.

So I'd been right all along, she didn't want to be seen with me, and yet I couldn't take my eyes off her. She clearly had no makeup on, but her cheeks were red and her face was bright.

"Where do you run around here?" I asked.

"There's a path through the woods, up that hill over to the other side. Then you get to a road and can come back around, through the lower soccer field and up by the main entrance to the school. It's about five miles."

Five miles, I could do that.

"Are you ready?" she asked, like she was doing me a favor.

"Sure," I said.

At the entrance to the path, she took off. After a few steps I realized I hadn't taken the time to stretch. Maybe she had stretched before she met me, I didn't know. I hadn't taken a run in weeks, and I had been sitting around so much.

"Hey, Vanessa," I called.

She turned with a look on her face that said I was bothering her.

"You asked me to come," I said. "Why are you acting like you didn't?"

Something shifted in her face.

"Do you mind if I stretch?" I asked. "I didn't realize we were in such a rush."

"Sorry," she said. "There's a spot at the beginning of the path. Follow me."

I walked behind her into the woods until we reached a clearing with a bunch of trees and logs at different levels that looked perfect for stretching. I went through my usual routine, but my eyes were already stinging. I shielded them for a minute, hoping it would be less bright as we got deeper into the woods.

"I stretched already," she offered, her voice much softer now.

"Okay, I'm ready," I said.

She looked behind me, down toward the campus, and then back at me.

"Let's go," she said.

I followed her. The path was too narrow for us to run side by side, so I ran behind her. I didn't mind that; I could hear her steady breath and could smell her soap or shampoo—something lemony and fresh. But as we got deeper into the woods, the path opened up and I came up next to her, relieved that I hadn't gotten totally out of shape in the last few weeks. I was pretty sure I could keep up, and so far my breathing was steady too.

"So that boyfriend of yours is really nice," I said.

"Yeah, he told me he met you," she said, her eyes focused on the path ahead. Luckily the tree cover was very heavy and the clouds had gotten a bit thicker, so my eyes were okay. I remember thinking that I had definitely made the right decision about my glasses.

"A real charmer," I said.

"Well, what do you expect?" she said. "He's a little possessive."

"A little?" I asked.

She looked at me out of the corner of her eye and then back to the path but didn't say anything.

"Why didn't you ask him to run with you?" I asked.

"Patrick is a bit competitive," she said. "He likes to see who can run faster. It's no fun."

"How do you know I'm not competitive?" I asked.

"Just a hunch," she said, turning her head and smiling at me.

"Well, what about your friends? Why didn't you ask them?"

"Usually I run with Celia, a girl on my floor, but she didn't feel well this morning," Vanessa said. "But I had to get out, and, like I told you, there's a policy that we can't run alone in the woods."

"Why?"

"Years ago," she said, "a girl broke her ankle and couldn't get back. She spent the night in the woods, and nobody even knew where she was. They did a big search but must have missed her. Finally, at, like, dinnertime the next night, she crawled out of the woods. She was so traumatized, she left school and never came back. Rumor is that her family sued the school for a pretty penny. Anyway, maybe that's a made-up story, but coach tells it every year. Legend has it that she put a curse on the school that every year a senior would leave for some unforeseen reason—drugs, failing, sickness, whatever. I looked it up recently in the archives of the school paper, and it seemed to be true for as far back as I could find. That's weird, don't you think?"

"Very," I said. To be perfectly honest, it gave me the creeps.

We were quiet for a minute, and I started to wonder how far we had gone. I hadn't realized how much wilderness was behind the school.

"That's the sledding hill," she said finally. "On really

snowy days, we come here. See how there are no trees right there? It's like a chute. Really fast. We haven't done it yet this year, but last year we did it twice."

"Is that allowed?" I asked.

"Not really, but that's part of the fun," she said, smiling.

We ran into a small field and the sun came out. I felt like I had been hit in the face with hot lava. Without thinking, I covered my eyes with my hands and bent forward, but I lost my balance and fell to the ground. Once I got up and turned away from the sun, I slowly opened my eyes. It took a few tries, but I was finally able to do it.

"Are you okay?" Vanessa asked, putting her warm hand on my shoulder. For a brief moment her hand was all I felt, but the pain in my eyes slowly crept back in.

"What's wrong?" she asked again.

"Oh, I, um, I get migraines, and I suddenly feel one coming on," I said quickly. I didn't want to tell her about my eyes. "It happens sometimes. I think I'm going to have to go back the way I came."

"Actually, the road is just up there. It might be closer to continue on," she said, feeling around in her pockets. "I don't have my cell phone with me. Shoot, I left it charging on my desk. Do you have yours?"

"No," I said. It hadn't even occurred to me to bring it.

"Sorry about this," I said. "I might not have the strongest constitution, but at least I'm charming."

She smiled and came closer to where I was standing. I looked behind us into the woods. It was brighter than it had been before, but I wanted to get back there; it was certainly dimmer than the open field and the road ahead. I saw a big rock and dragged myself over and sat with my face in my hands. She followed.

"Are you going to be able to make it back?" she asked. She seemed nervous.

"Yeah, sure, just give me a minute," I said. I felt like such an idiot. Why couldn't I just be normal?

Vanessa sat down on the rock next to me and started to rub my back. The pain was slowly subsiding, but I didn't dare uncover my eyes.

"So I lied to you," she said.

Without thinking, I looked right at her and the sun and then groaned, putting my hands back over my face.

"What do you mean?" I asked. My voice sounded muffled, but I was afraid to move again. I was starting to wonder how I was ever going to get out of there. Maybe I would be that girl—the example of why not to go into the woods alone— dragging myself back to campus for twenty hours, being traumatized, my life as I knew it over. Maybe *I* was going to be the victim of the curse that year.

"Well, it's true that we aren't supposed to run alone in the woods, but we aren't supposed to run in the woods with a boy either," she said. "The track team runs this path together, and sometimes a teacher will organize a morning hike, but this—what we're doing now—this is forbidden."

"Huh," I said, feeling a little flutter in my stomach. I should have been mad—I mean, she had lied to me and in theory I could be facing a lot of trouble, but the truth was, I liked it. . . . I really liked it.

"And I'm sorry about back there, when we first met," she said. "I was nervous about getting caught."

I wanted to thank her for lying, and tell her that I was nervous too, not so much about getting caught, just about being with her. But something made me hold back.

"Thanks for sending the note," I said. "But why didn't you wait until you saw me in the dining hall, or the library?"

"Patrick" was all she said. Though of course it wasn't really just Patrick, it was everyone—all her friends. She didn't want them to see her talking to me. Suddenly I knew Kyle must not figure too prominently in the social order or she never would have asked him to deliver the note. He probably wasn't the first boy she saw. He was probably the first boy she saw who didn't matter.

"I thought once I got back to school that I wouldn't think about you," she said. "But I *have* been thinking about you. I worried about you the whole way back."

"I can take care of myself," I said quickly.

"No, I don't mean that something might happen to you; I mean that I kept wondering why you didn't tell me you were coming here," she said. "And then I thought once I saw Patrick, everything would go back to normal, but . . ." Her voice trailed off. "So far it hasn't."

I felt another sharp pain and covered my eyes, pushing the palms of my hands into my closed eye sockets to counter the discomfort. At that moment, I was glad I couldn't look at her.

"So," she said. "What should we do?"

"I don't know," I mumbled. "Try to forget about the airport. I mean, the elevator."

She laughed, and somehow the sound shot relief through my head.

"No, I don't mean what should we do about that! I mean, what should we do about getting back?" she said.

I hadn't yet dared try to look up again, but I would have bet money that she was still smiling when she said that. I could hear it.

"Oh, I don't know. I think I'm starting to feel better," I said.

"How long have you had this?"

I was confused for a minute, but then I remembered what I had told her. Migraines.

"A few years," I said.

"That must be hard," she said. "I'm sorry you have to deal with that."

"Thanks."

"So, should I help you up?" she asked.

"I think I just need another minute," I said. I was much better but knew I would be hit again once I opened my eyes. *I deserved this*, I kept thinking. *I did this to myself.*

"I'm sorry Patrick was so mean to you this morning. He can be such a jerk," Vanessa said, taking me by surprise. "I told him about meeting you in the airport because I figured that was the best thing to do. Plus, I thought it might make me feel better. But he's being so aggressive lately, I can barely stand it. He told me he had a little fun with you."

"Huh," I said, not wanting to make her lose her train of thought.

"Last year was great. I mean, he was sweet and romantic, and I felt so lucky that he wanted to be my boyfriend," she said. "We spent every second we could together. Then his mother died. It was awful. I went home with him and then came back. He took a few weeks off from school, and then he came back too. At first, it seemed like he was going to be sad but nothing else. But he's been different. Angry. He started talking about going to college together. The thing is, his grades aren't as good as mine are, so that means either I will have to try for a less competitive school, which I don't really want to do, or we will have to find a big university that might have programs for both of us, like an honors program for me but a regular one for him."

"Did you find any?" I asked. I wanted her to keep talking.

"Some, but I still feel like I'm limiting myself. You know, I'd had a crush on him since ninth grade, and he never seemed too interested—in me, that is," she said. "He was plenty interested in the girls who were willing to do whatever he wanted. So when he wanted to be with me, I mean, I couldn't believe it. I was so happy. Did I tell you he's from Vermont? His dad still lives there. So all the colleges we've applied to are within an eight-hour drive of Vermont. I let him think I wanted this. I *did* want this when we started working on the applications, but now it seems like . . . Well, it seems so stifling. I'm rambling. I'll stop now, and you probably don't want to hear about this anyway. Sorry," she said.

As she had been talking, I slowly removed my hands from my face and opened my eyes. It was okay, I could stand it, though I couldn't wait to get back and make my room as dark as I could. I planned to sleep for the rest of the day.

"No, I'm interested," I said. She turned, and when she saw that my eyes were open again, she gave me a dazzling smile. I smiled back.

"Oh no, I'm just babbling. I'll tell you more later," she said. "What about you? Are you happy to be here?"

That was such a hard question. Now everything about the place was Vanessa—and when I say her name here, I am saying it in capital letters, the way she typed it into my phone. Attracting Vanessa and avoiding Patrick. Somehow I didn't expect to be so personally involved in anything this fast, or ever.

"Yeah, I'm happy to be here," I said. "Anything would be better than my last school."

"Why did you come anyway?" she asked. "I mean, why now? Why Irving?"

I wanted her to know everything. I did. But there was so much to say, and, really, I didn't want to have to actually state the obvious: that I couldn't fit in.

"My new stepfather went to Irving. He says it was the best time he ever had—until he met my mom, that is. And he's really good friends with Mr. Bowersox," I said. "He thought a little time at Irving would be better than no time here. Plus, he and my mom were moving, so it seemed like a good idea."

We were quiet for a minute. I am pretty sure she was waiting for me to talk more. When I didn't, she asked if we should head back.

"Can we walk?" I asked, calculating that that would take longer than running so it would give us more time together. At least I could make something work in my favor. The image of Vanessa in the hotel lobby popped into my mind after she recited the quote from *Macbeth*—something bad and something good.

"No problem," she said, getting up and brushing off her pants. She reached her hand out for me and I stood up slowly. We walked most of the way back in silence.

When we got close to the science building, Vanessa stiffened.

"You go ahead," she said, her voice back to how it was

when she first met me. "I can cut through there and come out by the back of the dining hall. Will you be okay?"

"Fine," I said a little coldly. How did she turn on and off like that? I felt like she was dismissing me. After everything she had just said, everything she'd shared, I had an urge to grab her and pull her toward me—maybe not kiss her, but connect with her physically somehow. But I think you're starting to understand, that is not usually my style. So I didn't.

"Okay," she said, turning. Then she faced me again. "What will you say if anyone asks where you've been?"

"That I went out for a walk in the woods," I said, looking her right in the eyes. "Alone."

"But it's against the rules, I told you—"

"Nobody has told me the rules yet," I cut her off. "So I can play dumb." I left out that I imagined they would feel sorry for the albino kid with the bad eyes and the bad headache, and I would probably get away with it—I usually did.

She grabbed my arm then, and I thought she was going to say something important.

"Maybe you should do something crazy before you're told the rules" was what she said. *Something crazy?*

She dropped my arm and moved gracefully around a cluster of trees and headed in another direction. As I watched her go, I wondered what she meant by *do something crazy*. Did she mean with her? Once she was out of sight, I followed the path up and around and walked back to my room. Nobody stopped me to ask where I had been or why I was late. I didn't have classes that day—the normal schedule still wasn't in place—so I went to my room and got right into bed, where I slept the afternoon away. Every now and then, I got a sharp pain in my eye that woke me, and each time it drew me away from a dream that was too good to be true.

CHAPTER FIFTEEN

DUCAN

MAYBE THIS WOULD BE HIS TURN . . .
IF HE DIDN'T KEEP SCREWING IT UP

Duncan lay on his bed wondering along with Tim what Vanessa had meant by *do something crazy*. He knew that trail in the woods too well, and he really didn't want to think about it, but he couldn't help it. It had been so snowy. He was among the handful of juniors who were allowed to come. There had been so much drinking. Duncan knew he shouldn't drink; it was so dark and slippery. He was a wimp and he knew it, but he didn't want anyone else to know. He accepted a paper cup full of scotch, or maybe it was bourbon, and made the motions of bringing it to his mouth and swallowing. When no one was looking, he poured a little into the snow and covered it up, worrying that the strong smell escaping into the air would give him away.

They were all getting ready to sled. He was scared. There were trees at the bottom, despite what anyone said, he could see that. Students from the Irving School had been doing it for years, they kept saying. They hadn't lost one yet.

When Duncan's cell phone rang, he had that awful feeling of being awakened from a bad dream. He had been trying hard not to think about that night—he hated thinking about it now. He found his phone. He didn't recognize the number but didn't care. He was desperate now for a distraction.

"Hello?" He knew he sounded groggy. He glanced at his digital clock—four-forty-five in the afternoon. That was embarrassing.

"It's Daisy."

He sat up so fast he felt dizzy and had to lie down again.

"Daisy, hi, where are you?"

"Listen, Justine told me you were looking for me."

"I was," he said. "I was worried."

"Well, don't worry so much, I'm okay," she said. He could hear beeping and something over a loudspeaker behind her. He imagined her in a hospital bed hooked up to an IV like he had been once after he got his tonsils out.

"Are you in the hospital?" he asked. He couldn't believe that he was talking to her, that she had called him.

"I'm at the hospital," she said flatly. "Not in it."

"Oh. Good," he said, louder than he needed to. "That's a relief."

They were quiet for a minute.

"Why are you there?" he asked. "Can I come help you or anything?"

"It's been such a long day," she said.

"Can you tell me about it?" he asked. "And I'm sorry I didn't let you in this morning. Did that have anything to do with why you're at the hospital now?"

She hesitated. "It might have made a difference," she said, a little coldly. He deserved it, he knew. But she had called him! Maybe he could help now.

"The minute you walked away, I tried to get you to come back," he said, not caring how silly or desperate that sounded. "I wish I could do that over again."

"I came by this morning to ask for your help. Amanda—You know her, right? She lives next to me. She's the quiet one with the bright blue streak of hair?"

Daisy waited for Duncan to acknowledge that he knew her, but he could not conjure up an image of her. Blue hair, Amanda—none of that rang a bell.

"Sure," he said. "I think I know who she is."

"Well, she was sick this morning, but she didn't want to go to the nurse and she was panicked about anyone finding out, even Mrs. Reilly on our floor. I told her Mrs. Reilly has seen it all—drinking, drugs, whatever—and she always helps. But Amanda insisted that after she helps, she gets mad or the student gets in trouble, and besides, school just started and she kept saying she didn't want to cause a problem so early in the year. She was fading fast, slurring her words. I knocked on everyone's door, but people were at breakfast or in the shower. So I ran over to you. But when you wouldn't let me in, I didn't want to risk bumping into Mr. Simon, so I left."

"Back up a minute," Duncan said. "Why were you at the exit door before you came to my room?"

"So you did see me," she said. "I thought you must have."

"Sorry," he said.

"I wanted to see if it was cold out, and it was, so that's why I knocked on your door. I thought that together we could get her to that door, that a little fresh air might help. But that was a crazy idea anyway, she never would have let us."

"So then what?" Duncan prompted her.

"I went back to my hall."

"I don't get it," he said. "I saw you in class."

"I know," she said. "When I got back, she had gotten into bed and was sleeping. So I thought she'd be okay. I pulled a blanket over her and got her some water that I left next to her bed and I went to class. That's why I was late."

"I feel terrible about that," he said. "Your being late, I mean."

"I do too," she said. "Anyway, after English, people started saying that they hadn't heard from her and that she wasn't answering her door. I said she was sick and probably sleeping. But I got worried. So I went in—even though you aren't supposed to do that without permission. And she was passed out. I tried over and over to wake her, but she wouldn't wake up. I thought she might be in a coma or something, so I went and got Mrs. Reilly after all. She called an ambulance, and I felt so guilty for leaving her that I came along, so I'm still here."

"Is she okay?" Duncan asked.

"Well, apparently, she took too many of her mother's Xanax that she stole from her medicine cabinet at home. She was so stressed about school starting that she took like half a dozen of them or something. They pumped her stomach, but she seems okay. I think she's spending the night here."

They were quiet again. Duncan thought of Vanessa and Tim sitting on the rock.

"So, why did you call?" he finally asked. It sounded a little snotty, and he hadn't meant it to at all. "I mean, can I help you in some way? I would really like to help you."

"I called because Justine said you looked pathetic," she said. "And it was a hard day, and I wanted to talk to someone."

"Let me make it up to you, for everything—not letting you in this morning, not calling you all summer," he said. "Please."

She hesitated. He clenched his eyes shut and waited.

"I'm going to take the bus back to town. I guess you could meet me," she said. It was another senior privilege that once a week, with permission, you were allowed to skip dinner at school and go into town. It was within walking distance of the campus, just down a big hill with the Hudson River in view the whole time. It would have been easy to say no, to hide in his room and see what happened next with Tim. But he was still bothered by that mention of the rock in the woods, and he didn't want to be like Tim, missing an opportunity to be with the girl he liked.

"Yes, definitely," he said. "I'll go sign out with Mr. Simon, and I'll call you back. Should we meet at Sal's Pizza in half an hour?"

"Sounds great," she said. "I'll just browse the bookstore in the meantime."

Duncan found Mr. Simon in the dining hall.

"How goes it?" he asked as Duncan approached him.

"Pretty good . . . No, great," he said, smiling. "I know it's early in the year, but I wanted to see if I could skip dinner tonight and head into town?"

"What is the purpose of your odyssey?" Mr. Simon asked, and Duncan smiled. A guy could get smarter just standing near Mr. Simon. He considered his question. There was a lot he could say—he needed socks, he craved pizza, he needed batteries.

"I want to meet Daisy," he said. "I don't know if you heard about Amanda—"

"I heard," Mr. Simon said, cutting him off. "I hear she's resting comfortably."

"Yes, that's what Daisy said," Duncan said. "But Daisy

was at the hospital all day, and she's hungry and tired and asked if I could meet her. What do you think?"

"You are the second senior boy to take advantage of the privilege tonight, so I say, 'Better three hours too soon than a minute too late.'"

Duncan just stood there looking at him.

Mr. Simon grinned. "That means go!"

"Thank you," Duncan said. "Really, thanks a lot."

Duncan pulled out his phone and texted Daisy as he walked out under the stone arch—thinking to himself *Enter Here to Find a Girlfriend.* Maybe this would be his turn . . . if he didn't keep screwing it up.

It was a beautiful September night, and the tips of the trees were just starting to turn yellow. The air was crisp, and he stopped to take a deep breath. Then he walked down the winding campus road to the main one and headed into town.

Daisy wasn't sitting in Sal's as he walked by. The best pizza in the state of New York, they always said, though as good as it was, everybody knew that wasn't quite true with all the pizzerias in the Bronx and Brooklyn and Lower Manhattan. But it was their favorite, hands down. There was just something about the thin crust, the perfect sauce, and the cheese. His mouth watered, but he kept walking to the small bookstore on the corner. He found her there, sitting in a big fluffy chair reading *A Thousand Acres.*

"Hi!" she said when she saw him, smiling.

"Hi!" he responded, feeling like he had been on a long journey and this was the place he had been trying to reach. He sat down on the chair next to her.

"What are you reading?"

"Oh, it's great," she said, sitting up a little. "It's Jane Smiley's version of *King Lear*. Mr. Simon told me I could read this or Shakespeare's version, so I picked this."

"When did he tell you that?" Duncan asked. "I don't remember hearing him say anything like that."

"I went to see him after class, even though he hates excuses of any kind," she said. "I mean, I could tell him that I had been sick and unable to lift my head for three days and he would say, *Well, that shouldn't stop you from reading or crawling to class!*"

Duncan laughed. "Yeah, that's true," he said. "But then he comes through somehow."

"So I told him about Amanda—that was before I knew what was really wrong with her and that the saga wasn't over yet—and he said I could read this or the play to make up for being late, and to think about it in terms of a tragedy, of course. This looks like it's going to be a really good book."

"Are you hungry?" Duncan asked.

"Starving!" she said, closing the book. "I barely ate anything at the hospital. It's true what they say about food there. Just let me buy this."

Duncan followed her to the register. He watched as Daisy pulled money from her small beaded purse. Her hands were so long and elegant. She had a tiny silver ring with a daisy blossom on her left pinky finger. When she caught him staring, he looked away.

"Do you need a bag?" the young man behind the counter asked.

"No thanks," she said, grabbing the book and tucking it under her arm.

They walked out together and without a word turned toward Sal's. They could smell the dough baking as they got close. Just as Daisy was about to reach out and open the door, he grabbed the elbow of her other arm.

"What? I thought we were eating here," she said.

"We are," he said. "But I want to do something else first."

She let him lead her around the corner and down a few blocks to the river. It was beautiful. The sun was setting and shining off the water, which was choppy because of the breeze. They could see the Palisades across the way. They kept walking, until they were as close as they could get to the river.

"I want to ask you something," he said, trying to keep his voice steady.

"Sure, anything," she said.

"Last year, in the dining hall, I just . . . Well, I have to ask, why were you suddenly so nice to me?"

She tilted her head to the side and looked right in his eyes. Her smile was big and open.

"Because you were nice to me," she said thoughtfully.

Okay, he told himself, maybe it could be that simple. He literally counted to three in his head—*One, two, three*—and then he took her soft face in his hands and leaned in to kiss her. She moved toward him, still smiling. He could hear cars driving by and the horn of what he guessed was a bus behind him. He could hear people talking and the last of the summer crickets chirping. But all he could feel were Daisy's lips, all he could smell was the scent of her skin, which was a cross between watermelon and vanilla, he thought. She was the first to pull away.

"What took you so long?" she asked, and the tone of her voice was so gentle and kind, he wanted to bury his face in her soft shoulder and stay there forever.

"Yeah," he said, smiling. "What took me so long?"

He grabbed her hand, wishing that they didn't have to eat and hurry back. They had an eight o'clock curfew, and if they missed it, this privilege would be taken away for the rest of the year. He didn't want that to happen, especially now.

"So who is Amanda again?" he asked.

"I knew you didn't know who I was talking about," she said, swatting him on the arm.

"I thought I knew all the seniors. I don't know why I can't picture her."

"Well, she was new last year," Daisy said. "And she *is* quiet. You know, she always wears straw hats and has the blue hair right here." She tugged the left side of her hair near her face.

"Oh, I know exactly who that is," he said. "You should have mentioned the straw hats sooner."

"Actually, I think more people wear straw hats than have blue hair," Daisy said. "I thought that would be enough to tip you off."

"Both my grandmothers have blue hair," Duncan said in his best fake-serious voice. "It isn't so special."

Daisy leaned her head into his chest and then turned it into a hug. Duncan couldn't believe it: somehow the hug felt even more intimate than the kiss.

"So, how was Amanda when you left?" he asked when he felt her start to pull away.

"Better," she said. "But I think she'll go home for a while. I heard her talking to her mom on the phone."

"That was nice of you," he said.

"Well, I don't know about that," Daisy said. "I shouldn't have let her sleep. I keep thinking, what if she'd taken more and she really had slipped into a coma? I mean, it could have been much worse." Daisy covered her face with her hands.

"Look, you did the best you could," Duncan said. "Sometimes that's all you can do."

"Since when do you have so much wisdom?" she asked as they approached Sal's.

He didn't answer. He hadn't meant it to sound that way. He, of all people, certainly didn't feel very wise. He reached for the door, but this time she stopped him. He looked at her.

"It's going to be different this time, right?" she asked.

He knew what she meant—of course he did. He also knew that a statement like that would have sent him running last year. It probably would have sent him running last week. There was so much he didn't trust about himself, and about depending on another person. But she was so soft and easy to be with. And she had every right to ask, he guessed. Still, he didn't know what to say.

"I mean, if we keep going with the same pattern, I'll see you again in December," she added.

He quickly calculated the timing. It *had* been three months, and, yes, it would be December in three more months. He was amazed that she had that information so available. It reminded him of Vanessa's thanking Tim for the last eighteen hours.

"Forget it," she finally said, and he realized he still hadn't responded to her.

"No, sorry, I was just thinking," he said. "I never meant for it to be so long. I thought about you—this summer.

A lot. I wondered what you were doing and if you were thinking about me." He could see her relax a little. "I want to see you, all the time. Would that be okay with you?"

"That would be great," she said.

CHAPTER SIXTEEN

TIM

WAS THIS THE ORDER OR THE CHAOS?

When Duncan returned to his room, he thought he would skip the CDs. He got ready for bed, read a little, and turned out the light. But he couldn't stand it. He wanted to lie there thinking about Daisy, but his mind constantly drifted back to Tim and Vanessa. He switched the light on again and slipped in the earbuds. His laptop was next to his bed. Then he closed his eyes and listened.

I'm not sure how much, if any, of this you might remember, or if you were paying attention to me at all, but it took about a week before people stopped looking at me like I was an alien. Most of you were actually quite subtle. You had been taught, I am sure, that it isn't polite to stare. But none of you were very good at it. You would keep your eyes down and then look up at the last minute, or pretend to be looking at something over my shoulder. Not you, specifically—I don't have any memory of you then—but everyone in general.

I tried to ignore it and jump into my classes, which, I have to say, I liked even better than I'd thought I would. I worried that despite what Sid had told me, the teachers would be uptight and the subjects would be boring, but that wasn't the case at all; it was the exact opposite. And then suddenly people seemed to be used to me.

I said I was focusing on my classes. That was really just another escape from something else: Vanessa. I began to settle into a routine. I went to classes and meals, and I overheard a lot of talk about the Game and what it should be. I started to wonder if there would ever be a decision made—or if they all just liked to talk about it and throw ideas around without ever settling on anything.

At first I was thrilled to find that Vanessa was in a few of my classes, including senior English. But after I spent the first two classes being completely distracted by her, I started to think it might not have been such good luck and forced myself to focus. It was during the third class that Mr. Simon started talking about the Tragedy Paper.

I knew about it, of course, because Mr. Bowersox had mentioned it to me in the car after he picked me up, and I had heard other students talking about it. But on that particular Thursday morning, Mr. Simon entered the classroom, stood up on a desk, and waited for the class to settle down. Has he ever done this in your class? I wonder if he does the same things every year.

Vanessa took a seat off to my right, and at the last minute Patrick swooped in next to her.

"Tragedy," Mr. Simon said loudly, and everyone groaned. He looked around the room, then rested his eyes on me. "Unfortunately for you, Mr. Macbeth, you do not have the benefit of having spent the first semester getting ready for this, the most important assignment of your young life to date."

A few people giggled; there were also a few snickers.

"Though with your name I would guess you are quite familiar with the subject of Shakespeare," he said.

Vanessa looked at me and smiled, and suddenly I was once again back at the airport hotel at the moment my life started to change.

"Would anyone here like to help bring Mr. Macbeth up to speed?" Mr. Simon asked, pulling me back to English class.

Apparently, nobody did.

"How about you, Mr. Hopkins?" Mr. Simon said. Patrick, who had been leaning over and writing something on a paper on Vanessa's desk, looked up, caught.

"Tragedy?" he said, his voice unsure. Mr. Simon nodded, and Patrick cleared his throat.

"Well," said Patrick, sitting up straight. "A tragedy is a

play or literary work in which the main character—that would be the tragic hero—suffers greatly and is brought to ruin. Usually this suffering and ruin come about because of the main character's own flaw or weakness and his or her inability to deal with the lot he or she has been given."

Patrick smiled the smuggest smile I have ever seen. I wanted to stare him down, but I couldn't. I looked at the ground, not sure why what he had said felt so personal. We were talking about plays written hundreds of years ago, weren't we?

"Very good, Patrick," Mr. Simon said, getting down off the desk and standing in front of it with his arms crossed over his chest. "Now, if you could please stop bothering your neighbor, we will get on with it."

Mr. Simon spent the rest of the period talking about the logistics of the paper, how long it should be, how it should be structured. He dismissed us with an assignment to begin thinking about the introduction and an outline. And then, "Go forth and spread beauty and light."

As we walked out the door, Patrick bumped me. His head was turned so it seemed like he didn't realize I was there, and then he stuck his elbow out and got me in the side.

I figured that was just how it was going to be. So it totally surprised me that the next time I saw Patrick, he was nice to me. But I still didn't trust him. I guess I never did. I noticed the way his face looked when he turned away from me. And I saw him with Vanessa everywhere—in the dining hall, on the quad, walking to class. But here is the strange part: somehow she always managed to find me at some point during the day—she must have known when Patrick would be out of sight—and she would make eye contact, or touch my arm gently. It was so subtle, and she was so good at it, like a fairy swooping in or a raindrop finding its way into a small space. She might pass me six times in a day and most of those times it was almost like she didn't know me, and then there would be that one time. I never knew when it would be, but I started to crave it. I realized pretty quickly, though, that I was making no effort to get to know anyone else. After that first week or so, people were nice enough to me, but honestly, I didn't care. It surprised me because that was all I wanted leading into my time there—to have a few friends and have a good time. But for me, even at that point, it had become all about Vanessa. And believe me, it wasn't always a pleasure when I did see her.

One day I was walking into the dorm and I saw Vanessa and Patrick talking, leaning against the doorway below the arch. He was facing me, her back was to me. As soon as he saw me approach, though he didn't meet my eyes, he leaned into her and started kissing her aggressively. I wasn't close enough to see her reaction, but I couldn't believe it. They were in public—anyone could have walked by. She was making tiny sounds. It was impossible to know if they were because she was happy or uncomfortable. I wanted to rip my ears off so I wouldn't be able to hear them. Patrick was moving his hands just underneath Vanessa's shirt. And then, as I walked through the door, she opened her eyes and looked at me. Her stare lasted long enough that I thought her eyes were saying she was sorry. Maybe that was just in my head; maybe that was what I wanted her to be thinking more than anything. But when Patrick nudged her, she closed her eyes again, and Patrick moved right back in, tightening his grip on her back. I forced myself to keep walking. I couldn't help myself—I looked back, and Patrick had stopped kissing her. He was looking right at me, smiling.

A few days later, on one particularly rainy afternoon when everyone was sitting around the halls with nowhere to go, she came up close to me, standing beside me as I sat on the floor with my back against the wall, and reached for something on the windowsill above my head. As she moved back, she brushed my hair gently, lingering for a minute, and then she was gone. I hadn't talked to her since I saw Patrick kissing her, and I wanted to be angry, but I reveled in her touch. Another time in the line at lunch—we were having macaroni and cheese that day made with local cheese from a self-sustaining farm in Pocantico Hills and the best fresh bread crumbs from a bakery in the Bronx— she somehow cut in behind me, and I didn't even know she was there until she moved her body up against mine. If I didn't know better, I could have mistaken it for a small push from someone behind her that made her get so close to me. But I was starting to know better.

And then things changed again and she started saying things to me, cryptic messages that I couldn't make any sense of, when we walked by each other.

"It's supposed to snow tonight," she said once as she moved by me in the main hallway.

"They're serving meatballs for dinner, Mr. Bowersox's mother's recipe," she said another time. "There'll be fresh Parmesan cheese on the condiments table, I hear."

Everything was so quiet, so impersonal, that it could have been missed or easily meant for another person. Even the brushes against me could have been taken as unintentional, a simple mistake. Or even a gesture of pity. Whatever they were, I started to look forward to them. They were always different and became my favorite moments of the day. I would go over and over them in my head, daydreaming in class, thinking about them as I fell asleep at night, always later than the other students because, as Mr. Simon had promised, I was never asked to turn out the lights at the specified time. I would leave them on, stare at the ceiling, and remember how green her eyes looked that day, or how soft her hand felt on my forearm, or how sweet her voice sounded when she talked about the weather or dinner or a book that was now available at the library.

It was during that time that I really started to shut out

my mother and Sid. I still don't know why. They had been so supportive, and so interested in how I was doing. We had set up a schedule to Skype once a week, and at first I looked forward to it. The first few weeks I used my microphone to record my voice, telling them about my schedule, my classes, what I was reading. Once I even took it along with my laptop to the dining hall so they could hear the deafening noise. Then I would burn all of it onto CDs, like I did for you, and send them to Italy. But then I stopped turning on my computer at the designated time, I never bothered to call them back, and I stopped making the CDs. My mom sent me worried emails, but I just didn't care. I could feel myself going into a cocoon, concerned that I might throw off the balance of the strange universe I was living in if I opened up to them. I didn't want them to know anything about it.

I started waiting for Vanessa to give me more, to ask me to go for another run, or to meet her somewhere. Sometimes I wondered what would happen if I asked her to join me for something. I would conjure up a scenario: Would she like to come into town with me to buy new running shoes? Or would she help me with a science project that required a partner? Sometimes I went for a run, even through the forbidden forest, with the hope of bumping into her. But I never did, and every time I almost had the nerve to ask her to do something with me, I would see her again with Patrick. They looked happy, holding hands or kissing when they thought no teachers were looking. So I didn't dare—I waited for her to come to me. I told myself that a few seconds a day were enough for me. And surely she would want to talk to me again at some point. But weeks went by and she didn't. You might want to ask yourself—was this the order or the chaos? I know what it was for me.

And then one day in February, she found me in the library. When I looked back, I realized that she had passed me that morning and muttered something about a new novel based on the *Odyssey* that was now available and could be signed out at the main desk. As usual, I enjoyed every second of her attention but didn't think anything more about it. It just so happened that that afternoon all the desks in the Hall were taken, so I ducked into the library, happy to have some quiet time where I could hide behind a book display.

Then suddenly she was standing next to me.

"Did you see the book?" she asked.

I had no idea what she was talking about.

"What book?"

"The one based on the *Odyssey*?" she asked. "The one I mentioned this morning."

"Oh no," I said. "I've done a lot of math homework, though."

My eyes had been giving me trouble lately. Sometimes they focused and sometimes they didn't, and I wasted a lot of time waiting for them to let me read or see the numbers on the page. On that particular day, my eyesight was so clear, and I honestly didn't want to waste any time. I wanted to enjoy it.

So when she asked me to take a walk with her, the thing I had most wanted for weeks now, I actually hesitated. I wasn't sure how my eyes would be in fifteen minutes, let alone after I got up, went outside, and then came back in. Why was she daring to do this now?

To be truthful—and I feel I need to be here—something had shifted for me. I had built up every gesture in my mind to mean so much, and I was now sure she had feelings for me. The reason she wasn't more open about it, I told myself, was because she didn't know how to get away from Patrick. I also imagined that, despite her feelings for me, she wasn't quite ready to face the humiliation of being seen with me in public. I was pretty sure people had gotten used to me—I rarely encountered one of those shocked expressions as I walked toward someone—but that didn't change anything. Patrick was tall and handsome with perfect skin. Everyone liked him, and people expected to see Vanessa with someone like that. That was the right world order (or should I say chaos?) at the Irving School.

Still, there was something.

That day in the library, I got up and followed her outside. It was windy and freezing. The sky was gray, and I was glad because the light was less harsh. She didn't stop but kept walking down toward the athletic field. I followed her even though I didn't have my coat. Of course I didn't have my glasses; I hadn't touched them in weeks.

She stopped behind the gym. She was wearing a lavender ski jacket and jeans. Her blond hair was down and was blowing everywhere—in her face, in my face. She kept trying to push it over her shoulders.

"Hi," she finally said.

"Hi," I said back.

"You never meet me when I ask you to," she said, her lower lip sticking out in a bit of a pout. There was some hair stuck to her upper lip, and I reached over and gently brushed it away.

"What are you talking about?" I said. My voice was gravelly. I cleared my throat, knowing I didn't talk enough during the day. I didn't have that many people to talk to—which, I will say now, was probably my own fault.

"Well, I say there's a book available in the library, then I go to the library and wait but you never come," she said. The wind was picking up, I could hear it moving through the treetops. "Or that time I told you about the meatballs and the Parmesan cheese at the condiments table, I wanted you to meet me at the condiments table!"

"How was I supposed to know?"

"Because I was giving you clues," she said, clearly exasperated. "I was trying to be clever."

A branch snapped above us and fell to the ground a few feet away. Vanessa jumped, then reached out and grabbed my wrist. It was like a tiny bolt of lightning ran up my arm. Then she pulled her hand back and shook her head.

"Sometimes I wish something would happen to me, like I would get hit on the head with a branch and then I wouldn't have to deal with any of this," she said.

"What are you talking about?" I asked. I was aware of my voice. It was confident and strong. I was still the same as far as the other kids went, but I knew I could be myself with Vanessa. It was such a strange feeling. I actually liked the way I sounded when I talked to her.

"You know, I told you, the whole college thing," she said. "Hey, have you heard about colleges? I never even asked you."

"I'm going to Northwestern," I said. "I got in early."

"Oh, cool," she said. "Right, 'cause you're from Chicago."

After she said that, she smiled a brilliant smile, and so did I. Like we were sharing an inside joke about Chicago and the airport.

"Well, yeah, but it's also a good school," I said. "And, actually, well, you know, my parents don't even live there anymore, so it has nothing to do with being from there. Except that my stepdad went there, and that helped me get in."

"Are you excited?" she asked. She was standing on the hill, twisting a long strand of blond hair around her finger by the left side of her head, with the most serious look on her face.

"Do you want to be a reporter or something?" I asked. "What? Why?"

"I don't know," I said. "Suddenly you're asking a lot of questions."

Two teachers walked by us at that moment and nodded in our direction. I think it made Vanessa nervous because she started to look around. Then she pointed to another spot up the hill but behind the chapel. It was that really pretty spot—you've probably walked by it a zillion times—that gave the illusion of being out of the way even though it wasn't really. You know, where that iron bench is? It was a gift from one graduating class or another. She sat down on it, so I sat down next to her.

"I feel trapped," she said. Then she looked at me. "I can't think of how to get out of this. I mean, if Patrick was simply being his usually pushy self, it would be one thing. But his mother just *died*. There's no way I can hurt him right now. I've tried a few times, and I honestly can't make the words come out of my mouth."

I didn't say anything. As I often felt with her, I was afraid she would disappear, vanish.

"Don't get me wrong," she said. "There are times I like being with Patrick. He can be very sweet when he wants to be."

I snickered and she swatted me on the arm.

"If it was just a matter of getting through to the end of the year, to graduation, I could do that, no problem. But four more years? I was hoping that the college thing would work itself out. That we would try to do what I told you. Do you remember?"

"Yes, yes, I remember," I said.

"So I figured we would try that, but in the back of my mind, I hoped it wouldn't work out—that we wouldn't get into the same school or even schools in the same city."

"What did happen?" I asked.

"Well, it turns out we both got into schools in New York."

"The same school?"

"No, but the same city."

"New York is big," I said, though I had very little actual experience with New York City. Still, you would have to live under a rock not to know that someone could get lost in a place like that.

"Now I worry it isn't big enough. I mean, I'll be uptown and he'll be downtown, but he's already talking about sharing an apartment somewhere in the middle," she said. "How did I get myself into this?"

"Just get yourself out," I said. "Is that the only school you got into?"

Her eyes lit up for a minute, and she smiled. And then she reached her hand across the bench and rested it on my thigh. It felt like a burning rock there. Everything around me stopped, and her hand on my leg was all that I could think about, all that I was aware of. She leaned over, kissed me on the cheek, and then she was gone.

I sat there for a long time. Feeling that kiss, wanting more, wanting Vanessa, wanting to be like Patrick, not wanting to be this lost-in-love albino whose eyes were getting worse by the day. I went back to the library and put my head down on the paper and went through every minute of what had just happened, wishing I could do it all over again, wondering when I would talk to her next.

At dinner that night I saw her sitting with Patrick looking as happy as anyone could look. There were no traces of wishing she could be somewhere else or feeling trapped—at least none that she gave away. I had taken to eating by myself at a round table in the back. On occasion one misfit or another would join me, and I was always open to that. But on this night nobody did; so as I spooned nutmeg-laced butternut squash soup into my mouth, I watched Vanessa and Patrick thumb-wrestle and laugh, and at one point, I think they were singing a song together. I lost my appetite quickly and headed back to my room.

The next morning Patrick cornered me in the bathroom again. I know I promised I wouldn't talk about the bathroom too much, but this one is important too, so bear with me.

As you can imagine, I immediately thought I was in for it, that he or someone else had spotted me with Vanessa the day before. I was at the sink trying to get the last of the toothpaste out of the tube, cursing myself for forgetting over and over to go to the school store when it was open, when I felt his hand on my shoulder. It wasn't just his hand, really; it was a tight grip like a claw. I jumped and my tube of toothpaste fell off the side of the sink into the garbage. He reached around me and pulled it out.

"Here you go," he said. I couldn't read his tone at all, but I anticipated the worst. "Sorry about that."

I took the tube from him, waiting for him to do something awful to me, but he just unloaded his stuff at the sink next to me and went about his business. I could barely stand to touch the tube anymore since I imagined all those dirty tissues and whatever else had touched it. I threw it back in the trash. Patrick looked up at me. Then he handed me his tube.

"Here, use some of mine," he said. I would have thought it was poisoned or something, but he had just used a squeeze and at that moment was messily brushing his teeth, so I took the leap of faith and pushed some onto my brush. We stood there like that for a few minutes, brushing side by side, and I kept waiting for him to explode, or shove me into a stall and dunk my head in the toilet, or say how ugly he thought I was, but he didn't do any of those things. He just hummed to himself and brushed his teeth.

"So, I've been thinking," he said very seriously.

"Yeah?" I said back, thinking *Okay, finally, here it comes.*

"This is going to sound crazy. We've never done anything like this before, but how about instead of a game we have an outing?"

I looked at him like he had just suggested we paint the bathroom red.

"I mean, a really great outing. A secret outing. Something that we're all in on, that we plan together." He kept talking, but it started to sound like he was really talking to himself, working out the idea in his mind. "Something that Vanessa will love. What do you think?"

I had been staring at him the whole time, thinking how perfect his hair looked even though he probably hadn't brushed it yet, how perfect his face looked even though he had nothing to do with it—he didn't work hard to make his face look that way, to make the pigment be there in his skin—so why should his life be so much better than mine?

"Whatever you think," I said, turning to leave.

"No, I'm asking what *you* think," he said, and for the first time he sounded sincere, not like a cartoon character of a high school jock from one of my comic books. "And there's something else. I'm . . . Well, have you talked to Vanessa lately?"

Now he was going to give it to me, I thought. I waited.

"I mean, I can't talk to her friends, and I doubt she would ever want them to think things were anything but perfect between us. But I'm sensing something—not exactly that she's less into me, just something," he said. "I figured maybe . . . Since she probably doesn't care what you think of her and you're sort of like a friend to her, I wondered if she said anything about me."

"No, I barely talk to her," I said. "Besides, why would she tell me what she thinks about you?"

He nodded. "I guess you're right," he said. "Must be my imagination."

"Must be," I said. "You guys looked pretty cozy at dinner last night."

He nodded again. This time he was smiling. "You're right," he said. "I don't know what my problem is. Girls love me."

What did he mean "girls"? Did he think Vanessa was just any girl?

"So, what do you think about my idea?"

"What idea?" I said. I couldn't get past the fact that Patrick didn't see Vanessa as the most incredible, beautiful girl on campus.

"About an outing instead of a game," he said, clearly annoyed that I had forgotten about that important question. "People are depending on me."

"I think an outing is a great idea," I said. I had no clue at that moment, of course, what I had set in motion.

CHAPTER SEVENTEEN

TIM
THIS IS TOP-SECRET

Duncan knew what Tim had set in motion. Why couldn't there be a big flashing red light that goes off when someone makes a bad choice, or in this case, a disastrous choice? A warning or something telling you to go back and try again. It was so frustrating that he considered throwing the CDs out his little round window and never thinking of them again. He'd lived through it once, why was he doing this to himself? The last thing he needed was to go through it all again. But it was late and Daisy was asleep, so there was nothing to distract him. And he could hear Tim's gravelly voice thanking him for listening. He didn't want to let him down again. He had already done that.

. . .

Notices started to go up and then they came down. This was how it was done, I gathered. A quick hit of information and then it disappeared. Then there was another one, and then that disappeared. The thing was, they made no sense to me. There was always one word out of place, or one word missing. The first notice said GAME IS CALLED OUT, EVERYONE MUST PLAY, CALLING ALL SENIORS, STAY TUNED FOR . . .

It was posted in the hall and in the bathroom. I read it, but when I went back later to get a better look, sure that I had missed something, it was gone. I looked in the hall where it had been earlier that day, and that one was gone too.

Two days later another one appeared: GAME IS OUT COLD, WALK THERE FOR FUN, PLAY ONE AND ALL, BLANK WILL BE DONE.

By then I was intrigued. The word *out* appeared in both, so that must have been code for outing. But it seemed so obvious. If I could figure that out, couldn't the teachers? On the other hand, they hadn't been privy to my conversation with Patrick in the bathroom. Maybe an outing was unusual and they would never think of it.

And then one night Patrick knocked on my door.

"Hey," he said, standing there wearing a white T-shirt with small holes all over it, his jeans, and Black Watch plaid slippers. I did my best to keep my expression neutral. I had no idea what he might have wanted from me.

"Hey," I said back flatly.

"You busy?"

"Not really," I said, and then I thought I shouldn't have given myself away so quickly. What if I wanted an out?

"Good," he said. "I could use your help."

"Doing what?"

"Making the invitations," he said proudly.

"What invitations?"

"For the outing," he said. "It's all planned. I just have to let people know where and when."

It seemed so strange to me that he would ask me for help. I mean, what about all his buddies? That covered pretty much every other guy living on our floor.

"Is everyone helping?" I asked, trying to get a better sense of what was going on.

"No," he said. "I think we can do it, just us. I thought I'd give you a little insight into what it's like to be popular, since you probably have no idea."

Until he said that, I was fairly sure he was playing a trick on me. Maybe he was going to lure me to his room and then tar-and-feather me or something. But after that comment, I knew he was just being his petty self, and I had to admit it, I was curious. And a little bored. I hadn't run into Vanessa at all that day. "Where do you want to make them?" I asked.

"My room," he said, gesturing with his arm that I should follow him. "I have all the supplies. But if you have any markers, bring them, okay?"

"Sure," I said, leaning toward my desk and picking up a Ziploc bag full of colored markers. I also picked up the scissors just in case.

I followed Patrick down the hall to his room. I had looked in sometimes when I walked by and his door was open, but I had never actually been inside. He opened his door and held out his hand, letting me know I should go ahead. His room was so much bigger than mine. It might have been double the size, and I wondered if he had the biggest room on the floor. He had painted the far wall, the one his bed was against, a kelly green color. He had a plaid comforter on his bed to match and a plaid rug. And then I noticed the pictures. They were Scotch-taped to the walls: one of Vanessa in the dining hall laughing; one of her outside somewhere, maybe behind the school; one of her sipping a milkshake adorably while looking off to the side. Patrick watched me but didn't say a word. I wanted to pretend I didn't care, that I didn't even notice. On the lamp by his bed, there was a picture of the two of them together: he was tickling her and she was trying to fend him off, but she was smiling, and I knew her well enough to know it was a real smile. I looked at Patrick as though to say *What now?* As though I didn't feel like a heavy cloak of loneliness had just been thrown over me that was making it hard to breathe.

"Hey, you've got to see this one," Patrick said then, pulling open his closet door. On the back was a picture that had been blown up not quite to poster size but bigger than a magazine cover. Vanessa was posing in a green bikini, her body lean and beautiful. I noticed the curves of the cups of her bikini top.

"It's a good one, isn't it?" Patrick mocked me. "It was taken last spring, right after school ended, when she came to visit."

I wondered briefly if that was before or after his mother died. It must have been after. Maybe she was trying to make him feel better. Then I wondered if she knew about that picture and how big it was, or if Patrick kept it in the closet so she wouldn't see it. I looked at Patrick without expression; I didn't want to give him anything. But he knew. A slow smile spread across his face, and then he shook his head.

"We better get started," he said, closing his door and putting a chair up against it, lodging the back of it under the doorknob so nobody would be able to get in if they tried. He must have seen my look of alarm.

"This is top-secret," he said, and then he opened the side drawer of his desk and pulled out a stack of colorful construction paper and markers. His were Sharpies. Maybe he was going to draw all over me—write things like "loser" and "idiot" before I could escape. I imagined for a minute having to walk through the halls with the writing on me and wondered if it would feel worse than I feel every day, but of course I knew the answer was yes. He gestured for me to sit on the floor.

"So, here's what I'm thinking," he said as he took a seat on the other side of a board he had pulled out of his closet. He crossed his legs like a little kid and inched a bit closer. "The invitations should be in the shape of feet. Like each person gets a foot under the door."

I stared at him blankly. Clearly he was serious about this, whatever it was.

"I keep forgetting, this is your first time," he said. "You're a newbie. Okay, so here's how it works. I'm the chairman—which you probably figured out already. It's up to me to organize the Game, which you already know is not going to be a game at all but an outing. The point is to bring the senior class together and invite a few juniors who will then carry the torch next year. Sort of like an initiation. You with me so far?"

I nodded.

"Oh, and I forgot to tell you the most important thing: while the teachers are of course expecting the Game to happen, since it does each year, the main point—the real measure of success—is to catch them completely off guard. They can't see it coming."

I nodded again.

"And with the outing, they're going to be completely thrown off, which I'm pretty excited about, if I do say so myself," Patrick said. Then he looked around like he had lost his train of thought.

"The invitations?" I offered.

"Right, so the invitations have to be great and cryptic, and I want them to catch everyone's attention, but the point here is to tell them about what we'll be doing without really saying it—so if, by chance, a teacher gets ahold of one, he or she will not be able to figure out exactly what it says."

"Sounds good," I said, reaching for a piece of green construction paper.

"Wait. First, we have to figure out what we want to say," he said.

I looked around the room to give the illusion that I was thinking, though the truth is I really didn't care. I was thinking about Vanessa. Where had she been today? Why hadn't I run into her at all? And then a terrible thought crossed my mind followed by a wave of misery: What if she had been purposefully ignoring me? What if she wasn't going to find me each day anymore? What if she had somehow changed her mind?

And then, miraculously, as though Patrick had been reading my thoughts, he glanced at the picture taped to the lampshade and said, "Vanessa was sick today. Eve on her hall said she was heaving into the toilet this morning, and then she went back to her room and I guess never left again. I hope she's feeling better; I certainly don't want to get it. I was thinking I should do something—she's probably expecting me to—you know, check on her or bring her some ginger ale and crackers or something. Maybe you could come with me after we're done here. I hate being around sick people."

Even Vanessa? I wanted to ask, but I didn't. "Yes, sure," I said instead, the feeling of relief still spreading through me. I felt energized—happy, even. She wasn't ignoring me! She still liked me! I wasn't sure how we were going to check on her, since her hall was off-limits, or where we were going to get ginger ale, but I figured Patrick had a plan for that. So now only the completion of the invitations stood between me and Vanessa.

"It might help if I knew what the outing was going to be," I said.

"Good point," he said, reaching over and making a pile of the paper neatly stacked by banging the bottom of it on the board. "I haven't run this by anyone yet, but here's what I'm thinking. One week from Wednesday will be the first night of March. I think we'll throw them off by doing it on a weeknight since usually the Games are played on the weekends. I want to have a midnight sledding outing— at that amazing hill in the woods. I figure I'll rent the sleds over the next two weeks, stock up on hot chocolate, we'll need thermoses, of course, and I want to get Kahlúa and some peppermint schnapps, and I have bourbon. Anyway—everyone will meet there when the clock strikes twelve, and we'll party until two. It will be the coolest senior event ever."

"How do you know there'll be snow?" I asked. Patrick looked at me thoughtfully, like that possibility had never crossed his mind. Then he nodded to himself.

"Snow will be icing on the cake," he said. "It's not about the snow. It's not even about the sledding. It's about having a crazy party."

As he spoke, he rearranged himself so he was in a kneeling position towering over me, and I realized again how much bigger he was. When he finished talking, he sat back on his heels and smiled.

"So, what do you think?"

What did I think? I thought he was crazy. But did I tell him? No. I knew he meant that hill Vanessa and I jogged by that day I was momentarily blinded. The truth was, I didn't care. Sledding, a game of tag, a keg party—it was all the same to me unless I could be alone with Vanessa.

"Sounds cool," I said. "Do you think we should make the invitations in the shape of a snowflake or a sled?"

"No," Patrick said kindly. "Too obvious. I was thinking Bigfoot."

"Bigfoot?" I asked.

"Like big feet in the shape that Bigfoot would have," he said, looking very pleased with himself. "And this is what I think it should say. They all have to be exactly the same."

He took out a black Sharpie and started writing, being very careful to turn the paper this way and that. When he was finished, he held it up.

"Okay, picture a foot. A three goes here," he said, pointing to the big toe. "Write 'Best Prize,' which everyone knows means 'number one,' here. So that's March first." This time he pointed to the center of the foot.

He was so close to me, I could smell his breath—a combination of Gummi Bears and mint with a hint of something dark and evil. I inched away as subtly as I could. He didn't seem to notice.

"Okay, they already know it's an outing from my other notes. We need to figure out a way to make clear it's at midnight."

"How about we draw a pumpkin?" I said. "Would that work?"

"Yes!" Patrick said enthusiastically. "Great idea."

"Thanks," I said, surprised to find myself smiling.

"We have the day and time. I think if we write a hill like this," he said, leaning over a piece of paper and fixing a small hill he had already drawn, which really looked like an upside-down *U*. "The truth is, they're allowed to ask me for details privately, so I think this is just enough info."

"Okay, then," I said, thinking the whole thing was a bit ridiculous and the effort we were putting into this could probably be better spent some other way, but so what? I'll say this now, in case you didn't get it, but whatever airs I was putting on here, there's no question that I was happy to be in on something.

We were quiet for a long time while we started to cut

out the feet. After a few minutes, Patrick put on his iPod, which was connected to a pair of tiny speakers. Journey's "Don't Stop Believin'" came on.

"We'll need to cut out fifty-three of these," Patrick said, talking over my favorite part of the song, the part that goes *born and raised in south Detroit.* I don't know why I like that so much. Well, I guess I do know. I have cousins from the Detroit area. Not actually Detroit but a small town called Farmington Hills. When I was younger, we would go visit them. There was a time when my mother thought it was really important for me to know my cousins. I think that started when it dawned on her that I was going to be an only child. So about four or five times a year, we would drive from Chicago to see them. I always liked it, but after a few years my mother got tired of it and realized they were never going to make the effort to come to see us, even though my mother invited them all the time. We stopped going. I could never really figure out why we stopped going altogether—why we didn't just scale it back to one or two visits a year.

After that, I ended up seeing my cousins at Thanksgiving and sometimes on a summer trip my grandparents organized. But I remember those visits, and I remember being down in their dark basement, the one my uncle had redone with indoor-outdoor carpet and a stereo that was brand-new in 1970, before any of us were even born. We would turn out all the lights and blast the music. Nobody could see me. I told myself they were my cousins and they had to accept me no matter what. I think that was why I always hoped for a brother or sister, because they would have to accept me no matter what. But on those nights, with my cousins in that dark basement where nobody could see anybody's face, we would wait at the beginning of the song and all yell that line—*born and raised in south Detroit*—at the top of our lungs. I know this is really pathetic and sad—but looking back, that is one of my best childhood memories. Sorry to get off track; let me get back to that night.

Once I forgave Patrick for ruining my favorite part of the song, I asked why we needed fifty-three. There were exactly forty-three members of our graduating class. I knew that number by heart; it was something that was said over and over in one way or another. There were forty-two before I arrived. I made lucky number forty-three.

"Because," he said, not looking up, "as I mentioned earlier, we invite a few people from the junior class to join us. You have to start paying better attention if you want to learn anything around here."

"Okay," I said, knowing without having to be told that Patrick was one of those people, one of the members of the junior class who was chosen to play with the seniors last year.

"Who decides which juniors will be included?" I asked.

"I do, sort of," Patrick said.

"How do you decide?" I asked.

Patrick thought for a minute. He seemed to take my question very seriously.

"You'll see," he said.

CHAPTER EIGHTEEN

DUNCAN

FIVE DAYS—FOUR FULL ONES, REALLY

So that was the big question, Duncan realized. And he also realized that maybe he really didn't want to know. Before Tim had a chance to continue, Duncan took that CD out of the computer, added it to the stack, and put them all on the hidden shelf in his closet.

"Now, stay there," he said, and then felt silly. Who was he talking to? Tim? If he could, he would apologize for not following through and listening to the rest of the story. But, he decided, he was doing exactly what he'd said he wouldn't do: he was letting the events of last year ruin this one. He was done. He was sorry, but he was done.

The rest of the fall could only be described as blissful for Duncan. October especially. The air turned cool and then colder—but the students refused to pull out their winter coats. Instead, they wore sweaters—each week thicker and bulkier. It became a thing, really, something that Duncan didn't remember from years past but sort of liked. He and Daisy were together constantly—spending as little time in their rooms as possible. When they did go to their rooms, they spent the night texting each other, planning when and how early they could meet the next morning.

"7 more hours," Duncan would text as soon as he got to his room.

"2 long," Daisy would text back.

"Should we make it 6?"

"How about 5?"

"No, u rest," Duncan wrote. "I don't want u 2 be tired 2morrow."

"I love u."

"I love u 2."

Duncan always tried to be the one waiting at the bottom of the stairs in the morning. He loved how Daisy's eyes would light up when she saw him. It became a game to see who could get there first. When she beat him, he would always feel a twinge that he was letting her down in some way.

On the day before they left for Thanksgiving break, he set his alarm for five in the morning. When it first went off, he thought about just ignoring it and going back to sleep, but the images of Tim's missed opportunities ran through his mind. He didn't want to come close to making the same mistakes Tim had. Already he was certainly doing a million times better than Tim had done, but he felt a constant nagging that he could do more. He owed it to himself, and to Daisy—and when it came down to it, he felt he owed it to Tim and Vanessa.

He forced himself out of bed. He had been planning this morning for a while, so once he was up and out of his warm bed, he was full of energy. He had borrowed a small plug-in hot plate from a kid down the hall, even though they were illegal in the dorms. The day before, he had gone into town to shop. The best he could come up with was oatmeal with brown sugar and cream, which he carefully kept on ice all night. He knew Daisy liked that because she always ate it when it was available in the dining hall, but she complained that they had no cream to put in it—only milk. Duncan made it, put it in a pretty flowered plastic bowl he had also bought the day before in town, and then he texted her, asking her to open her door. It took a minute— he expected that she would be fast asleep—but then the "OK" came and he went.

As he rounded the corner, he could see her waiting, sleepy in bright yellow pajamas. She didn't say a word but let him come inside and shut the door. They turned and looked at each other. He was certain in that moment that he would never have feelings like that for anyone else. Ever. They started to kiss. She was warm and smelled so good. He realized it was the first time that he was with her before she had a chance to shower or brush her teeth, and he held on to that idea, thinking that's how married people are.

Then she got into bed and pulled a blue-flowered comforter up to let him know she wanted him to join her. The oatmeal was long forgotten on the desk. He couldn't believe how sleepy he felt suddenly, like he wanted to shut down and stay there forever. And then instead of spending the next hour fooling around, they fell asleep. It was the most peaceful sleep Duncan had ever experienced.

When they had to say good-bye the next afternoon, it was so much harder than Duncan imagined it would be. Five days—four full ones, really—shouldn't be so hard to get through. But Duncan felt like every second away from Daisy was almost painful.

Once he was home, he tried hard to enjoy himself, but it was impossible. Duncan called Daisy every day in Connecticut, had even sent letters to her home that were perfectly planned to arrive each day she was there. They emailed and texted constantly, but he loved the idea of the letters showing up at her house, letters that he had touched a few days before.

When they got back to Irving, they started dreading the big holiday break that loomed in front of them. First they had nineteen days together, then eighteen, then seventeen. Neither of their parents thought they should take time away from their families to visit during the almost three weeks of break—they spent enough time together at school, the adults seemed to agree. But they vowed to call every day—twice a day—maybe even three times a day. And they realized that as much as they dreaded the countdown they were on to the vacation, when they got home, they could start at the same place and count down to being together again—nineteen lonely days, then eighteen, then seventeen.

During that time, Duncan never went back to Tim's story. He was too busy, for one thing. Between squeezing in every last second with Daisy, hanging out with the guys, showing off his math skills, and reading Aristotle and Shakespeare, he simply couldn't find time to sit and listen. But it was more than that, and Duncan knew it. The last time he'd listened to Tim's tale, it made him feel awful. It made him remember things he didn't want to remember. He left the CDs in the secret compartment of his closet and tried not to think about them or what listening to the rest of Tim's year might mean. He had a moment every now and then when he thought he would tell Daisy about them, about everything, but then something would happen, or he would flash forward and be unable to imagine her reaction, and he would decide not to. So he never did.

January turned to February, and then one day while the guys were up late in Tad's room listening to some music that

Hugh's brother had recorded himself, hoping to make it big, Ben turned to Duncan and changed everything—again.

"So, what about the senior Game?" he asked. "I trust you'll have a better handle on it than Patrick did last year."

The words pierced Duncan. Nobody had mentioned the senior Game to him. Partly that was because it wasn't supposed to be talked about openly, but privately, among friends, it was allowed. Still, until that point, Duncan thought it had been on purpose that the subject was never brought up. Nobody talked to him about what had happened. It wasn't unusual for him to come upon a conversation, especially at the beginning of the year, and feel like he was interrupting something, and he would know they were talking about it. But he felt like his friends had really protected him from it, and he had gotten used to that. He knew he couldn't avoid it, though there was a tiny bit of him that hoped the Game would be canceled for good, considering everything. Of course, outings were now forbidden, that was a definite, but an easy game of tag or capture the flag should be okay, the administration seemed to agree.

"Yeah, Dunc, what about the Game?" Tad chimed in.

Duncan swallowed. He was glad at that moment that the lights were out. He was sure that his face was turning an ugly shade of red. He was certain last year that it had all been a misunderstanding. Maybe not a misunderstanding so much, but something that could be switched back, that was never validated. Especially after what happened, there had really been no question in his mind. But if the guys were waiting for him to plan the Game, then the rest of the senior class was also waiting.

"I'm on it," he said, with as much confidence as he could find. "You can count on me."

CHAPTER NINETEEN

TIM

HOW AM I GOING TO GET OUT OF HERE?

That was when Duncan started listening again. He pictured pulling the CDs out of the closet and wiping dust and cobwebs off them, that was how far away he felt from them, but they were as clean as they had been when he hid them. There was no way he could plan his own Game without knowing the exact details of last year, of Patrick's Game. How else was he going to be absolutely sure he didn't make the same bad choices? So once again he traveled back to last year, leaving the current one behind.

Patrick and I spent hours making the invitations. It was well after lights-out when we were finished. They looked great, I had to admit.

"Now let's get them out there," Patrick said.

"Now?" I asked, glancing at the clock by his bedside.

"Yeah, it's as good a time as any. Plus, we want to surprise everyone, right?"

"I guess so," I said halfheartedly. It was so late. I had to be up in three hours, four if I really pushed it. I still had work to do for Mr. Simon's class in the morning. More work than I would ever be able to do even if I worked from then until the class. The first ten pages of the Tragedy Paper were due in the morning. The first ten pages! I had written three bad ones and was going to ask for an extension that I was sure I would get. After all, everyone else had a full semester's head start on me. Mr. Simon had been pretty nice about it so far.

"Come on," Patrick said, turning to take a quick look at himself in the mirror. He smiled and then turned back to me. I avoided the mirror with all my might.

"How do we do it?"

"Okay," he said, handing me a stack of Bigfoot invitations. "Let's do our hall first. You do that half and I'll do this half," he said. "Just slip one under each door."

We took about ten minutes, and I realized Patrick was right—this was the perfect time to do it. Quiet, no teachers. We met back in the middle of the hall.

"Now we have to go to the girls' side," Patrick said without any hesitation. He said it the way you would say *Now it's time to buy milk* or *brush your teeth*.

"Are you sure?" I asked.

"Very," he said, again without hesitation. "But let's go

down to the dining hall first and see if we can get some crackers and ginger ale for Ness."

The use of her nickname gave me that awful, lonely feeling again, like Patrick had something that I wanted more than anything but would never be mine. I had heard it in passing, but it had never been used in direct conversation with me. To me, she was Vanessa.

"Are you kidding?" I asked, and it occurred to me again that this could be some sort of trick. Maybe he had the dining hall booby-trapped and I was going to get caught up in it.

"No, I mean, the dining hall is no big deal. They have that sick station, you know," he said. I shook my head. "In the far back corner, there's that refrigerator with Gatorade and ginger ale and crackers, ice chips, I think. It's meant to be taken—in case someone gets sick in the middle of the night or something. It is totally within our rights."

"Huh, I didn't know about that," I said.

"Follow me," he said. "There's a lot you don't know."

Have you ever been in there at night? It's creepy. The floor was icy cold, and I wished I had put my slippers on. There were shadows everywhere. I followed Patrick into the back corner of the dining hall, where he grabbed a cold soda from the fridge and a few packets of saltines. I took a Styrofoam cup and scooped chipped ice into it, looking to see if there was anything else there that might help her.

"Come on," he said, and I did. This time back up the stairs, and at the fork we went to the right. I held my breath, but the hall was as quiet as could be. He handed me another stack of big feet and nodded toward one half of the hall. Wordlessly, we started at the ends and slipped an invitation under each door. We met back in the middle, and I wondered if he was going to skip giving the stuff to Vanessa, but then he handed me the leftover invitations, walked toward her door, and knocked softly.

"What if she's asleep?" I whispered urgently.

Patrick looked at his wrist. There was no watch there, but he acted like there was.

He waved me off and knocked lightly, so lightly I couldn't hear a thing. We waited.

"Maybe she went to the infirmary," I offered. That was a possibility. I knew from a time I went to get Advil for one of my headaches that it was pretty nice there, with a cot and a TV.

"No way," Patrick said. He knocked again, this time a bit louder. I started to get nervous. Someone was likely to see us or hear us. Someone was bound to go to the bathroom.

He knocked again.

"I'm going to head back," I said. "If she's that sound asleep, she'll be okay without this stuff until the morning. Or maybe you could leave it outside her door. Just put it there; she'll find it when she wakes up."

Before Patrick had a chance to answer me, the door creaked open, first about an inch and then two inches. It was so dark inside, I couldn't see anything. I took a step back. But then the door opened all the way, and I could see it was Vanessa, her hair as crazy as I had ever seen it, literally standing up in the front and the back. Her face was pale, her eyes red. She was wearing gray sweatpants and a red bulldog shirt that I had never seen. She groaned quietly and then opened the door even wider, indicating that we should come in. Patrick walked in but I hesitated.

"Please," she said in a raspy voice that I couldn't refuse.

"Okay," I said, coming into her tiny room.

As soon as we were in far enough, she closed the door. That was when the horrible smell hit me. Even when I told myself that whatever I was smelling came from her, it didn't help. I crinkled my nose, then I tried to tuck it into my shirt, then I just put my hand up to cover it completely and tried to breathe through my mouth.

"Whoa, what's the stench?" Patrick asked.

Vanessa had already gotten back into bed, her head on a flowered pillowcase that looked old and I would have bet came from her childhood bedroom. I saw the stuffed monkey thrown off to the side of her pillow. She was breathing heavily and groaning a little.

"Here," I said, pushing the cup of ice toward her. She reached out weakly and took it but let it rest on the bed next to her. I was fairly sure she was dehydrated. I moved toward her with the intention of helping her eat some, and that was when I saw where the smell was coming from. She had moved her bright green plastic trash can over to her bed, and it was almost full of vomit. I had to look away for a minute, feeling the urge to retch myself. Patrick saw my reaction and had the same one, but he wasn't subtle about it. He made a huge gagging sound and started to back toward the door.

"I'm sorry you're so sick," he said, his hand on the door-knob. "I think Tim was right, we should let you rest."

"Wait," I said, and reached toward him for the crackers and the soda. He gave them up happily, taking the rest of the invitations from me, and opened the door. The fresh air from the hall was the best air I ever smelled. He walked into the hall and waited for me. But I didn't follow.

"You got this?" he finally whispered, having gotten himself under control but not willing to risk coming back in.

"Sure," I said, seething because he was going to leave her when she needed him and yet she wasn't willing to leave him. "She looks like she could use some help."

He hesitated then, I could see it. Vanessa's eyes were closed. I wasn't even sure if she was awake. Maybe he could leave and she would never know. Maybe she was so out of it she wouldn't remember our coming in the first place. Maybe this was how he got through life—lucky omissions.

He took a step toward us again, but was immediately re-pelled by the vomit. He might be the better-looking guy, he might be the more popular guy—on a basketball court, he'd

191

probably crush me—but in this arena of vomit, I was the stronger man and I wanted to see if it counted for anything. Also, I could never leave her there like that. I just couldn't do it.

Patrick didn't say anything else. He left and I went into action. The first thing I did was open the window. At that point I considered dumping the vomit out the window, but it only opened so far and that would have been incredibly messy. So I picked up the trash can, holding my breath, and carried it out the door and to the girls' bathroom. I was relieved to find it empty.

I dumped the vomit in the toilet and immediately flushed. Then I took the trash can to the shower, poured in some shampoo that had been left behind, and cleaned it. When I got back to her room, the door was still open. I shut it and waited to be hit again with the wave of stench, but it wasn't so bad this time. Vanessa's eyes were still closed. I sat next to her on the bed. Then I pressed the wet towels I had in my hand softly to her forehead.

She stirred and slowly opened her eyes. I reached for an ice chip and tried to ease it into her mouth. At first she kept her lips shut and weakly shook her head, but then she accepted it and I waited. I don't mean to draw this out, but you have to understand that I like to relive this; being there with her that night was like nothing I had ever experienced. I could have sat there forever, to be perfectly honest. The smell was gone. I was in Vanessa's room. She was in bed. I was sorry she was sick, of course, but I couldn't imagine wanting to be anywhere else. It was four-forty-five in the morning and I knew there would be no sleep for me that night, but I stopped caring about that. Then she moaned again, and I picked up another ice chip to give her. I noticed that her lips were dry, so I brushed the ice around a bit and let it melt first. I did that for a long time.

When I looked at the clock again, it was seven-thirty. I had fallen asleep next to her. The cup had dropped from my hand and there was a wet puddle on the floor, reminding me of the melted snowballs.

When I turned to look at her, she was looking back at me. And then she smiled.

"Can you give me a bit of that ginger ale?" she asked.

"Sure," I said, jumping up and getting it. It wasn't cold anymore, but that was probably better for her anyway.

"Wow, I feel so much better," she said, drinking from the small bottle.

"Not so fast," I said just as there was a knock on the door.

"Vanessa?" a girl's voice called.

"Hi, Julia," she called weakly. "I'm still in bed but feeling better. Will you let Mrs. Reilly know I'm going to skip breakfast but try to go to class?"

"Sure thing," the girl called through the door. "Do you need anything?"

Vanessa looked at me and smiled.

"No, I'm good," she said.

Vanessa put her head back and closed her eyes. She wiggled a bit in bed, trying to get more comfortable.

"How am I going to get out of here?" I asked. "Not only am I nowhere to be found on my hall, but there are so many people out there. I'm screwed."

"I can't believe what you did for me," she said, ignoring my question. "You actually dumped my throw-up?"

"Someone had to do it."

"Not really," she said. "And you rehydrated me. I was going to die in here."

"Not literally," I said. "You would have been okay."

"Well, I felt like I was going to die."

"For the record, I'm glad you didn't," I said. "Now, can you help me? Do you have any ideas?"

"Can we just sit a little?" she asked. "I'm still really dizzy."

How could I deny that request?

"So, I think this might go down as my most embarrassing moment," she said after we were quiet for a minute.

"If that's the case, then you're doing pretty well. This wasn't so bad," I said, meaning it.

"What's your most embarrassing moment?" she asked. I should have expected it: the admission of an embarrassing moment is usually followed by that question. And yet, I was completely thrown off-kilter. Did I tell her? Did I make one up? Did I pretend I didn't have any? Or I could have just said the obvious—that my life was a string of embarrassing moments.

"When I was little," I said, looking around her room—we were safe and alone; I felt like I could say anything—"I thought that my being an albino was a superpower."

I waited but she didn't move, didn't flinch away.

"I've always loved superheroes, even now, which might be considered embarrassing because I'm so old, but I figured, many of them were mutants, right? It made perfect sense to me that my affliction was really something good. I spent so much time trying to figure out what my power was, but nothing ever revealed itself. So one day, I told this kid in the cafeteria—I was in first grade, about seven, I think—not to mess with me because I had superpowers, and he said, very loud, 'Yeah, your power is being the ugliest kid in the school.' Looking back, that may have done more damage than the reality of how I look. Needless to say, I do not have a superpower, and this, my skin and lack of pigment, is nothing good, only bad."

She turned to face me, and this is what she said: "I disagree with that, and I am not so sure you don't have superpowers."

We both looked at the clock at the same time.

I was so torn—not wanting this moment to ever end and at the same time feeling like I was about to be caught. How in the world was I going to get out of this one? Part of me didn't care. Short of not graduating, what were they going to take away from me? My social life? Not much to miss there. But still.

"Well, since I can't scale buildings and I can't make myself invisible, what is your suggestion for how I should leave your room without being seen?" I asked. What I really wanted to say was *Can I stay here forever?*

She pushed the covers off and eased herself up.

"Look in my closet," she said, pointing. "There's a pink-checked hooded sweatshirt that says 'Spread the love' in embroidered letters. It's really big. I think it will fit you."

I looked at her like she was crazy, but I forced myself up and walked to her closet. I was bombarded with a palette of the brightest colors I had ever seen all in one place. I smiled. The closet was full, packed. There wasn't room for one more thing, and I certainly wasn't going to be able to find a sweatshirt in that mess. But I tried. I looked through the hangers, and combed through the shelves.

"It's on a hook, to the right," she said.

Sure enough, it was there. A pink gingham sweatshirt that looked big enough to fit two of her inside. I held it up so she could see.

"That's it. Now put it on," she said.

"What? Are you kidding?"

She quickly looked at the clock. "In about seven minutes, this hall will be quiet. Everyone will be at breakfast—believe me, I know. I will bet money that you won't run into anyone. But just in case, put that on, pull the hood up, and go the back way, toward the fire stairs. Before you get to your hall, take it off and leave it there. I'll come get it later. You'll be home free."

I considered her plan. It was a good one. And I had nothing to lose. Now I had about five minutes.

"Do you really think you'll be able to go to class?" I asked. I wanted to go back and sit on her bed, but somehow standing up and devising our plan made me feel like I couldn't do that anymore.

"Those first pages of the Tragedy Paper are due, and you know how Mr. Simon is," she said. "I think I'll feel better after a shower."

"Good, I hope so," I said. Now we had three and a half minutes.

"Did you finish the pages?" she asked.

"No," I said. "I still need some time to work. I'm going to talk to Mr. Simon before class."

"Do you want help?"

I wanted to accept her offer without hesitation. "Maybe," I said. "I'll let you know if it doesn't go well."

"Okay," she said. "I owe you one."

We were down to two minutes. There was almost no noise in the hall anymore. I could still hear a few stragglers, but the rush was over.

"Put on the sweatshirt," she said. "And when I say go, go."

"You sound like you've done this before," I said.

Vanessa looked down.

"Get ready," she said, almost whispering.

I pulled the sweatshirt on and zipped it up. I pulled the hood up. We had less than a minute left together.

"Stand by the door," she said.

I did as she said, as much as I didn't want to. There was no noise at all now; it was as quiet as it had been at four in the morning.

"Now," she said. "Go."

I wanted to go over and hug her. But I turned the doorknob and, without looking back, headed out of her room, turned right, and walked fast. A part of me hoped I would be stopped, that I would be questioned and that we might get into trouble together. But there wasn't a single person in the hall, and my path to the boys' hall was clear. When I got to the tiny space that was neutral territory—not the girls' hall and not the boys'—I took off the sweatshirt. I thought about dropping it and just leaving it there as she'd told me to do. But I couldn't. Instead, I folded the sweatshirt in half and tucked it under my arm. I glanced down my empty hall and walked unnoticed to my room.

CHAPTER TWENTY

TIM
EVERYTHING IS CONNECTED

Duncan liked that idea, using a big hoodie sweatshirt for a getaway. Maybe he could try it to escape from Daisy's room one morning. Why hadn't he thought of that before? It was so obvious and yet so brilliant at the same time. He realized then that Tim wasn't saying anything, so he glanced at his computer. There was a pop-up message warning him that there was no battery power left. He must have forgotten to plug his computer in after he rushed back to start listening. He leaned over, straightened the cord a bit, and stuck it into the socket. Immediately his screen brightened. He sat down on his bed with his back against the wall and waited for Tim to start talking again.

• • •

I stayed in my room for about ten minutes. I couldn't decide what to do first or what would seem the most normal—if anyone was paying attention. I was missing breakfast, but that was okay—I did that sometimes when Mr. Simon brought me something to eat. The only problem would be if Mr. Simon noticed I was missing on a day when he didn't bring me something. But that was unlikely, especially on this day when all the seniors had a Tragedy Paper deadline. He lived for that kind of stuff. He was probably already in his office, waiting.

There it was, I had my answer. I would get myself together and go talk to Mr. Simon about an extension. If I seemed frenzied or off-kilter, he would hopefully just attribute that to my concern over missing the deadline. In fact, all of this could work in my favor.

I took off my clothes, knowing they were dirty—gross, even—and at the same time thinking how close I had been to Vanessa when I was wearing them. I put on clean jeans and a T-shirt, grabbed my backpack and my way-too-thin Tragedy folder, and pulled open the door. Patrick was standing there.

My first thought was to run, or slam the door shut. It made sense to me that he was going to be very angry with me. I showed him up. I did a better job than he was able to do. He wasn't going to let me get away with that.

But when I looked at his face, I saw immediately that I was wrong. He looked great, fresh and clean and ready for the day. He looked relaxed.

"How is she?" he asked, but he asked like he already knew the answer—that she was okay because I took care of her, I did his dirty work.

"Okay," I said. "Better."

"Are you just getting back now?" he asked. Maybe it was starting to dawn on him how much help she had needed.

"Yeah," I said, feeling a bit trapped and—dare I add—proud. He knew. Obviously, he had been looking for me. But the last thing I wanted to do was make him jealous and feed the anger I imagined was waiting to explode.

"Were you . . . with her . . . this whole time?"

I could have lied. I could have said no, I had gone to the Hall to study or write as much as I could of my Tragedy Paper. I could have said I took a walk, or sat on the quad thinking. But I didn't.

"Yes," I said. "I cleaned up a little, and I gave her some ice chips. And then I fell asleep. I didn't mean to. I was shocked when I woke up and it was after seven. But she knew exactly how to get me back. It involved waiting until just the right moment, when the hall was empty, and putting on a pink hooded sweatshirt."

Patrick nodded, a smirk on his face.

"That's an old trick." he said. And then he looked me in the eyes and smiled. "I can't thank you enough, man. I mean, I couldn't hack it. I couldn't stand that smell. But you did it—you stepped in for me and you did it. I owe you one. Oh, and I'd really appreciate it if this could be our little secret, okay?"

I was dumbfounded. And then I remembered what I looked like, something I hadn't thought about in hours. Of course he didn't see me as a threat. He never did. And that pissed me off.

"I didn't do it for you," I said. "I did it for her."

It was a bold move. Something I wouldn't normally do, but how dare he think I was filling in for him, that I was his cleanup man, his helper? I was done with that. But something clicked in me and I thought, *Why not let him think that?* He looked so confused and surprised. It wasn't going to last long.

"But you're welcome," I said quietly. "There's no denying that smell was horrible."

"Yeah, I mean, who would ever think such an awful smell could come from such a hot girl?"

I had to let it go. I just nodded, trying not to look as offended as I was.

"I've gotten some feedback already from a few of the guys on the hall," Patrick said, running his fingers through his thick hair. "Everyone is psyched about the outing. Now we have to get things ready."

"Really? Already?" I asked. I was starting to worry that I wouldn't be able to keep up with everything.

He patted me on the back and turned toward the bathroom. I was relieved. I couldn't take any more banter with him. I would wash up later.

I headed in the other direction, toward Mr. Simon's office.

The halls were quiet, with everyone enjoying the cinnamon buns they were serving for breakfast. It was a nice time at the Irving School, one I never really took advantage of, and for a brief moment I thought about how lucky I was to be there.

Mr. Simon was looking through a huge stack of files when I peeked in his office door, and I worried for a minute that those were the files of all the seniors who turned in their work early or, worse, did more than they had to. The files looked pretty thick.

Mr. Simon wore one of those Norwegian sweaters from L.L.Bean, the kind that is navy blue with white flecks, the kind that you never see a student wearing. He had on faded jeans and his hair was neatly combed.

"Excuse me, Mr. Simon?" I asked.

Mr. Simon looked through me for a minute before registering my question.

"Yes, Tim, of course, come on in," he said warmly.

"What is all that?" I asked.

"These, my friend, are the best Tragedy Papers from over the years. I keep them locked in my desk drawer, but on exciting days like this, I can't help but take them out and read through them. Listen to this," he said, looking through the pile of folders and grabbing one. "This is how it begins: 'On October third of last year, a restaurant called Flying High burned down. It burned to the ground, killing six employees inside. It was the day the restaurant was to celebrate its seventy-fifth anniversary. There was a party planned. People were going to arrive in a matter of hours. What they found when they got there was a charred mess, ambulances waiting to see if anyone had been overlooked in the chaos, and the owners sobbing in the parking lot. Was this a tragedy?'" Mr. Simon stopped reading and looked out the window. I followed his gaze to the quad, where the leafless trees blew in the mid-February wind.

"Wow," I said, because I had no idea what to say. That wasn't what I had in mind at all.

"'Wow' is right," Mr. Simon said, coming back to face me. "I love that question, 'Was this a tragedy?'"

"Was it?" I asked.

"Ah, you don't think it is as easy as that, young man, do you?" he said. "But, for the sake of our discussion, what do you think?"

I actually wasn't sure. "Do you mean, was it a tragedy in the literary sense?"

"I'm glad you came to our school," Mr. Simon said, surprising me. "It's nice to have a new mind, a different perspective, join the class. That is an excellent question. Was it a tragedy in the literary sense, and what would another sort of tragedy be?"

"A tragic happening?" I offered. I'd been to class. I was getting to know his lingo.

"Yes! And is there a difference? Can you separate the two? Is there any reason to?"

He sat back. The halls were getting busy. I glanced at the clock. Class began in nine minutes. Mr. Simon shook his head.

"What can I do for you?" he asked. "I have a feeling this isn't what you came to talk to me about."

"Well, in a way it is," I said. "I feel . . . overwhelmed by this assignment. I think I'm lagging behind."

"That's understandable," he said kindly. "The other students have about a four-month jump on you. I take this to mean you aren't ready for today. Am I right?"

"Yes," I said, suddenly feeling like I really hadn't tried hard enough. I was disappointing him.

"Okay, clearly you're thinking about this stuff," he said. He gathered the files and put them back in his bottom drawer. He took a tiny key out of his front pocket and locked the drawer, then slipped the key back into his pocket. "Can you get the first five pages to me by Monday?"

It was Wednesday. That would give me the whole weekend. That was much more than I could have asked for.

"I absolutely can do that. . . . That would be great," I said.

"Let me leave you with a few parting thoughts, and then we should get to class," he said. "I'm not saying this is right or wrong, necessary or not, but here are some things to consider. You've heard me talk about them a bit in class, but you missed the real push in the fall. Pity and fear. A tragic flaw. A reversal of fortune that might or might not come from an error in judgment. Irony. Catharsis. Monomania—do you know what that is?"

"Being obsessed with one goal?" I said. I wasn't even sure where that answer came from.

"Yes!" he said, one hand waving in the air like he was conducting an orchestra. "Also keep in mind the move from order to chaos to order again," he said.

"Like that restaurant fire?" I asked. "There was order—the planned celebration, their daily activity—and then chaos with the fire and the deaths, and then, was there order again? How did it turn out?"

Mr. Simon stood.

"Oh, and there was a clear reversal of fortune there too," I said excitedly. "I mean, they were ready to have a party, to celebrate everything they had built, and then it all burned to the ground. Am I right about that?"

Mr. Simon smiled.

"Maybe later, after you've turned your paper in, I'll let you read that one to see how it turns out, to see what conclusion that student drew," he said. "But I will say that I liked her basing it on real life. That was a restaurant in the town where she grew up. She ate there all her life."

"But the paper has to be about literature too?" I asked. Things were becoming clearer than ever and at the same time more confusing. "The assignment is to consider a written work, right?"

"Yes it is," Mr. Simon said. "But don't get lost in that.

Everything is connected, my friend, everything is connected. And let me leave you with one last word, and then we must be on our way. This one is a big one. You've heard me mention it in class. Are you ready?"

"I am," I said, not so sure.

Mr. Simon took a deep breath.

"Magnitude," he boomed. "Can you define *magnitude* for me?"

"Great meaning?" I offered.

"Yes, and so much more," he said, smiling again and putting his hand on my back to guide me out of the room. "So much more."

CHAPTER TWENTY-ONE

DUNCAN

THIS TIME THERE WAS NO GOING BACK

Duncan had held it together so well, but now he began to worry he was losing his grip on what was important. And then hearing that word—*magnitude*—made him start to question everything. He became paralyzed by decisions: Did his choice of socks in the morning hold any magnitude? Would it change anything if he wore different socks? Or the path he took, did that choice hold magnitude? If he went one way, maybe he'd trip and break his leg, or maybe he'd run into someone he didn't want to see. Texting Daisy became a problem because he couldn't settle on what words to use. It was impossible to decide where to go and what to say. It was hard to know what had magnitude and what didn't.

So he decided again that he had to stop listening to Tim. This time, though, he didn't hide the CDs away but simply left them casually on the corner of his desk, trying to pretend they didn't hold any more importance than the pencil with the bad point that sat next to them. He told himself he was very busy now, with Daisy and everything else, so why waste his time sitting in his room listening to a sad guy tell a sad story? Was he really going to learn anything that would make a difference?

But not listening didn't make things any better. He was tense when he was with Daisy, he knew that. The easiness of their relationship started to slip away. And then there was that night. He came up the stairs and walked toward his room. There was a guy lingering at the door before his, a guy he hadn't seen before, who looked like Tim from the back. Was it Tim? His mind was bursting, and then the boy turned around. It was a junior. He didn't look anything like Tim. He wasn't even an albino. For the rest of the night, Duncan felt like he'd seen a ghost.

The lines were blurring. He tried to focus on the task at hand. All he had to do, really, was come up with the most benign, easy game. Not even try to hide it from the teachers. What if they played a Scrabble tournament in the dining hall? What if they played a rousing game of hide-and-seek? What if he invited the faculty to play along? But every time he thought, *Okay, that's what I'll do,* he knew he couldn't. He just knew it.

One rainy night, Daisy was off with her friends having some "girl time." It was sort of a relief. Duncan was getting tired of trying so hard to pretend things were normal. He went to his room to finally hash out the Game. It had to take place sometime before spring break—that was the Irving School tradition—and it was getting close. He still had time, though, especially if he wasn't going to do some crazy secret event.

When he sat down at his desk, he saw the CDs and realized how much he missed the mesmerizing sound of Tim's voice. It actually occurred to him that moving through the rest of his story—at least this part that he had avoided—might be a welcome relief from his own life. He hoped so anyway. He started to listen again, and this time there was no going back.

CHAPTER TWENTY-TWO

TIM

NEVER FORGET—WHAT HAPPENS IN VEGAS STAYS IN VEGAS

I didn't see Vanessa that whole day; she wasn't even in Mr. Simon's class. I seriously thought about sneaking to her room, but it was one of those things that could never go as well the second time. I didn't want to take away from that first time, which in my mind had been a strange and wonderful moment. Dare I say it had magnitude? I hope so, but to be perfectly honest, I wasn't sure at that point—at least if it held any for her, which was really what mattered most to me.

Speaking of magnitude, I ran into Mr. Simon again that day, and he asked me to come back to his office. I was worried: Had he found out that I'd snuck into Vanessa's room the night before? Was I in trouble? I could barely eat my lunch, so I just cleared my tray and walked to his office. He was there waiting. Right away I knew it was okay, he wasn't mad, he didn't know.

"Tim, come in," he said. "I've been thinking about our conversation this morning, and I wanted to give you something."

I couldn't imagine what he wanted to give me, short of the stack of perfect Tragedy Papers to peruse. As I was thinking that, literally just then, he handed me a key, and I thought, *Wow, he really is going to give me access to those papers.* But he wasn't.

"Have you noticed the bookshelf in the round room outside the dining hall?" he asked. I had. It stood out and looked like a collection of random old books. "If you're interested, which I think you might be, use this key to open the case. There's a big black book on the bottom. It's the book of Irving traditions. They're all in there. Some of them might seem silly to you, but I've come to believe that the traditions are what keep this place alive, they connect us from year to year. Most of them go back to when I was a student here."

I was amazed, and interested.

"I'm honored," I told him, reaching across his desk and taking the key. "Thank you."

"The only thing I ask is that you pass it along to another student when you're finished with it, someone else who might benefit from it. Is that a deal?"

"Yes, absolutely," I said. I was beyond eager to get to the book, but I had a feeling I should wait until things quieted down.

"Now go forth," he said, "and spread beauty and light."

For some reason I felt empowered by that. When I saw Vanessa's friend Julia at dinner, I walked right up to her. Normally I would have pretended I didn't see her. When she saw me coming, she actually smiled.

"Hi," I said. I had seen her so many times. It would have been ridiculous for me to introduce myself at that point. So I didn't. Of course she knew who I was.

"How's Vanessa?" I asked. I wanted to get right to it. I wasn't sure how long I would have her attention.

"Much better," Julia said, "We made her go see the nurse this morning. It was pretty funny, actually. She was all dressed and ready to go to English. You should have seen her—she was so weak she could barely brush her hair. But she kept insisting that she didn't feel sick anymore so she could go to class."

I smiled and nodded. I couldn't believe she was talking to me like I was just a regular person. I didn't want her to stop. She told me how they tricked Vanessa into thinking they were walking her to class but instead took her to see the nurse.

"Is she still there?" I asked.

"No," Julia said. "She spent most of the day there, though. Now she's resting in her room."

"That was nice of you guys," I said, shifting my tray to my other hand. It was getting heavy. "To take care of her like that."

"You know how it is at school—we're her family," Julia

said. She was quiet for a few seconds. "I hear you were pretty nice to her too," she added.

I looked down. Had Vanessa really told her friends about that? The pull to go talk to her was so strong, but at the same time things had never been better—all the way around. I didn't want to ruin anything.

"Did the nurse say what made her sick?" I asked.

"No, a virus probably," she said. "I mean, we all eat the same things, and nobody else got sick. It sounded awful."

I nodded again. It looked and smelled awful too, but I didn't say that.

"I'm gonna sit down and eat," she said. "Do you want to join us?"

I was still eating at the back table alone.

"No thanks," I said. "I already put my books over there."

"Well, if you change your mind, the offer stands," she said.

"Thanks."

I made my way over to my usual table, and had just taken a big bite of a chicken leg, when Patrick came over. I swallowed fast and hard, almost choking, having no idea what he wanted from me now. Before he started talking, he looked behind him almost like he wanted to see if anyone was following him.

"We didn't finish last night," he said quietly.

"We didn't?"

"No. I mean, all the senior invitations are out, but we still have to pick the junior officer and the extras."

I was as shocked as I had been the day before that he was still going out of his way to enlist my help—again. I'd forgotten all about the junior officer and the extras. To be honest, I hoped he'd move on to another newbie. I was fairly sure I was the only one who dared like his girlfriend. It was becoming clear to me that he enjoyed watching me squirm.

"Sure, I guess so," I said, wondering if I was ever going to get to eat.

"Can you come by my room after dinner?" Patrick asked. "Around seven-thirty?"

Did I have a choice? "Sure," I said.

"Great," he said. "See you later."

By then I had pretty much lost my appetite, though I realized it would be the second meal I would skip that day. I was going to be starving.

When I was finished, I left my tray on the table and went up to my room to lie down. My eyes had been killing me for days. It was getting harder and harder to focus. One night I woke up with such a bad headache that I wasn't sure how I was going to make it through until morning.

I didn't want to admit it, but I was having moments of complete blackness. So far they had happened only in my room, which was so lucky because I worried about what would happen if I was walking around. I guess I would just stop until my eyes readjusted. It usually took only a few seconds, thirty at the most, and then light would come back in and I could pretend everything was okay for a while longer.

Back at my room, I got right into bed. I wished Vanessa could be there and take care of me like I'd taken care of her. It seemed to me that her smile and the soft touch of her hand were so powerful they could make it all go away. Maybe I should tell her about it. Maybe she could help. I was so tired, I had to fight sleep. I must have lost the battle, because the next thing I knew, there was a knock at the door.

I jumped up, feeling a stab of pain in my right eye along with some dizziness. The clock said eight-fifteen.

It was Patrick.

"Are you okay?" he asked.

"I think so," I said, trying to shake it off. "I guess last night's lack of sleep caught up with me. I'm sorry. I'll come right over."

"Your eye is red," he said, pointing.

I glanced in the mirror. It was. It looked like someone had painted the white of my right eye with red paint.

"A blood vessel must have popped," I said casually. "No big deal."

"Maybe you're getting sick," Patrick offered. "Maybe you're getting that nasty bug that Vanessa had."

"No, I'm okay," I said. "This has nothing to do with Vanessa."

"I hope you're right," he said. Then, "But just to play it safe, try not to touch anything in my room. Getting sick is the last thing I need right now."

When I shut the door, I took a better look at myself. I knew things always looked worse on me than they would on other people because of my intense whiteness. Cuts and bruises looked especially terrible when on someone else they might barely be noticeable. When my eyes got bloodshot, they got really, really bloodshot, but this was something I hadn't seen before. I shook it off. With all that exhaustion and the headaches, it was probably nothing, just tiredness. Plus, with all my rushing around the night before cleaning Vanessa's trash can and ducking off her floor this morning, maybe I really did pop a blood vessel or something. If it didn't get better by the time I went home that summer, I told myself, I would talk to a doctor about it.

I ran my hand through my hair, smoothed my shirt, and headed out. It seemed like days had passed since I sat on Patrick's floor making invitations.

I knocked.

He pulled open the door, and I was shocked to see a roomful of guys. Last night I had been so surprised that I was the only one he chose to work with him, and now I was equally surprised to see other people there.

"Hi," I said, hoping, as usual, that it wasn't some sort of trick.

"Hey," they all said, echoing each other.

"What's up with your eye?" asked Peter, the one who had been in the bathroom the first time I met Patrick.

"I'm not sure," I said, raising my hand to my eye. The sharp pain had gone away, so it couldn't be that bad, I told myself. "I burst a blood vessel or something."

"Come in," Patrick yelled from the back of the room. I counted—there were eight guys plus Patrick. The pictures of Vanessa were still there, and a few had been added. I could see Patrick looking at me. I was sure he wanted me to notice the pictures, and I was starting to wonder how much of it was for him and how much was for me. Unlike last time, though, I was able to look away. Patrick hesitated for a minute.

"Everyone take a seat," he finally said. "Let me explain how this works, even though most of you already know. Basically, it's a lottery. We choose one name from the bunch—which I will put in my most favorite hat—to be the junior officer. Then we will also choose nine extras. All ten will get an invitation to the outing but will not be told who the officer is—until that night. A bulldog handkerchief is quietly slipped into his or her pocket at the beginning of the event. Then it is up to him or her to begin the outing. That person starts everything. It's symbolic."

For the first time that night, I noticed Kyle, the guy who

had brought me the note from Vanessa asking me to meet her to run. He had always been friendly enough. I was glad to see him. He cleared his throat.

"I checked and there are forty-seven members of the junior class and not a single one of them has the same name, so I just wrote down the first names," Kyle said. I had been right about him. From what I had observed, he was definitely on the outskirts of popularity—a bit closer to that golden ring than I was, for sure, but still not quite there. It made me wonder again how the decision was made about who would be in on this.

Kyle held up a plastic bag full of scraps of paper. It was a little ripped on one end, and I wondered if any of the names fell out. I considered saying something, but since I had no idea what was going on and I didn't really care that much, I decided to let it go.

Patrick smiled.

"Any questions?"

I raised my hand.

"I don't mean to ask the obvious, but I have missed a lot of the buildup," I said. Patrick nodded. "How was *this* group picked?"

"Oh—that's easy. Last year I was the officer, clearly. Everyone else here was an extra. Sydney was an extra too, but she didn't come back this year. The rules say we have to invite the new people to fill the openings. . . . It's a way to make them feel welcome, I guess, so—welcome!" Patrick said in a surprisingly patient tone. What he said made sense, but there seemed to be something off about it. Could it really have been a coincidence that the most popular athlete in the school just happened to be picked out of a hat to lead the senior class in this way? I doubted it. I wondered about the insertion of the handkerchief into his pocket during last year's Game. Had he been excited? Did he expect it? And it also seemed suspicious to me that everyone in the room was male, considering they chose from the entire class. Shouldn't the ratio have been more like five to five, three to seven at the outside? But nine to one? I strongly doubted it.

Patrick moved to his desk, where he picked up what looked like a black magician's hat. I had expected something along the lines of a Yankees cap, so I was surprised to see it. He tapped the top, then turned it over and walked across to Kyle with the bowl of the hat ready to receive the names. Kyle slowly counted each scrap of paper he put in, making sure they were all there. They were.

"Tim, would you like to do the honors?" Patrick asked.

This was getting weirder and weirder. I thought I might tell Vanessa about this whole thing—I could imagine how her face would look when I told her. I hoped I would have a chance to. Just then one of the recently added pictures caught my eye. She was twirling on the quad, her bright skirt dancing around her, lilacs in the background. I swallowed.

"Sure," I said, reaching up and fishing in the hat for a name.

"Wait!" Peter called, putting up his hand. "We didn't take the oath."

"You're right," Patrick said. "Okay, Tim, hold on a minute. We have to take the oath."

I had already settled on a piece of paper, but I let it go and pulled my hand out, wondering how this would change the fate of the draw and ultimately of next year's senior Game. The word *magnitude* ran through my mind again, and I realized I was becoming brainwashed. All that talk of tragedy—maybe it wasn't so good for people our age.

Patrick opened his closet door, got down on his hands and knees, and dug to the way back, through a huge pile of what must have been dirty laundry. He pulled out a bottle of liquor and a stack of tiny plastic cups. He handed each of us a cup and filled it with a bit of liquor. When he got to me, I could see the label said bourbon. I had never tasted anything as strong as that—a beer here and there, a sip of wine with my mother and Sid, but nothing that resembled hard alcohol. My head was starting to throb, not just near my right eye but everywhere now. I knew the bourbon would only make that worse.

Once everyone had a cup, Patrick put down the bottle and the rest of the cups and held his out.

"Repeat after me," he said.

"I hereby promise that everything that transpires in this room will remain secret," he said.

We repeated it.

"And that any decisions made, choices agreed upon, and names uttered will never be discussed again—with anyone."

We repeated that too.

"And never forget—what happens in Vegas stays in Vegas."

I started to laugh, but the rest of the group repeated it, so I stifled my laughter and said the rest of the words.

"Now drink," Patrick commanded. And we all did, quickly. The burn was overwhelming. I was still trying to recover when I noticed everyone looking at me, waiting for me to pick up where I had left off. I quickly reached into the hat, not even bothering to sift through the choices, and grabbed a name. I held it up, wanting more than anything to lie down.

"Read it to us," Patrick said.

I unfolded the name and could see thick black writing, but it was so blurry. I held it close to my face, then pulled it back to see if that would be better. Everyone laughed, I guess thinking that the alcohol had already had an effect on me.

"Can *you* read it?" I said to Kyle, sounding a bit pathetic.

"Sorry, man, house rules: he who pulls reads," Kyle said.

I kept looking, and slowly the letters came into focus. I made out a *D* and I was sure the last letter was an *N*. Finally I was able to see it.

"Duncan," I said, sitting back.

"No way, that guy's such a loser," a mean-looking kid named Justin said.

"I've never even heard of him," Peter said.

"Now, now, gentlemen," Patrick said. "I've thought this through, and this is exactly why we took the oath. We'll pick all ten and then decide who will best fit the job."

I don't know why, but to me it seemed like breaking the rules. Also, I want to apologize here for being so frank, but you'll see I have to be to tell the true story. At this point, I've got to tell the whole, honest story or this would all be a waste.

The hat moved around the room, and everyone but Patrick got a chance to choose a name. Jake, Celia, Arthur, Henry, Kate, Lily, Abigail, Keith. For some reason, the rules state that the officer doesn't participate, so the hat came back to me for the last pick. I just shook my head. I couldn't go through it again. Nobody pushed me. Peter reached in and chose a slip, most likely not the one I would have chosen if I hadn't refused my turn. I mean, it would have had to be different, right? There was a small chance another hand reaching in would grab the same slip but much more likely it would settle on a different slip altogether.

Peter unfolded the slip. He read out the name: "Janie."

"Now we vote," Patrick said.

"Is this how it happened last year?" Kyle asked, like it was finally dawning on him. "I thought the first name was the officer, no questions asked."

Patrick smirked. "Well, you can vote that way—that is completely within your rights—but no, there is always some wiggle room."

"So, who was pulled first last year?" Kyle asked, and I got the sense he was pushing something that he should have left alone. Or at least that Patrick thought he should leave alone.

"I don't know. I wasn't there," Patrick said, but the look on his face said he did know.

"Fine," Kyle said, looking away.

Everyone was a bit antsy and kept glancing toward the door. It seemed like nobody really wanted to be there anymore.

"So, let's vote," Patrick said. "I'll read a name, and if you want that person to be the officer, you raise your hand. You can vote only once. After the first round, we'll see where we are."

This is where you come in, Duncan. I'm sorry for what you're about to hear, but I have to be honest—otherwise, what's the point? So, he started reading the names in the order they were picked. Duncan? Kyle's hand went up. I didn't know you, so I had no opinion, but I realized you were the first one picked—you were the rightful winner, if you could call it that—so I raised my hand too. The response in the room was as though nobody had voted for you. Patrick barely even looked up. He went through the rest of the names until he got to Janie—the one I didn't pick, the one Peter picked for me—when eight hands, including Patrick's, went up.

"In the end it has to be unanimous," Patrick said. "So

there are no questions or disputes later." I detected a hint of annoyance in his voice.

It occurred to me to ask about each of these people: Who were they, what did they have to offer, what were they expected to do anyway? Why weren't we just going with the first name picked—your name? But my eyes were killing me. My right eye kept going in and out of focus. I started to wonder about a possible stroke. I needed to lie down.

"Let's do this again," he said, like he was talking to a five-year-old.

"No, no," I said. "I can just tell you. I vote for Janie."

"Great," Patrick said. He looked at Kyle.

Kyle shook his head. "Fine. I don't care that much. I change my vote to Janie."

"Good choice," Patrick said, and for some reason I hated him more at that moment than I had since I met him. "So, now we just have to get the invitations to these ten, and that's that. Who wants to distribute them?"

There were no volunteers.

"Everyone take one," Patrick said.

"Can I have a close one?" I asked. "My eyes are really bothering me."

Patrick looked at me and shook his head. "You know what, man, you go back to your room. I'll take yours. They are all in the same building anyway. I can do it. It'll be easy."

"Thanks," I said, wondering just how pathetic I looked to be getting sympathy from such a monster.

But I couldn't sleep. I tried, I needed it, but I just couldn't. In so many ways, Mr. Simon's timing couldn't have been better. It was like he knew somehow. There are times when I wonder if he did know. But I tell myself there is no way he would have let it go so far if he really knew, so I must be wrong about that. When I was sure everyone was asleep, that Patrick and the other guys were back from distributing the invitations, I got up and walked down to the bookshelf outside the dining hall. Before I opened it, I went to the sick cabinet and got myself a few packets of graham crackers and ginger ale. I unlocked the glass case and read until the sun came up. As I expected, the book confirmed everything I thought and feared.

CHAPTER TWENTY-THREE

DUNCAN

IT'S TIME TO MAKE THE DONUTS

Duncan walked slowly down the stairs to the senior donut breakfast—one of the best events all year. A local donut maker came in, let the students help prepare the batter and top the donuts themselves. Throughout the dining hall there were huge plastic bowls filled with powdered sugar, cinnamon sugar, cocoa, and glazes like honey, vanilla, and chocolate. The seniors spent the morning there, making donuts, eating, and—best of all—drinking coffee. It was the one time all year the delicious, rich coffee was served to the students in the dining hall. There was a line leading up to the coffee urn, next to which was a chalkboard sign saying it had been roasted in a town across the county called Mamaroneck, and a stack of Irving mugs they were allowed to keep. It was a long-standing tradition and symbolic of their move toward adulthood.

Duncan had been looking forward to it—before. In fact, he had fantasized about it on more than one occasion, to be at the donut breakfast with Daisy by his side and all of his friends there. He had heard that in years past the seniors sometimes spent all day in the dining hall, in their pajamas, playing long games of cards or Monopoly or Scrabble. It was one of those days when anything went, when the seniors could skip class and not get in trouble.

But that morning Duncan didn't feel so well. Daisy was at the bottom of the stairs, wearing navy-blue sweats with pink and yellow flowers embroidered on them and a yellow bulldog T-shirt. Her hair was swept up in a high ponytail with a yellow gingham ribbon tied tightly around. Duncan had thrown on jeans and a plain gray T-shirt. He could see Daisy's disappointment immediately.

"Morning," he mumbled as he got close to her.

"Hi, good morning," she said, still trying to be upbeat. "Did you sleep well?"

"Not so great," he said.

"Well, it's time to make the donuts," she said.

Duncan could barely manage a smile or a small laugh. He felt rotten.

"Are you okay?" Daisy asked.

For a brief moment, Duncan considered confessing everything—telling her about Tim's story and what he had just heard. He considered talking through the various scenarios of what might have happened if things hadn't gone the way they did, how things might have been different. But he looked at her and saw his carefree girlfriend in her pajamas, and he decided he couldn't do that to her.

"Yeah," he said, putting his arm through hers. "Just tired and stressed about my Tragedy Paper."

"Me too," she said, sounding relieved. "Who isn't? But let's not think about it today. Today is a day off."

"Okay," he said, wanting more than anything to go back to bed, to keep listening to Tim's words and get through the worst of it. He knew where it was going, of course, but there were some details he couldn't place, some moments only Tim could let him in on, was already starting to let him in on.

The dining hall was amazing. It was set up like a donut shop, with streamers and balloons everywhere. Trays of warm, sweet donuts sat on tables all around, and there was a workstation for those who really wanted to get in on the action. The dining room was theirs today: the other students had been allowed to have breakfast on their halls—small boxes of dry cereal and milk. And then they would have picnic lunches throughout the school for the rest of the day— some in the library, others in classrooms.

Duncan was able to forget for a little while. He had fun playing Uno with Daisy, and the food was delicious. He particularly liked the chocolate-glazed donuts, which Daisy seemed to love to make for him. He was relieved that there were no questions about the senior Game. It was an unspoken rule to not talk about it openly, and nobody took him aside. But days were slipping by, and he was as stumped as ever. In the time he sat at the table, cards moving back and forth between them, he thought of six different ways to proceed, knowing that choosing the junior officer and extras was at the top of his list of what bothered him. Maybe they could just play a game of Ultimate Frisbee on the quad—out in the open in the middle of the day. What could go wrong there? Or maybe an indoor game of sardines in a can—that could be fun. But that also might involve too much hiding, too many out-of-sight moments. What about another version of the donut day? he wondered to himself. Perhaps a cookie-decoration day or a cake day? He knew that wasn't the answer. By that time, it was nearly eleven. They had spent hours already making and eating donuts, and nobody seemed to be going anywhere. Duncan couldn't stand it any longer—he had to get out of there.

"I'm sorry," he said to Daisy. "I'm really not feeling too hot today. I think I'm going to take advantage of the loose schedule and head back to bed."

The look in Daisy's eyes cut through him and made his stomach sink. He wanted to keep it together, he kept telling himself. He didn't want to ruin everything he had built—everything he had achieved. In the end, what difference would it make, really? He couldn't change things that had already happened.

"Can I come with you?" Daisy asked, her eyes pleading. It was so unlike her to want to break the rules or miss such a big event that again he was tempted to let her in on everything.

"No," he said, reaching out and rubbing her arm in an attempt to let her know this truly had nothing to do with her. "I think I just need to be alone. Maybe I'll come back later."

She nodded. He could tell she was close to tears.

"Have fun with everyone," he said.

She nodded again. He had a feeling she was afraid to talk.

He stood up and gave her a quick hug. Then he walked through the big double doors, telling himself he would come back. Maybe an hour was all he needed. But as it turned out, he didn't come back that day, since Tim took him almost to the end of his story.

CHAPTER TWENTY-FOUR

TIM
VANESSA FOUND ME LATER, AS PROMISED

I slept for a few hours, and when I woke up, I quickly realized three things: I had missed Mr. Simon's class. My head didn't hurt anymore. And my eye wasn't nearly as red as it had been. I breathed a huge sigh of relief and went to the bathroom to wash up. Because classes had already started, it was peaceful and I enjoyed every minute of washing my face and brushing my teeth and glancing at my eyes and seeing they looked close to normal.

I went back to my room, got dressed, grabbed my books, and headed for the nurse's office. It was the only way I could get a pass for missing English, and I thought that even though I was feeling much better, a few Advils wouldn't hurt.

I was surprised to see Vanessa sitting in the waiting room. It was the first time I had seen her since I had been in her room two days before, and she looked great. Her color was back to normal, her hair was shiny and beautiful, and she was wearing faded jeans and a turquoise bulldog shirt. I had never seen the shirt in that color before and wondered how many versions there were altogether.

"Hey!" I said, walking directly to her and sitting in the seat next to her.

"Hi!" she said with a big smile.

"How are you feeling?" I asked, wanting to get as close to her as I could, wanting to kiss her. But I didn't. I knew I couldn't.

"I'm much better," she said, reaching up to play with a strand of her hair. "All better, really. Nurse Singer just wanted me to come in for a follow-up, so that's why I'm here."

We sat quietly for a minute, each of us looking at our feet. Vanessa was wearing turquoise Chuck Taylors. I loved that. I was wearing typical old sneakers that, as I looked at them, became more and more dorky by the minute.

"Why are you here?" Vanessa said suddenly, as though it had just occurred to her that there might be something going on with me.

"I overslept," I said, which she would understand. She was the one who told me the trick to getting away with over-sleeping was a quick trip to the nurse's office. "And I had a headache," I added.

"Do you still?" she said, looking at my eyes more closely now. Even though they were so much better, they still weren't quite right, I knew that.

"What?" I said, distracted.

"Have a headache?" she asked.

I considered it for a minute and realized I did. It was coming back.

"A little," I said.

Just then Nurse Singer came out to greet us and called Vanessa back with her. I waited in my seat, willing my headache to not get any worse.

It took only a few minutes and they were back, smiling.

"Keep drinking fluids," the nurse said kindly.

"I will," Vanessa said. Then she looked at me. "I especially like ginger ale."

"Perfect," the nurse said. "And water. You can't go wrong with water."

I wanted to add to the banter and say "And ice chips," but I refrained.

As Vanessa walked by, she reached out and touched my wrist. "Thank you," she said.

Nurse Singer was just standing there, waiting for me.

"You're welcome," I said.

And then Vanessa said the magic words. "I'll find you later."

I nodded, probably more seriously than I should have, but what more could I ask for, hope for? She'd find me later. That was better than hearing *You'll win the lottery later*.

"What's going on?" the nurse asked once I sat down on the edge of the exam table. At first I thought she was asking me what was going on with Vanessa. I almost started to tell her, but I realized she was simply asking me why I was there in her office.

"I had a bad headache last night and slept in," I said. "It's much better now, but I didn't want Mr. Simon to be mad, and I could use some Advil, or Tylenol, or whatever you think might help."

I was hoping she would just take my word for it and give me a few pills and let me go. But she went to the cabinet and found my file, standing for a while to read through it. Then she took out her light and looked in my ears, and then my mouth, and then my eyes. She looked in my eyes for a long time.

"Have you had pain in your eyes?" she asked.

"A little," I admitted. "But nothing too bad."

"Have you been wearing your glasses?" she asked, pointing to my file. "Especially in the sun?"

"I was," I said. "But I lost them," I lied.

"Do you sometimes feel dizzy?" she asked, slight alarm showing in her eyes.

"Sometimes," I said. "But not often," I lied.

"I'm going to send you into town later today to see an eye doctor," she said. "Your eyes don't look good, and that coupled with the headache you're complaining of makes me think it wouldn't hurt to see someone. Plus, he can give you a new pair of glasses."

The way she said it—that it wouldn't hurt—told me I

had a good chance of talking her out of it. So I did: I told her I was stressed about the Tragedy Paper and that was what was causing my headaches. I told her that I got an eyelash in my right eye last night and rubbed it way too hard, that I would be more careful. And I told her that I did have another pair of glasses, a pair I didn't like as much. I promised I would take them out and wear them. I also told her that I couldn't lose any time this afternoon, that I planned to work on my paper, and that if I didn't, it would just add to my stress. She thought for a minute and nodded.

"Okay," she said slowly. "But if anything changes, or you experience any severe pain or dizziness, I want you to come back right away—I don't care what time of day or night it is. And either way, I want you to find me early next week and let me take another look. If I don't like what I see, I'm going to drive you to the eye doctor myself. Is that a deal?"

"Yes," I said, hopping off the exam table. "It's a deal."

She wrote a few sentences in my file and scribbled a separate note that she handed to me, which said I had a legitimate excuse for being late to class.

I followed her to the locked medicine cabinet. I stood as she unlocked it and pulled out a huge bottle of white capsules. She shook out two long pills and handed them to me. She turned and pulled down a plastic cup, leaned over a water cooler to fill it, and handed me the cold cup.

"Thank you," I said again, taking the pills.

"Now get to class," she said, smiling.

Class was the last place I wanted to go but I had no choice, and by then, there were only about fifteen minutes left anyway.

Vanessa found me later, as promised. Now, at this point I am pretty sure you just want to get on with it. I'm sure you have figured some things out and simply want me to confirm them. But I have to tell you about that afternoon—which I look back on as the worst and best afternoon of my life for a bunch of different reasons, some I didn't even consider until very recently. You might remember at the beginning of my story I said Vanessa was the only other person who would hear this story. It's true—I sent her the same CDs I had Kyle leave on your desk. I have no way of knowing if she did or ever will listen to them, but on the off chance that she does, I have to take my time with this. I want her to know how much it meant to me. I want her to understand my thought processes that week—how I thought one thing, then another. Dare I use the word *monomania* here? Obsessed with one goal? Well, it depends on what that goal would be. And if I am allowed to be more liberal with the meaning of the word and look at it as obsessed with one thing—well, then, maybe.

Vanessa found me at lunch. I was starving and feeling pretty good. The pills that the nurse had given me that morning were like a miracle drug. The menu that day was grilled cheese and garden tomato soup. As I was dropping the tiny round crackers into my thick red broth, trying not to splatter it on my flannel shirt, Vanessa came up behind me. I had expected one of her usual brushes in the hall, a muttered word that I would spend the rest of the day trying to figure out. But she walked right up and said hi.

"Hi," I said back.

Her hands were empty, so I assumed she'd just arrived.

"Are you going to eat that?" she asked.

I glanced at my tray: the crackers were starting to soften in the soup, just the way I liked it.

"I was planning to," I said.

"Would you consider not eating it and come with me?" she asked.

I hesitated, but only for a second. Food or Vanessa—seriously?

"Sure," I said. "Just let me put the tray away."

As always, I wondered if it was some kind of trick, but I dropped off my full tray, hoping nobody would notice how much food I was wasting, and I walked back to her. She was just standing there waiting for me and smiled even wider as I got closer. When I was about a foot away from her, she turned and walked out. I followed. She walked through the main room and toward the door, under the ENTER HERE TO BE AND FIND A FRIEND arch, and out onto the quad. I followed, thinking it was going to be freezing since neither of us had our coats. But I was surprised by the balmy late-February air. It was mild and breezy, and I closed my eyes and breathed it in.

"Where are we going?" I asked as I followed her down the path toward the lower school.

"You'll see," she said. I liked walking behind her. I could watch her—the way she walked; the way her ponytail, fastened with a turquoise rubber band, swung back and forth; the way she placed her feet on the ground with her toes turned slightly outward—but feel completely protected because she couldn't see me. I was quiet as we made our way through the playground and into the main building. She walked right to the office and said we were there, reporting for duty.

I had no idea what was going on but went along with it. I liked seeing the little kids around me. I liked being away from our familiar life for a short while; it's something we don't get to do very often at a boarding school.

"They asked if we wanted to do art or writing, and I chose art," she said.

"Art or writing what?" I asked.

"To mentor the little kids," she said. "I do this a few times a year, and I thought you would like to come with me. It's fun."

I nodded, holding back the question that was forming in my mind: why didn't she ask Patrick? But I knew the answer to that. This was probably the last thing he would want to do. He was way too busy being cool and playing sports and putting together—or should I say "fixing"?—the senior outing.

A teacher greeted us. He looked so young I wondered how he could possibly have finished enough school to be qualified to teach here. But when he spoke, I could tell he was older than I thought he was. Vanessa introduced us. I loved hearing her say my name.

"Thanks for coming, you guys," he said. "The kids love having older students hang out with them. You'll be working with the second graders. They're seven and eight years old—that's the age you asked for, right?"

Vanessa nodded, a bit sheepishly, I thought.

"Great," he continued, leading us down a long hall covered with kids' art projects. There were spiral paper mobiles hanging from the ceiling, what looked like decorated body outlines hanging on the walls, and the floor was covered with different animal prints.

"The project we had in mind is a winter collage," we were told. "They've already walked through the woods and picked tons of things to work with—dried leaves, pinecones, pine needles. But I want you guys to decide what materials to use from the art room to enhance the collage. Anything you find there is fair game."

"Sounds good," Vanessa said confidently. The teacher stopped walking and gestured toward an open door. Inside, there were about twelve kids spread between two big square tables covered with brown paper, smiling. I hoped I wouldn't freak them out. A few waved when we walked in. Others called hello. I didn't notice anyone doing a double take or staring at me. If anything, they couldn't take their eyes off Vanessa.

"This is Vanessa and Tim," the teacher said, and I realized he'd never told us his name. "Be nice to them if you want them to come back." He turned to us. "They're all yours."

Vanessa jumped right in. She asked one kid at a time to come up and look through the bins and choose one type of item that would be placed on the table for everyone to use. That way, she explained, they could each make a choice and benefit from everyone else's choices. I was amazed by how easy she was with the kids. I stood back, unsure of what to say or do. I had spent so little time with young kids, they were like alien life-forms to me.

One girl chose feathers, explaining that they could symbolize the birds in the woods; someone else chose colorful rocks; a third child picked green confetti. "For rain," he said.

"That's a great idea," Vanessa said. "Because even though it gets really cold, there are still warmer days in the winter, so it does rain. That gives me an idea. Can I make my choice now and put it on the table?"

Everyone nodded, mesmerized.

"I'm going to pick the white confetti," she said. "Do you know what that can represent?"

"Snow!!" everyone called out.

"Yes, snow, my favorite."

It was at that moment that a little boy I hadn't noticed before peeked up from behind the far table. His hair was a shocking white, and his skin was like paper. The other kids didn't seem to be aware of him at all. Maybe he always hung out below the table. He stared at me, and at first I wanted to run; I didn't want to be connected to the little kid who was too scared to come out from behind the table. That had been me—my whole life! But the farther he lifted up his head, the more amazing he looked to me. He was the same size as the other kids, but he seemed more compact. His eyes were a pale blue.

"I like snow," he said, his voice a bit deeper than I would have expected. "Do you?"

He was looking right at me. Without thinking, I walked over to him. There was an empty seat next to the one that was his but he hadn't been sitting on. I sat down.

"I do like snow," I said. "But not as much as Vanessa does."

That did what I hoped it would do, put the focus back on her. She led the class through the activity. I sat quietly next to the albino boy, who told me his name was Nathan.

"I'm a little like snow," he said after a while. "So are you!"

"Yes, we are," I said. "And snow is a pretty special thing, I guess."

I spent the rest of the time sitting with Nathan. I figured that was what Vanessa had had in mind, so I don't think I was letting her down. Although when I look back to that day and remember her face, I realize that when she looked at us from her place in the front of the room, her expression was one of surprise and concern. The collages at the end were amazing—they each looked like they had been done by kids far older than the ones in that class. I wasn't sure I was even seeing them all that clearly, to be perfectly honest, my eyes were so bad by then. I was fairly sure I was missing a lot.

We were thanked over and over again by the teachers as we left. Vanessa started heading back to school.

"Do you want to take a walk?" I asked. The sun had come out and the sky was as blue as I could ever remember seeing it, I thought. "I don't have any more classes today. Do you?"

"No," she said. "Sure, let's take a walk."

"Where to?" I asked.

"How about the lower school nature trail?" she asked. "It's really nice."

As soon as we were about twenty feet in, I took her hand. She let me and I was grateful for that. Her hand was soft and full of energy. I hoped mine felt the same to her.

"Thanks for coming with me," she said. "I like little kids. Sometimes I think I'd like to be a teacher."

"You'd be a good teacher," I said.

"Do you think so? Really?" she asked. It was so uncharacteristically insecure of her that I laughed. She didn't need me to tell her she'd make a good teacher. Still holding her hand, I turned and pulled her toward me. She didn't resist. I leaned in and kissed her. She kissed me back, for a long time. It was better than our kiss in the elevator. It was better than any kiss I had ever had and, I fear now, any I will ever have again.

And then she pulled away slightly and nuzzled her face into my neck. I drew her closer, and we stood there for a long time. My eyes were stinging in the bright sunlight, but I didn't want her to notice; I wanted to stand there forever. She stepped away and, still holding my hand, moved back out toward the playground. She didn't say a word. When we were within sight, I dropped her hand and we quietly walked back to school, across the quad, under the ENTER HERE TO BE AND FIND A FRIEND arch, and into the main, paneled room. I was going to keep walking up the stairs, but she stopped me.

"I just want to say—" she started. Suddenly her eyes moved behind me, and I turned and there was Patrick. I expected Vanessa to take a step back or make some excuse, but she didn't. She waved to Patrick and he joined us, standing next to both of us, completing the circle.

"See you later," I said after we made a little small talk. She hesitated, I saw it. But there was no point anymore. There would never be a point. Whatever she had meant to achieve with that little teacher stunt—no matter how good-hearted it may have been—it told me only one thing.

For Vanessa, Patrick would always come first, and she would always see me as an albino—that was all I would ever be to her.

Duncan sat back on his bed, then he lay on his side and curled up. He faced the wall and waited to see what came next. It was too much to process, and now, more than wishing he could talk to Tim, he wished he could talk to Vanessa. She truly seemed to like Tim, way more than Patrick, or at least on a much more important level than she liked Patrick. Would she ever take Patrick to mentor the little kids? He bet not. And was it only because there was an albino boy there that she took Tim, or was that just a coincidence?

Duncan knew girls like Vanessa. Or maybe he didn't and just thought he did because the way she was behaving, or at least the way Tim described it, was far beyond what he ever would have expected from her. But why keep Patrick around, then? Because under all those layers there was still nothing more than a superficial girl? Even as he thought it, he wasn't sure he believed it. His mind flashed to Daisy, in her pajamas, looking so sad. He pushed himself up to sitting, thinking he would go find her, but when he glanced at the clock and saw there was still so much day left, he gave up. He just couldn't pretend to be happy for that long.

CHAPTER TWENTY-FIVE

TIM

SOMETIMES IT'S HARD—IMPOSSIBLE, EVEN—TO KNOW HOW MUCH MAGNITUDE A CHOICE HOLDS UNTIL IT IS ALL OVER

I couldn't get it out of my head—the image of that little albino kid peeking up from behind the art table. That poor kid, having to go through life with everyone staring at him, wondering what's wrong with him. And he was so young, he had so many years of that ahead of him. I knew I should have befriended him, but I simply didn't have the energy to do it.

On Wednesday night, Patrick knocked on my door after lights-out. I had been lying in bed, in boxers and my first bulldog T-shirt—I chose black—trying to will away my headache. It had turned into a low-grade nuisance, no longer a sharp pain, but it came back exactly four hours after I had taken the painkillers from the nurse.

"Is everything okay?" I asked as he slipped into my room.

"Yeah," he said casually. "I just wanted to fill you in. I was out at the site."

"The site?"

"You know, the site for the outing. The big hill," he said a bit impatiently.

"Right," I said, nodding, wishing I had pretended I was asleep.

"I need about six, seven guys to help me, and I want you to be one of them," he said. "I already talked to Kyle and Peter."

"What sort of help?" I asked, stalling. But really, I was getting used to being in his inner circle. Who wouldn't like that?

"Are you in?" he asked, looking so huge in my room.

"I didn't say that yet. I want to know what sort of help you need before I decide," I said. "Do you want to take your coat off and sit down?"

"Sure," he said, doing both. He sat cross-legged on the floor in front of my bed. And then he looked around like he couldn't quite remember what he was doing there.

"You need help?" I prompted him.

"Oh yeah," he said. "The thing is, I can't let you in on the details unless I have your word that you're in. It's too risky."

"Why is it risky?" I asked.

"Are you in or not?" Patrick asked. His voice was still kind, but I got the feeling I shouldn't push that anymore. I knew I was going to say I was in, but there was a part of me that worried I wouldn't be able to do what he asked of me—literally. At this point, I was starting to be concerned about basic things like walking to class and participating in gym.

"In," I said.

"Great, good," he said, moving an inch closer to me. "You know how we need sleds?"

I nodded.

"And we need them to be there when everyone arrives. I thought about having people drag them in that night, but there is no way that will work. First of all, where would we store them in the meantime? And second of all, it will make way too much commotion and noise. So they have to be there, at the top of the hill, waiting. I'm thinking we'll need at least ten."

"Why can't you just have them waiting at the entrance to the path and as everyone comes by, they can pick one up?" I asked.

"I thought about that," he said, running his hand through his hair, messy from the hood he had just had on. "But there is too good a chance they will be found. Teachers jog on that path; kids walk there even though they aren't supposed to. You know how it is. And," he said, gearing up like he was going to tell me something really great, "the best news is that I was in town this afternoon and I talked to a guy at the toy store. He actually graduated from the Irving School—in, like, 1979 or something—and I told him about the outing. Turns out he was second-in-command for his class Game— I guess they did it a bit differently then—and, get this, their Game was musical chairs! Apparently, they thought they were being really cutting-edge when they took all the chairs out of the Hall and set them up on the quad. Then they brought out big speakers and played musical chairs. He seems like a sad sack wanting to relive his high school glory, but I think that's going to work in our favor. When I told him that I was this year's senior officer and about the plan we came up with, he was blown away with excitement. He offered to do whatever he could to help us. So he's going to drop off the sleds at the entrance to the path on the far side of campus, you know where I mean? If you walk through the woods?"

Again, I nodded.

"He's going to drop them all off there on Monday night—two days before the event. Hey, did you hear—there's supposed to be a big storm over the weekend?"

"Cool," I said. "So what do you need me to do?"

"Oh yeah," he said, smacking his forehead with his palm like he was an idiot. "I need you to help me lug the sleds in from the road."

He said it like he was saying *I need you to grab an extra burger for me at lunch.* Like it was no big deal. I could have— I should have—said no, I wasn't feeling great. I know I keep saying this, but it is important so you understand why I did some of the things I did: for the first time in my life, I was a part of something, The Event. And I wanted to be. As stupid or shortsighted as that sounds, I didn't want to say no. Also, I figured, the busier I was, the less time I would have to think about Vanessa.

"Sure," I said.

"So, Monday night after lights-out, we'll walk to the road and pull the sleds to the top of the hill."

"Great," I said, thinking that at least it would be dark, so I wouldn't have to worry about the sun hurting my eyes.

"Sleep well," he said, opening the door quietly and peeking out before he made his getaway. He pulled my door shut without a sound, and I was left there, wide-awake, wishing I, instead of he, could be with Vanessa.

It did snow that weekend. We woke up on Saturday to a few inches that had already fallen. It was beautiful and I felt hopeful. For a very brief moment, it made me think I wasn't being fair to Vanessa when it came to that little albino kid. Maybe I should give her a chance to explain, or maybe I could just loosen up a tiny bit. I told myself I would try. I would try anything for Vanessa.

I planned on using the entire weekend to work on my Tragedy Paper. I had done some research, and thought a lot about what made something a tragedy. I had no idea if I was on the same wavelength as Mr. Simon, but I was beginning to think it didn't really matter all that much as long as I was on some wavelength. I could hear lots of noise in the hall, so I pulled on jeans, left on the T-shirt I had slept in, and walked out.

"There's an omelet bar!" Patrick yelled down the hall to me. Omelet bars were special, apparently. "Come on!"

The dining room was already way busier than a usual

weekend day, when it's open from eight to ten and people trickle in when they wake up. The snow really had everyone excited.

Before we entered the craziness, Patrick stopped walking and pulled me over to the window.

"What's up?" I asked. I started to wish I had at least washed my face and brushed my teeth. When he leaned in and starting talking quietly, I closed my mouth and tried not to breathe. But I was feeling good. I had decided to take my pain management into my own hands. I had come up with a plan, and I was going to be ready to help Patrick with those sleds.

"I've decided to change the outing to tonight," he said. "With this snow, it's too good to miss."

"What? Are you kidding? All that planning and now you're going to change it? How will you let everyone know? How will you get the sleds in time?"

"I have most of that covered," he said. "Right now Kyle and Peter are telling each and every member of our class, and then they'll move on to the ten juniors. But I still need your help with the sleds. I called into town, and just as I thought, the guy is happy to work with us. He said he can have the sleds here by about two. Look at it out there, man. This is so freakin' awesome."

The word *magnitude* popped into my head, and for the very first time, I think I understood it. Well, to be perfectly honest, I don't think I fully understood it until everything was over. But still, I kept thinking, this decision had more magnitude than Patrick realized. I just felt it. But isn't that always the case? Or at least often the case? Sometimes it's hard—impossible, even—to know how much magnitude a choice holds until it is all over.

"Okay. Great," I said. "Whatever you need."

"Meet me on the quad at about one-thirty, and we'll head out."

"It's snowing really hard," I said, looking out the window in the round room. "Are you sure this is a good idea?"

"Yes, I'm sure," he said, turning. I followed him into the dining hall. There were three omelet bars with a person behind each one dressed in a chef's coat and hat. They looked just like the ones I've seen in hotels, with lots of choices for fillings. I could see cheddar cheese, mushrooms, peppers, onions—all grown or made locally, no doubt. But my appetite was gone, so I grabbed a bagel and took it back to my room.

I gathered my books and went to the Hall, which was completely empty despite the deadlines racing toward us, and I tried to write. My mind was blank. All I could think about was magnitude. So I made a list of all the things I thought had magnitude. I wrote a big number one, and after that I wrote: "That I was born albino." And then I was stuck. It seemed like everything for me was based on that—it was certainly the biggest defining thing in my life—but I had a feeling I was missing the point. As much as I would like to change that, I knew that being an albino was not a tragedy. A tragedy was something else. I could almost feel it, but I couldn't get it down on paper.

I gave up and headed back to my room to get ready, noticing that the wind was blowing and it must have snowed at least another six inches since we woke up. I dug into the back of my closet and pulled out my glasses. I knew I had been pushing my luck, and I hoped I'd be so covered up anyway that nobody would notice. I stuck them in my pocket and trudged downstairs, marveling at how good my head and eyes felt, patting myself on the back for having taken care of that problem.

Man, it was amazing out there. There were kids everywhere, and I wondered where all the teachers were. You know how there were always a few adults milling around wherever we were? But on that day I didn't see any, I think. The entire campus was covered with thick, bright snow. The treetops were blanketed in white. And the tiny flakes were still coming down, swirling around. It was like the night at the airport, the night Vanessa and I built our igloo together.

There were so many people on the quad, throwing snowballs and making snow angels, that it took me a minute to realize Patrick was already there. I walked over to him.

"Hey," I said.

"Oh, good, you're here," he said.

He turned and started waving people toward him. Kyle was there, and Peter. It was mostly the guys from the meeting in Patrick's room plus two or three more. Everyone nodded and smiled at each other, and I felt, all covered up as I was, that I belonged. I would have done pretty much anything to hold on to that feeling.

My glasses were still in my pocket as we turned and walked across the quad, but my eyes felt so good I just left them there. I stayed in the back of the group. It was slow going, and by the time we reached the science building and the path into the woods, there was so much wind and icy snow that I decided to pull them out and put them on anyway. They shielded me from the wind and the pelting flakes.

"Onward," Patrick said, and I hoped he wouldn't make us stop and talk because I knew I would feel compelled to take my glasses off. We all looked behind us as we entered the woods, surprised that nobody was following us or asking where we were going. I'm sure everyone had the same thought I did: this seemed way too easy.

I tried to remember where I had been with Vanessa that day when she asked me to jog with her, and kept my eye out for our rock, though I never found it in all that snow. I started thinking I had been wrong all along. No, maybe that wasn't what I was thinking. Maybe it was more that I should put aside my silly convictions for the day and enjoy it and everyone here, including Vanessa. Maybe if I wasn't such a monomaniac—I was the one obsessed with being an albino—maybe things could be different. If I could let it go, even for one day, maybe I could be happy. I could slip in another kiss. The thought of that and my clear, pain-free head made me feel like Superman walking through those woods.

About halfway along the path, Kyle started to slow down noticeably. At first, I thought he was adjusting the zipper on his coat or something, but then he leaned against a tree and started moaning.

"I hate this." He said it to himself, but I heard him anyway.

"Are you okay?" I asked.

He looked up, startled. He must have thought he was last in line. For a minute his face looked almost normal, but then he leaned behind the tree and puked. The rest of the group was about twenty feet ahead, maybe more, trudging through the snow.

"You guys coming?" Patrick called back, annoyance in his voice. "We have to keep going."

Kyle started to move forward, then he turned to the side and threw up again.

"I think I must have eaten a rotten egg."

I put my hand on his shoulder. After what I'd been through with Vanessa, Kyle's vomit didn't bother me in the least.

"Kyle's sick," I yelled ahead to Patrick. "Do you have any water or anything?"

Patrick wasn't much of a leader, I have to say. He just stood there for a minute and then shook his head.

"You'll feel better if you keep walking," he said. "Try not to think about it."

That was all the support he offered before continuing on. A few guys lingered and muttered things, but they seemed afraid to be left behind, so they followed Patrick. I stood next to Kyle in the snow and waited. My eyes were feeling better than they had in days. I know I keep saying this too, but the feeling was amazing. My glasses gave me a sense of protection, and I was sorry I had so fully rejected them, though I did know this was far different from wearing them in the bright sun with no hat or bulky coat.

"I know the path," I said gently. "We're closer to the road than if we headed back the way we came."

Kyle didn't respond.

"I'm going to be sick again," Kyle said, stepping away from me and heaving into the snow. I grabbed a handful of snow when he was finished and offered it to him.

"Use a little of this to wash out your mouth," I said. "And put some on the nape of your neck if you can, and your wrists—it might help."

About five minutes went by, and Kyle seemed to feel a bit better.

"What do you want to do?" I asked him.

"Stay here until they come back, and then head out," he said seriously. "What else can I do?"

"That's not going to work for a few reasons," I said. "First,

I'm not even sure they'll come back this way. And the longer we wait, the weaker you're going to get. Plus, it's really cold out here."

Kyle nodded. I was afraid he'd say he was going to be sick again, but he didn't. He reached down and lifted some more snow into his mouth.

"Come with me. I'll go slowly. When we get to the other side, I'll ask the guy who's bringing the sleds if he can drive you back. What do you say?"

Kyle looked unsure.

"Do you want to at least try to go?" I asked.

Kyle nodded, and then took a step. We walked quietly, and after a while I could hear a car idling, which turned out to be a huge bright red pickup truck full of sleds. When we got closer, I could see they were long, made of wood with blades on each side and a steering mechanism at the front. It wasn't what I had expected. I thought they would be inner tubes or plastic rings.

Patrick was talking to the man through the driver's side window. Then the man got out, shook Patrick's hand, and started unloading. I couldn't help but think Patrick was using him the way he used all of us for one thing or another.

"I can't do it," Kyle muttered.

"No, no, of course not," I said. "You're sick. I'll ask him to drive you back."

Kyle seemed to have second thoughts.

"No. You know what, the guys are going to think I'm a wuss," he said. "I'm going to stick it out and walk back with everyone else."

I looked at him. He was pale and trying not to shiver.

"Look," I said quietly, "you just threw up three times and still walked through the woods. If anyone thinks you're a wuss, so be it, that's their problem."

I walked over to the man and explained the situation. In minutes he had Kyle set up in the warm cab of the truck. I promised Kyle we would do this as fast as we could.

One by one the sleds were taken off the truck. They were big and heavy. Why in the world they had to be wood with blades I didn't know. But the man said they were the best he had and he wanted to provide only the best for the senior outing.

There were exactly twelve sleds on the truck. I did the math: that was going to mean two trips. The first trip was okay. It took about thirty minutes to get to the top of the hill. I was surprised by how high it was up there.

The toy store man—I never got his name—wondered out loud if it was going to snow all day and night, would the sleds be buried? Patrick thought for a minute and decided we should stand the sleds up against trees, which added to our time and energy drain. When we got back to the road for the second round, everyone was exhausted. I checked on Kyle, who was warm and cozy in the cab listening to the radio. This time it took almost an hour to reach the spot. We had brought no water or food, and I actually started to worry. I was relieved to return to the truck.

"I think we should say good-bye here," Patrick said to the sled man. "We'll head on back."

"Wait," I said. "Can't you drive us?"

"Hell, yeah," he said. I thought more than anything he probably wanted to be invited to the outing tonight. But that wasn't my invitation to extend. "My truck is big. I can drive you all back."

Patrick shook his head.

"If we all show up on the quad in a truck, we're going to get caught," he said. "We can't take that chance."

"I got you covered, guys," the man said, pulling his cap off and on again. He looked to me like he hadn't had this much fun in a long time. "I'll drive you around and drop you off on the road by the gym. It will be fine, and you'll have a ten-minute walk as opposed to an hour or whatever it will take you to get there in this deep snow."

"That should work," Patrick said, looking gratefully at me. I smiled.

A few guys piled into the cab next to Kyle, but I was happy in the bed of the truck.

The ride went fast. When we got back, it was like we had never left: there were still tons of people playing and no teachers in sight. We all nodded to each other but said nothing about what we had just done as we started to go our separate ways.

"Thanks," Kyle said after the group dispersed. "I owe you."

"No problem," I said. "I'm glad you're feeling better."

As I crossed the quad, I caught a glimpse of a lavender ski jacket and turned. Vanessa was with all her friends, and they looked very busy. My eyes were strong, and I loved how her colors—lavender and dark purple—were even brighter next to the snow. I realized what they were doing. They were building an igloo and Vanessa was directing. I wanted to go to her, but Patrick was coming up behind me. And maybe I was still mad about the little albino kid and everything else. So I didn't. I turned and went inside. As I walked under the arch, I could hear her laughter glide toward me across the snow.

I went right to my room, thankful for the tiny window so I could feel far away from the activity and the storm. I got into bed and slept for the next four hours.

CHAPTER TWENTY-SIX

TIM

WHY ARE YOU BAREFOOT?

Duncan wondered for a minute where he had been then—it would have been about four in the afternoon on that awful day. He was probably playing in the snow, he realized. He and Tad had gone out back, instead of out front to the quad, because there was a cool hill leading down from the dining hall to a parking lot. It was really fast, and once, he remembered suddenly, Tad had crashed into one of the parked cars. But he was okay; they laughed it off. He hadn't thought about that at all, there had been so many other things to think about after that night.

Duncan stood up and went to the tiny window, the one Tim had just mentioned. He wished for a minute that it was a time portal and could take him back to that snowy afternoon, hours before everything happened. He would look out and see the blanket of white, and Vanessa would be there, in her bright jacket. And he and Tad would be just on the other side of the building. He wanted to go back to that time, not because he wanted to relive it, not at all. But because those were the last few hours he would ever have without the terrible image in his mind that he feared he would spend the rest of his life running from. But there was no snow out there today. That snow could only be found in Tim's recording.

When I woke up, my clock said it was eight o'clock. I had slept through dinner and I was starving, so I headed to the sick cabinet for a few crackers. I'm sure you remember dinner that night—how they put out sandwiches because of the storm. I was happy to see there was still plenty of food and I wouldn't have to brave the wilderness with only a few crackers in my stomach. I hadn't expected to stay, so I had just socks on, which got soaked from all the melted snow. I pulled them off before I got my food and left them on a chair. I gathered my dinner, and when I got back, Kyle was on the chair next to my socks, a cup of tea in front of him.

"Hi. What's going on?" I asked. He looked up and smiled.

"Hey, thanks again for helping me today," he said. "I can't believe how quickly I got sick. I think I'd still be out there if it wasn't for you."

"No you wouldn't," I said, smiling back. "You would have been okay."

"Well, it would have been much worse, if that's possible, I know that," he said. "Vanessa was looking for you, by the way." I had just taken a bite of my sandwich, and I had to work hard to swallow it.

"She was?" I asked.

"Yeah," he said. "You just missed everyone. They were all here. Vanessa and Patrick and everyone else. I think Patrick must have told her the story of the sleds, and must have said how I got sick and you helped me. I could hear him telling some of the story, and he was sort of laughing. I know he was being mean to me, and to you, like we were wimps who couldn't just go out into the woods and be manly. He said something like I had to throw up and you were at the ready to help. I don't know. He can be a total jerk. But then Patrick got up to get some hot chocolate. I think there's still some over there, and they have real whipped cream. Anyway, as soon as he was out of earshot, she asked if I'd seen you. It seemed pretty urgent."

I willed myself to take a second bite of my sandwich because I didn't want to look like it was such a big deal. I chewed, not tasting the food at all.

"So, what did you tell her?" I finally asked.

"That I hadn't seen you since we got back."

We sat quietly for a minute.

"I thought I'd slept through dinner," I said, trying to change the subject. "I can't believe there's still food out."

"That's because of the snowstorm," he said. "This happens

sometimes. The full kitchen staff can't get in, so we have a simple sandwich night. I think Mr. Simon actually made the brownies."

"Well, it works for me," I said, finishing off the first half of my sandwich. "Is the outing still on?"

"Yeah, everyone is psyched," he said.

"Are you psyched?" I asked.

"No, I'm going to skip it," he said. "I still feel pretty queasy, and to be perfectly honest, I have a really bad feeling about tonight."

"It stopped snowing," I said, pretending not to hear his last comment.

"But there's, like, a foot of snow out there," he said. "I'm fine with it. If Patrick makes fun of me, so be it. It just isn't my thing."

"Okay," I said, thinking he was probably the only smart one around. "I get that. But do you know, is the plan still the same? It's so quiet around here."

"That's on purpose," Kyle said. "Patrick told everyone to pretend they're so tired from playing outside and act like it's going to be an early night. Honestly, I haven't seen a teacher or anyone in charge in a while. I think almost everyone has turned in for the night. I don't think there's going to be a problem."

I nodded. That seemed like too much of a statement to take on, even though I knew what he meant.

I wondered at that moment if I should do what Kyle was

going to do and opt out. I could just not show up. I could somehow get Vanessa's attention and beg her to stay back with me. But I knew I wasn't going to do that. I was feeling physically better than I had in a long time—my eyes felt good, and I was still managing my headaches perfectly. I had finally found the answer to that problem. I was going to take advantage of it.

"Why are you barefoot?" Kyle asked, looking at my feet, which I realized were cold. Instinctively, I reached down and rubbed them.

"My socks got all wet," I said. "I hadn't planned on hanging out so long."

I pushed my chair back and stood up.

"If you change your mind about tonight, I'll watch your back," I said, not sure why I cared if he came or not.

"I know you would," he said. "But I've made up my mind."

We walked up the stairs together, and he stopped at the door to his room.

"I hope it goes well," he said. "I'll see you tomorrow."

"Thanks," I said, reaching out to shake his hand, something I don't usually do. He took my hand and shook, looking me in the eyes. I turned and walked back to my room. I didn't hear a sound, but I started to feel the energy building: somewhere it was growing. I smiled. Maybe it was going to be a good night after all.

CHAPTER TWENTY-SEVEN

DUNCAN

TO BE OR NOT TO BE? TO PLAY OR NOT TO PLAY?

Duncan turned off the CD. He had been in his room all day listening. At one point he slept for an hour. But when he woke up, he went right back to it. It almost felt to him like he was reentering a bad dream, but he couldn't help himself. He had to hear more.

In the middle of the afternoon, Tad knocked on the door to see if he was okay. Later he came back with a note from Daisy asking him to come down and meet her. He ignored the note. He knew he was acting crazy, but he just wanted to get through it.

He told himself he was doing important schoolwork, that this was all for his Tragedy Paper. But he knew it was much more than that. Still, as he listened, he took notes. *Order to chaos to order,* he kept writing, but he could never quite figure out which was the order and which was the chaos. *Reversal of fortune—bad to good to bad?* he wrote. Or was it just good to bad? He wasn't sure. Magnitude, magnitude, magnitude. He knew that was a big one. But he still couldn't identify which things held the greatest magnitude and which didn't matter at all. Monomania? Was this his own personal version of monomania?

He glanced at his desk and saw the paperback version of *Hamlet* that Tim had left for him in the secret compartment. *Don't miss the point,* the Post-it note said. The point? And then Duncan knew: it had to do with the Game, he thought. Because it couldn't have had to do with Daisy. To be or not to be? To play or not to play? His mind was playing tricks on him and he knew it. He listened to Tim's voice tell him about the journey into the snowy woods, and that's when he turned it off. He didn't want to listen to it alone anymore. He could still feel those snowy woods. He took a quick look at himself in the mirror, running his hands over his rumpled hair. He could see sleep in the corners of his eyes, and he took a minute to work it out. Then he went in search of Daisy.

He found her in the Hall, working on her Tragedy Paper. He was so relieved to have finally made the decision to tell her everything that he felt like he was going to cry. He had to stand for a minute before he could talk, pretending he had gotten something in his eye.

"Can you come with me?" he finally choked out. "I want to show you something."

He thought about correcting himself and saying he wanted to play something for her, or he wanted her to hear something, but decided he'd explain when they got to his room.

She smiled, sensing he might be breaking through the shell he had been putting up lately, closed her books, and stood. He took her hand, and they walked back through the long hallway to the stairs leading to the dorms. He didn't hesitate, so she followed, and at the top of the stairs, he tugged her hand, and she went, without asking if it was okay or if they might get in trouble, to the boys' hall. They held hands as they walked the long way down to his tiny room—they didn't see a single person—and then they slipped inside, and he closed the door.

The first thing he did was kiss her. He took her into his arms and kissed her in a way he had wanted to for so long. They had shared great kisses, but other than that one amazing pre-Thanksgiving-break morning, there were always people somewhere around, or the possibility that they would come at any moment and interrupt them. They kissed for a long time, but when she indicated that they should lie down on his rumpled bed, he shook his head gently, nicely.

"I really do want to share something with you," he said. "Something that has nothing to do with us or our being together. Is that okay?"

"Sure," she said. He couldn't tell if she was insulted or not, but he moved to his desk and pressed Play. It was Tim's voice, but she didn't know that yet.

CHAPTER TWENTY-EIGHT

TIM

THE FIRST NAME PULLED IS THE JUNIOR OFFICER—NO QUESTION

As you know, the plan was to leave at eleven-eighteen. That was Patrick's idea, and at first it seemed completely random, but when I thought about it later, it sort of made sense. When nobody made a move by eleven, anyone paying attention probably thought everyone was settled in for the night. Then the next obvious time to meet or plan an activity would have been on the half hour. So to schedule the departure at eighteen minutes after eleven was pretty smart. At the very least, it is a number I will always remember.

Slowly and quietly, people emerged from their rooms dressed for a sledding expedition in deep snow. Somehow, despite all the bulk and the potentially noisy snow pants, it was silent. People filed out and down the stairs like zombies or robots or something. I followed. On the quad, we made a single line shuffling across the campus, down toward the science building and then into the woods. Patrick was at the head of the line, and as we went, the ten juniors who had been asked to join us filed into line. If anyone had looked out the window at that moment, it would have been a crazy sight, but there was no indication that anyone did.

I was toward the middle of the line. Vanessa was in line behind Patrick, and I could see her lavender ski coat and pants, a bright purple hat and scarf to match. I recognized her brother's gloves from our time at the airport.

As we moved into the woods, people started to relax and talk a little. Flashlights were brought out. I looked around—it was beautiful and I remember thinking how lucky I was that my eyes were working so well at that moment. It was much brighter than I expected it to be, but not bright in the way it would have been during the day, requiring me to shield my eyes. It was perfect for me, actually.

I stopped trudging for a minute and realized I was feeling something I very rarely felt—I was happy. I took a deep breath and walked on, following the person in front of me. He was a junior, I knew that, but I didn't know his name. He was wearing a bright green ski hat, so I kept my eye on that and moved forward.

At the bottom of the hill, the line broke apart and everyone started forming groups and talking. I could see Vanessa ahead talking to Patrick, holding his gloved hand with her own and leaning into him. But I wasn't going to let that bother me. No way. People brought out Dixie cups and filled them with what I guessed was scotch or bourbon. I accepted a cup and sniffed it. I slowly took a sip. It was shocking and strong but also warm and crazy-feeling. There was only about an inch in the bottom of my cup, so I chugged it and put the folded cup in the pocket of my jacket.

Patrick came toward me. I felt cozy and untouchable, and I remember wondering why I didn't drink more often.

"Hey," Patrick said, beaming. "Thanks for your help."

"Happy to help," I said, not quite sounding like myself. At that moment, my vision did a weird thing, and I had to blink to get it back in focus, but I told myself it was the liquor and not my eyes. I had that under control.

"I have a final job for you," he said, leaning in so nobody would hear. Vanessa was up ahead with her friends. She looked so happy. Her beautiful blond hair was falling over her shoulders. Julia said something to her and she laughed, swatting her on the arm. She covered her mouth and said something else. They all laughed harder.

"The new guy gets the honor of naming the junior officer—says so in the book. I figure I've fudged enough of the rules, this one seems easy enough to stick to," Patrick said, handing me a folded blue handkerchief. It was stiff and small. There was a tiny bulldog on the corner. As usual, I wondered if it was some trick. Why was he bothering to follow the rules now? "You know who she is, right?"

I shook my head. I didn't know any of the juniors.

"Okay, see that girl over there in the bright pink hat and

gloves, and the white coat?" he asked, talking through an almost-closed mouth. "That's Janie. You just have to slip the bandanna in her pocket. It's okay if she sees you. They're all expecting it, or hoping for it. If she doesn't notice, it's always better, though, more of a thrill. And don't forget, don't tell anyone. It's supposed to be secret."

He nodded urgently at my hand. I was still holding the fabric square out in the open, so I quickly put it in my pocket.

"Okay?" he asked.

"Okay," I said.

"Good. The first chance you get—just do it," he said, his eyes wandering back to Vanessa. "Now, let's have some fun." He patted me on the back and walked away.

You know what happened next.

I still had no idea who you were—that you were the boy in the green hat walking in front of me into the woods. In fact, I had to ask. Your name was rightfully pulled first. I had read the book, I knew the rules. I'm not sure if you've found the key ring yet, in the back of the hidden compartment in the closet. If you have, and I bet you have, then let me just tell you that the skeleton key opens the bookshelf I told you about. It's worth taking the time; it is fascinating.

Some of the book's pages were so scribbled and full, I could barely make anything out. But that page was clear: the first name pulled is the junior officer—no question.

It made me realize there was no way Patrick got so lucky. No way. Why didn't anyone else call him on it? What were the chances that out of fifty people, the most popular one would be picked? Not so good, really. But I wasn't going to let the same thing happen. I don't know why I was so determined. It seemed like everyone was happy with Patrick's choices so far. But I couldn't help wondering whose name had been picked first last year. What if it had been that quiet guy who always ate alone at the table next to the one that I now considered mine? He looked interesting and he was good-looking. But he didn't seem to connect to anyone. Maybe that would have made all the difference for him. These people were in charge of the social order of the school, and it just kept repeating itself. I wasn't going to be a part of that.

So I asked around. I walked up to Peter and casually asked him to point out all the juniors and tell me their names. He had been standing alone, looking like he couldn't quite find a way to break into one of the groups, so he was more than happy to talk to me. He pointed everyone out—starting with Janie Cottage and ending with you: Duncan Meade.

I waited. You were standing in a group of about six people, holding a cup in your hand. You looked nice, approachable. That reinforced my decision. I was going to make things right. I was going to give you what you deserved.

Everyone was waiting for the fun to begin. And for a moment, you turned away from the group. I saw you pour out some of the liquid in your cup. I watched it spill into the snow, and then you saw me looking at you. I walked toward you at that point. My plan was to be perfectly subtle about it and slip it into your pocket, but as I got closer to you, my eyes, which had been feeling so good for days, did a strange thing. It was almost like I felt something pop in my right eye and then my left. I stood still for a minute and it didn't happen again, so I kept coming toward you. But I didn't dare wait around for the ideal moment anymore. Instead of slipping the square into your pocket, I slipped it into your hand. You looked shocked, like I had just fired a stun gun at you. I kept walking, hoping nobody would see. Just then my eyes popped again, and I almost went down. I know you noticed, you were looking right at me, but somehow I stayed on my feet, and once again my eyes were okay. You looked down at the handkerchief, hesitated, and pushed it into your pocket. I took that to mean you had accepted it.

Everything was set in motion.

Patrick, of course, was waiting for Janie Cottage to take over. He was watching her. But she was clueless and making no move toward the top of the slope. Meanwhile, slowly, you made your way around the back and climbed. Everyone was getting antsy; it was taking a long time for the sledding to begin. But people were still having fun.

There you were, at the top of the hill, getting on a sled. You seemed unsure, but I was still certain I had made the right decision. That was when Patrick saw you. He looked so angry, even in that first moment of recognition. You screamed, "Let the sledding begin!" You said it loud, but I could hear the nervousness in your voice; I heard it crack a bit. You were coming down the hill, and we all started running up. I might not have run so fast, but I could feel Patrick behind me, coming to talk to me—to yell at me, probably. Once the bulldog handkerchief was given, it could not be taken back, I knew that. I had read the book.

So I ran. And it was chaos, let me tell you. People were slipping and sliding and laughing and pushing. The pain in my head started so slowly I barely noticed it. It was in front of my eyes, in the usual place, but I was running so fast it didn't sink in until I stopped at the top of the hill. But I still ignored it.

People were going too fast down the slope. They were jumping on two at a time, sometimes three at a time, not realizing they had to steer until they were already moving, racing down. I grabbed a sled. My eyes were going in and out of focus, but I thought that it was fear, that I was afraid of Patrick. I set my sled at the ready, looking behind me. Vanessa was there, an arm's length away. I reached back and grabbed her hand. Patrick was already mad—I didn't even care about making him madder. I pulled Vanessa toward me. She got on the back of my sled and wrapped her arms around me, in front of everyone. I was flying high. I was better than I had ever been. I pushed off. We started slow at first. Then we were going faster and faster. There were people everywhere. Sleds and people. And trees. There were all those beautiful linden trees. The trunks came up toward us and I steered by them. Once, we were so close that Vanessa yelped. I loved it. When we got to the bottom, I was going to tell her how I felt. I was going to ask if she felt the same way about me. I was going to let her explain why she took me to the lower school. It wasn't that I was just an albino to her. I could see it now. It was that she thought albinos were special. She had found another albino person, and she wanted to point him out to me. It took a long time, but I could see it all so clearly.

And then I could see nothing at all.

CHAPTER TWENTY-NINE

TIM

AND THEN MY EYES STOPPED WORKING FOR GOOD

Daisy hadn't moved from the moment Duncan pressed Play, but now she stood up suddenly. Duncan had been sitting at his desk the whole time. He hadn't meant to—he had meant to sit closer to her—but it was like Tim's voice had paralyzed them. Now he also stood and went to her. He wasn't sure if she was going to run. Maybe she couldn't take it any more than he could. But she grabbed him and then, without a word, took his hand. Together they sat down on the bed, side by side, looking straight ahead, and braced themselves.

My eyes went out a few seconds before we hit. Totally out—I couldn't see a thing, no images, no shadows, not even the flashlights. Vanessa's yelps turned into terrified screams as she held on to me so tight. I felt the impact. It was hard and unforgiving. And then everything was quiet.

Here is one of the really cruel parts. Even though I was in the front of the sled and I should have taken the brunt of the hit, I didn't. Obviously, once my eyes went out, I was steering blindly, crazily. So there was no way to avoid those big trees. But at the last minute, the back of the sled swung around and hit one hard. That was what eventually stopped us. After a minute or two went by, when people started moving again after they were frozen in shock, my eyes turned back on. It didn't last long, but it was long enough to see that Vanessa had hit the tree: she was lying in the snow, and there was blood—a lot of blood.

"Does anyone have a cell phone?" I heard someone shout.

"Get help!" someone else yelled.

"Is she dead?" I heard a terrified voice ask. It was familiar, and it came closer to us. Patrick was leaning over her, starting to touch her.

"No, don't move her," you said. It was you, but other than my being so determined to make you the junior officer, to uphold the rule the others wanted to break, you meant nothing to me yet.

Patrick didn't listen; he slipped one arm under her back. You know, you were there. You grabbed him. You stopped him. And, really, because you were the junior officer, you were now in some club together: He was supposed to listen. He had to listen.

"You could hurt her more," you said. My eyes were going again. I tried to hold on, but I was so tired. For a minute, I wondered why nobody had come to me, but I quickly realized people were around me. People I didn't really know. They were asking me questions, but all I could hear was what was going on around Vanessa.

"A bunch of people ran for help," I heard you tell Patrick. "If you move her, you could do more damage."

She was so still. There was so much blood—bright red on white. And then I heard the best noise I have ever heard. I would have given anything for that noise. That was what I was thinking, actually: *Please let her make a noise. I will do anything if she would just make a noise or move. Anything.* I got my wish. She groaned. I could literally hear everyone breathe a sigh of relief. Patrick moved back a bit, as though he was agreeing not to injure her further. I saw you pat him on the back. And then my eyes stopped working for good.

I never lost consciousness. I don't have the luxury of saying *The next thing I knew, I was waking up in the hospital.* Or, *The next thing I knew, it was two weeks later and we were both fine.* No. I couldn't see anything. But I could hear everything. I'm not sure which is worse.

It seemed like forever before help came. I could hear Vanessa making tiny noises, which told me she was not dead, but the longer they went on, the more tortured they sounded.

Finally, we heard shouts and then Mr. Bowersox's voice. That made me feel more terrible than anything. He had been so nice to me, he had welcomed me to the Irving School, and I had done the worst thing possible. I had caused this accident. He came over to me first.

"Tim, can you hear me? Can you speak?" he asked. Until then, everyone had just kept talking at me, not really giving me a chance to respond. But he waited, and when I realized he wasn't going to say anything else until he figured that one thing out, I answered weakly, "Yes."

He patted me on the thigh. "Help is on the way," he said, and got up and went to Vanessa. He did not ask if she could speak, which confirmed my fear that she was in much worse shape than I was. I heard some whispers but couldn't make them out. In the distance, there were sirens. We were in such deep snow I had no idea how the paramedics would get to us. But it didn't even take long. They brought boards, not gurneys, and they were surprisingly fast. Of course, I couldn't see, but there seemed to be a lot of them. Once they came, it was hard to have any sense of what was going on with Vanessa. People swarmed around me; someone held my wrist feeling for my pulse, then lifted my eyelids; they asked me questions, which I answered as best I could.

"Can you talk?"

"Yes."

"Does anything hurt?"

"Not really."

"Can you see?"

"No."

I heard them talking to each other, saying that even though they weren't sure, I must have hit my head since I couldn't see. I didn't tell them—I have never told anyone—that my going blind had nothing to do with the accident. It *caused* the accident. But let me move forward, and I will get back to that in a little while.

After that, they treated me like I had a head injury. They eased me onto the board, strapped me on, and carried me out. I felt so bad. I could have walked if someone would have led me through the woods. But they never would have let me, and I didn't want to give up my status of a person who needed help.

It took longer to get Vanessa out. She had to be stabilized, and they tried to stop the bleeding. It was coming from her head, which apparently bleeds a lot. I was put into an ambulance and driven away before she was. We were taken to the same hospital, but it took so long to get any information. Since I couldn't see anymore, I had no idea what time of day it was, if it was dark or light out. I was completely disoriented. But it was because of my blindness that they kept me there. I didn't hit anything, really. I was completely fine. It took a little while, but I knew that. My blindness was a long time coming, but in the end, I had caused it with my own hand. That key ring again, the silver key? It opens the medicine cabinet in Nurse Singer's office. She had a bunch of keys in a drawer. I wasn't sure if it would fit, but it looked like the one she used, so I slipped it into my pocket later that day after the pain medicine had worked so well. I stick out, I've said that all along, but nobody ever thinks I would do anything bad. I don't know why I never appreciated that. What a waste. It was easy to slip into her office and take one of the keys, and then later that night I went back to see if the key worked. It did. I took a bunch of pills from the bottle. I think now I might have taken them from a different bottle, I was rushing so much. I don't know if it would have made a difference. The one I grabbed had aspirin in it. I'd been taking it every four hours for days. Sometimes I would only wait three hours between doses, and eventually, it caused internal bleeding. I figured it out from what the doctors said and the tests they did. In the end, though, it was really all their unanswered questions that clued me in. They never, ever suspected that I did this to myself. But I know it without a doubt. I haven't told a single person besides you—and, if she listens to these CDs, Vanessa.

I was released from the hospital five days later. Vanessa was still in a medically induced coma. Her chances of making a full recovery were about fifty-fifty, depending on how the swelling in her brain went. If it started to go down, she had a great chance. If it kept swelling, well, then, she could be in big trouble. They'd had to do surgery once already to relieve some of the pressure. I was pretty sure at least some of her beautiful hair was gone. I hated the thought that now her color combination was white and white.

My mother and Sid came immediately, of course. They took the first plane they could book from Italy and got to me quickly. It wasn't lost on me that it was right around the time that I was supposed to be visiting them in Europe. Nobody mentioned it. They were worried and horrified and sad that I had gone blind. Everyone blamed it on the accident. Even they didn't question it. I thought for sure the school nurse would put her two cents in, suggesting that this was a problem waiting to happen, but she didn't. Maybe she thought I had suffered enough. Or maybe she didn't add things up. People can be pretty stupid. There is the chance she knew exactly what happened and didn't want to be implicated, or figured there was no point to it now. I will always wonder why those keys were so accessible. Though I have a feeling they aren't any longer.

Once it was determined that I was okay except for my blindness, we shifted gears. There were about two months of school left. We had to figure out what to do with me. I was that close to finishing high school. I was completely healthy except for my eyesight. My mom wanted me to stay with her. I had already been accepted to college, I've told you that, so what difference did it make? But I insisted I wanted to go back. I had to be near where Vanessa had been. I worried I would never have that chance again.

Had there ever been a blind student at the Irving School before? Mr. Bowersox assured us that there had. At some point, I was going to have to learn a whole new set of skills:

how to get around, how to read Braille, how to type with-out seeing the keyboard, though I was still using the old one. Once in a while I started with the wrong key and it was all gibberish. But usually whatever I wrote turned out just fine. At least I think it did.

Now I was an albino blind person coming at you with a cane and a good chance that I might bump into you. I didn't have an ounce of caring about me anymore. I was gone. My parents and I stayed in a hotel in New York City for a few weeks; the apartment they planned to make their home when they returned from Italy was being sublet. I saw a bunch of rehab people. I know what they were doing: they wanted the time to go by so I could graduate and move forward. Nobody blamed me for anything. I just didn't get it. They all felt sorry for me.

Kyle kept calling. He was so nice. He's the only friend I have right now. And so when there were just two weeks of school left, I went back. Kyle agreed to help me get around. He walked me from class to class and place to place. He fetched my tray for me. All I could think about was how stupid I had been, how different things could have been.

Seeing Vanessa lying in the snow with red blood slowly overtaking the white is the last image I will ever have of her, and I have never been and will never be in her presence again. But we both know that she is okay. That her brain stopped swelling. That despite some short-term memory loss, she is her old self. I know this because Mr. Simon told me. But she never went back. She was the senior that year who was maimed and traumatized and didn't finish her year—the curse the long-lost jogger put on the school so many years before. It came true again. She finished her senior year over the summer, and the Irving School sent her a diploma.

She never had to write her Tragedy Paper. I asked Kyle to find that out for me, and somehow he did. I guess they figured she'd lived enough tragedy that year for any single person. Sometimes I'm surprised they didn't cancel the assignment altogether. All those ideas of tragedy hanging over everyone's head the whole year. But I know that isn't the point; I've talked to Mr. Simon a number of times, and he stands by his senior-year curriculum as much as he ever did.

I worried about running into Patrick when I went back. I realized, though, that I wouldn't even know if I did. I wouldn't see him, and I couldn't imagine he would want to talk to me. So I tried to relax. But on my third day back, something happened. I was so out of sorts, always waiting for someone to help me get around, obsessing about Vanessa and wondering, every second, how she was. I was starting to think coming back to school might have been a mistake. Why was I putting myself through it? I made a point of trying not to stay in my room all the time, but on that afternoon I was ready to give up. I meant to shut my door—I planned to just sit in my room and give in to my misery—but when I heard Patrick start to talk, I realized it was wide open. I didn't want to draw attention to myself, so I just sat there and listened.

He was a few doors down. The sound of his voice was so startling, it was hard to believe it still existed in the world as it had become. I mean, it made sense that it was there before, but how could that carefree, selfish voice not have changed after what he had seen? After what he had a hand in causing? Well, let me tell you, it didn't.

"Did you see that hot sophomore today at lunch?" he asked someone. I wasn't sure who he was talking to at first.

"Which one?" It was Peter.

"The one with the long black hair," Patrick said. "It makes me sorry I'm graduating. Maybe I still have a shot, though. There are what, ten days left of school? I've decided to try something different now. I'm done with blondes for a while. Maybe a brunette would do me some good."

Peter laughed and Patrick joined in. It took me only a second to react. I didn't even know what I was doing. I stood up, somehow made it through my door without bumping into it, and walked in the direction of their voices. They saw me. They were quiet, but I could hear them breathing. I must have looked wild—my pale skin, the blank stare in my eyes that I still can't really imagine. I put my arms out in front of me and started shoving as hard as I could. I made contact.

"Hey," Peter said.

I turned, and I know I was flailing my arms, desperately trying to find Patrick, to hurt him. He grabbed my hands with one of his, and I felt a strong blow to the left side of my lower rib cage. It knocked the air out of me, but I didn't care, I didn't even stop. I was struggling to get out of his grasp, but suddenly he let go of my hands. I waited for another punch. The first one was starting to ache; I wondered if he broke a rib, but I still didn't care. If anything, I liked it. I hadn't felt anything in a while; the pain was a relief. I smacked and slapped and punched, and he just stood there. Nobody came to stop me. Actually, there could have been a crowd and I never would have known, but I don't think there was.

"I hate you," I spat at him. I was exhausted. I knew in that moment that I was never going to really hurt him and that he wasn't going to hurt me again, not physically anyway.

And then, to my surprise, he leaned in. I could feel his hot breath on my ear.

"I hate you too," he said. It was a mumble, barely audible, but I heard it.

What else was there to say? I stopped fighting and stood still as they walked away. I heard them on the stairs, their voices rising as they moved down.

"Freak," Peter said.

"Always was, always will be," Patrick said.

I stumbled back to my room, rubbing the pain in my side and not minding that it was getting worse by the minute. That was when I started to wonder, was this it? Had order been restored? We've been over it again and again, but I keep coming back to it: there was order, then chaos, and was this the order again? And if it was, what did that mean for me? For Vanessa?

I never said another word to Patrick. Only a few kids other than Kyle bothered to talk to me. It was probably easier not to than to have to say who they were and then wait for me to remember. But you did. That last Friday. Classes had ended. I was sitting at a table in the dining hall. I would say it was my usual table in the back, but the truth is I have no idea what table it was. I heard your footsteps, and I thought they would go by, but they stopped. I waited. I figured it was Kyle with my lunch. You know what you said—that it was you, that you were sorry, that you should have stopped me somehow, that it was all you could think about. When I didn't say anything, you touched my hand and walked away. Later, I wished I had said something. I can't believe I was actually given the chance. That was why I worked so hard to get this to you. It saved me, talking to you. It got me through the summer. Kyle brought it to your room. Mr. Simon helped him get onto the senior floor the day before you arrived—I don't think that had ever been done before, except maybe for the animals, since all treasures are supposed to be left on the last day of school. But Mr. Simon agreed to help—he did this for me, and maybe for you.

As far as I know, Vanessa is still at home with her parents. That's where I sent these CDs. It was my only way of reaching her. She never responded, and I can't imagine she ever will. But I wonder so many things. How is she? Will she go to New York City? Do you think she has forgiven me?

I want to tell you about the last key on that key ring. I got that one by sneaking around too, and it wasn't hard either. It opens the top drawer to Mr. Simon's desk. He left it sometimes in another drawer. I was able to get it one afternoon and take it into town to have a copy made. I had it back in his drawer before he ever knew it was missing. It was a risk, sure, but not a big one. These are things I will never be able to do again. I'm glad I did them when I did. The drawer you now have access to is where all the best Tragedy Papers are stored. It will give you insight nobody else has ever had before writing the paper. Use it wisely. And if I might, I want to thank you for listening. You deserve to be the senior officer. You do. You were not responsible for anything that happened last year. Not for a single thing. I am. I accept the entire burden. Please let it go. In Mr. Simon's words, I bid you to go forth and spread beauty and light. It's too late for me, but it is not too late for you.

CHAPTER THIRTY

DUCNAN

DUNCAN
YOU HAVE TO FORGIVE YOURSELF

They sat that way for as long as it took to get through to the end, then Daisy wanted to go back to the beginning and hear the whole thing, but Duncan said no, they could do that some other time.

"Is this why you've been acting so weird?" she asked.

"Yes," he said. "I mean, I've been listening to this since the first day of school, so yes and no. But as he got closer to that night and people started asking about this year's Game, I guess I freaked. And it is the weirdest thing, because in some ways hearing these CDs made me more open with you; so much of what he talks about is how things didn't work out with Vanessa, or how he had chances to be with her that he didn't always take. He didn't believe in himself. I have to say—with all this tragedy vocabulary going around—that I can see it so clearly now. His tragic flaw was that he didn't believe in himself."

Daisy nodded. Duncan took a deep breath.

"And I was so worried about that, about making the same mistakes he did, about losing my chance to be with you."

"But you didn't. We've been together."

"I know, but I've been distant lately, and I want to tell you why. I mean, I know why now. I couldn't stand myself. I knew there was something wrong with Tim. I knew it. I had been watching him that night; he was hard to miss. But even if he hadn't been, he was the one who gave me the handkerchief. You heard him: he made that decision. When he came up to me that night, I was so startled. I never thought I would be the officer. I knew how that worked. Everyone knew they decided. It wasn't random, I don't care what that book of traditions says. I don't know why, but Patrick never seemed to like me much.

"When Tim came up to me, he could barely see. It was so clear. He almost walked into me, and he seemed almost confused about what to do with the handkerchief. I thought he'd been drinking—that made the most sense. But I wasn't certain. Then, when I watched him walk away, he was so unsure of his footing. Now I know that he realized his eyes weren't right. But they must have gotten better, or he stopped caring, because suddenly he was moving with confidence, and I told myself I had been wrong, he was fine. That's when I climbed to the top of the hill to start the sledding."

Duncan was exhausted. He could barely go on. Daisy sat quietly, waiting.

"I have never told this to anyone," Duncan said. "I think it was part of the reason I didn't follow through with us last year, or over the summer. I spent so much time thinking about that moment, thinking that I could have stopped the accident."

"Everyone's okay now," Daisy said.

"But Vanessa's senior year was ruined, and Tim is blind," Duncan pleaded.

"But that had nothing to do with the accident," she said. "He was overmedicating himself, he didn't take care of himself—you had nothing to do with that. Maybe you're too close to realize, but I just heard him tell you what he thinks of that night and how he clearly doesn't blame you."

"I should have done something," Duncan said quietly.

Daisy shrugged. But the look on her face was patient.

"A wise man once said to me, 'You did the best you could,'" Daisy said. "'Sometimes that is all you can do.'"

Duncan looked up, startled. He remembered, he'd said that before their first kiss. He was referring to that girl on Daisy's floor who overdosed on Xanax. How could he not have made that connection? Maybe he *had* made the connection, without even realizing it; maybe that was what gave him the courage to move forward with Daisy. And then something else occurred to him: that girl, Amanda, she never came back. She left after the day she took the Xanax. There was some discussion that she just needed a break, but she ended up staying home and finishing her senior year at her local school. So she was the one who didn't return. That person had already been decided. As sad as it was for Amanda, it took a huge weight off Duncan. He realized at that moment that he had been terrified he would cause someone's ruin at this year's Game.

"I always wondered about that night," Daisy finally said after Duncan was quiet for a while. "There were so many times I wanted to ask you about it, but I didn't dare. I mean, no one ever mentioned it to you, but I could see you tense up whenever it seemed like someone might."

Duncan nodded. He was grateful. That might have pushed him away.

"You have to let it go," Daisy said gently.

Duncan looked up.

"You have to forgive yourself," she said. "Besides, after hearing Tim talk, I don't think there would have been a way to stop him. Did you think of that? You could have asked if he was okay, or suggested he shouldn't sled, but do you think he would have said, *You know what, you're right*? I don't think so."

"But I can still hear that sound of the sled hitting the tree," Duncan said. "Of Vanessa hitting the tree. She could have been killed."

"But she wasn't."

At that moment, there was a knock at the door. They both froze. Duncan thought of telling Daisy to hide in the closet or under the bed, but that seemed worse if the person outside had heard them talking. When they first started talking, it had been in hushed tones, but they had forgotten about that and had started talking at a normal volume.

"Who is it?" Duncan called out. *Please let it be Tad,* he thought to himself.

"It's Mr. Simon. I've been experimenting with scones, and I wanted to see what you think."

Duncan glanced at Daisy, mouthed "I'm sorry," stood, and opened the door. Mr. Simon smiled, held out the plate he was carrying, then looked around him at Daisy sitting on the bed. The expression that crossed his face was full of confusion and disappointment, but it seemed like they all stood frozen for a few minutes before he spoke, as though it took that long for him to switch gears.

"What's going on here?" he asked, letting the plate drop to his side, no longer offering Duncan the treats.

"We were just talking," Duncan said. "Please, I know she isn't supposed to be here but . . ."

"Miss Pickett, go to your room," Mr. Simon said. "I will come find you later. Mr. Meade, follow me to my office."

Duncan couldn't help it, he started to cry. He felt such a cathartic release from sharing everything with Daisy, and maybe she was right, maybe his tragic flaw was going to be that he couldn't let it go. Everyone had a tragic flaw, it seemed. But now he had gotten Daisy in trouble. It was more than he could stand. Mr. Simon and Daisy looked at him for a minute, both surprised by his reaction, and then Mr. Simon turned and started walking toward the stairs.

Duncan grabbed Daisy's hand and squeezed it; then he followed Mr. Simon down the hall, down the stairs, and into his office, where Mr. Simon closed the door and locked it.

CHAPTER THIRTY-ONE

DUNCAN

SO, AM I IN TROUBLE?

Duncan told Mr. Simon everything. He cried through most of it. Looking back, the crying probably helped, though Duncan couldn't have planned it or forced it if he had to. His tears were real.

Duncan figured he was in for it, he might even be expelled, so he had nothing to lose. As he talked, he used the words that had been swirling around in his head: *magnitude, tragic flaw, chaos and order, catharsis.* He told Tim's story and his own; he intertwined them with Vanessa and Daisy. He referred to *Hamlet* and *King Lear* and *Romeo and Juliet.*

When he was finished, he sat back. He had stopped crying. Mr. Simon sat looking at him, a stunned expression on his face. Duncan wondered what Daisy was doing. If she was terrified of what was going to happen to her, if she could lose everything.

Mr. Simon cleared his throat.

"I need some time to process all this," he finally said.

Duncan hesitated. Again, he felt he had nothing to lose.

"Daisy and I weren't doing anything," he blurted out. "It wasn't like I lured her to my room for sex."

As soon as he said it, he couldn't believe he was talking to a teacher that way. But he needed him to know.

"I was young once too" was all Mr. Simon said before he stood, unlocked the door, and waited until Duncan walked out. Duncan heard the door close behind him and the lock turn.

Of course he wanted more than anything to go to Daisy. But he didn't dare. He didn't even dare text her in case that could be used as some sort of evidence later. So he sat on a window seat in the round room outside the dining hall and waited. He thought about working on his Tragedy Paper—he could run up and get his laptop—but he decided that would be a waste of his time if he really was going to be expelled.

People walked by and said hello. Duncan said hello back but barely took his eyes off the stairs, hoping to see Daisy. He longed for her.

Finally, finally, Mr. Simon came toward him. At first he made a move to go up the stairs, but he caught sight of Duncan at the last minute.

"Will you come with me, please?" he asked, his voice much kinder than it had been before.

"Sure, where?" Duncan stood up.

"To Mr. Bowersox's office," Mr. Simon said.

Uh-oh.

"What about Daisy?"

"Daisy is fine," he said nicely.

"Is she in trouble?"

"No," he said.

Duncan felt such a wave of relief, he thought he might have to sit down again, but he managed to stay on his feet.

"Thank you for telling me that," he said, following Mr. Simon in the other direction beyond the dining hall to the administrative offices. Mr. Bowersox was there to greet them.

"Hello, Mr. Meade," he said. His voice too was kind. Duncan couldn't figure out what was going on.

"Hello, Mr. Bowersox," he said.

"Please, come in," the headmaster said.

Duncan waited for Mr. Simon to choose a seat, and then he sat next to him. He felt numb, resigned. As long as Daisy was okay and not in trouble, he could handle anything. It seemed like a long time before anyone talked.

"Mr. Simon has filled me in on everything," Mr. Bowersox said, looking right at Duncan. Duncan nodded. He was sure that meant that he had snuck Daisy into his room. He had—there was no denying that.

"Mr. Simon is concerned," he said slowly, in his headmaster sort of way.

Again, Duncan nodded. Of course he was concerned. That made sense to him.

"Mr. Simon, do you want to talk, or should I?" Mr. Bowersox asked.

"I guess you can," Mr. Simon said. "I'm not sure what to say."

Now Duncan was getting confused. He would have thought that Mr. Simon would know exactly what to say. Surely he had dealt with this type of situation over the years. Duncan looked at Mr. Bowersox.

"Very well, then," Mr. Bowersox said. "Mr. Simon is concerned that he pushed the tragedy theme too far."

Duncan looked from Mr. Bowersox to Mr. Simon, who was sitting with his hands together in front of him and his head slightly down.

"What do you mean?" Duncan asked.

"He told me about your conversation, and, yes, I know there is more to discuss, but his feeling was that this idea of tragedy may have become too ingrained in your thought process."

Duncan didn't know what to say. This wasn't at all how he had expected this conversation to go.

"He told me about your involvement with Tim Macbeth, your relationship with Daisy Pickett, but most disturbing to him was the way you were able to use those words, the ones associated with a tragedy or a tragic happening, so easily, as though you have been really thinking about them, living them. Do you think this has become a problem for you?"

Duncan thought for a minute. It had been Tim who

planted the idea of his story being connected to the idea of tragedy, not Mr. Simon. And it wasn't the fault of the Tragedy Paper that those things happened last year. He had the strongest urge to speak to Tim; he wished he could ask what he thought. Maybe he could call him. He could track down his parents' phone number and try to reach him. But he knew that would take too long; he had a hunch that this concern of Mr. Simon's might dissipate with time, and right now he was getting the feeling he had the upper hand. He liked that.

Besides, he realized he didn't have to actually talk to Tim. He was pretty sure he knew what he would say.

"This has been a great year and a hard year, and of course the Tragedy Paper has been looming over me, over all of us, since the first day of school," Duncan said. "But I don't blame Mr. Simon or the things he taught us for any of the bad stuff that happened. If anything, I think he's an amazing teacher who helped me sort some of this out, make sense of it."

Mr. Bowersox smiled. "My sentiments exactly," he said.

Mr. Simon looked up. "Thank you," he said. "And, if it is okay with Mr. Bowersox, I would like to accept our conversation as your Tragedy Paper. It was as good as defending a dissertation, in my book."

Mr. Bowersox nodded.

"So, am I in trouble?" Duncan asked.

"No," Mr. Simon said. "Don't ever invite Daisy to your room again, and I don't want to hear you've been to hers, but we have decided to let that slide in light of everything you've been through."

"Thank you," Duncan said. He couldn't wipe the smile off his face. He would wait at the bottom of the stairs until Daisy found him. He would tell her how much she meant to him and make sure to every day. If she let him, he would help her write her own Tragedy Paper—apparently, he was an expert, however accidental that was.

CHAPTER THIRTY-TWO

DUNCAN

"DON'T STOP BELIEVIN'"

There was one CD Tim had left for Duncan that he had never listened to. He knew the story was over; there was nothing more to say. So he had overlooked it. But when he gathered the CDs together to slip them into the secret compartment of his closet for the rest of the year, he noticed it.

It was different from the others. Instead of having a date scrawled on it—like *Jan. 5 thru Jan. 15*—as the others did, this one had messy musical notes on it. Duncan hesitated, then slipped it in and listened. It was a compilation of Journey songs—"Don't Stop Believin'," "Wheel in the Sky," and "Faithfully," among others. It was the music Tim had promised he would leave him with. Duncan decided to keep it out.

Duncan finally got around to choosing the juniors. He

did it openly—anyone who was interested could come—and he followed the rule. The first name picked was the junior officer—no question.

In the end, he planned a great senior Game. He took the idea from the man who had provided the sleds last year and arranged a megagame of musical chairs. This time they snuck all the chairs out of the dining hall and set them up on the quad in a long oval. The music he used was Tim's.

There was some discussion about inviting last year's senior class to join in, to let them have a positive senior event. It was Daisy's idea and Duncan loved it, but they decided in the end to make it about their class.

During the Game, Duncan looked up at his tiny round window and thought of Tim's words: *Well, I bet you're thinking a lot of things, but at the top of your list is probably that this room sucks. It doesn't.* He wondered how long it would be before he didn't hear Tim's voice at every turn. Maybe it would take leaving school, or maybe it would take more than that. He turned his gaze back to his classmates and smiled at all the white bulldog T-shirts. Without much discussion that had become the color of their year. Whether it was in honor of Tim or the snow, Duncan didn't know. But it seemed fitting, and he liked it.

Mr. Simon had given Duncan a pass on his Tragedy Paper, but Duncan couldn't get it out of his mind. Finally, on the morning after the senior Game, Duncan knew what he needed to do.

He went to the Hall and found a free desk in the back. Words were running through his mind, and he started to write them down. There were so many words. The first words were Tim's: *The day I went to Irving, I was the last one to leave my house, and I don't mean for the day. I mean forever.* He kept going in that direction for a little while, but he knew it wasn't right. He didn't care about his grade any-more—he had already been given an A, and he knew that would stand no matter what he wrote. But this was it: this was his chance to move forward. He took a deep breath and finally wrote: *As I walked through the stone archway leading into the senior dorm, I had two things on my mind: what "trea-sure" had been left behind for me and my Tragedy Paper.*

MR. SIMON'S TIPS ON AVOIDING A TRAGIC ENDING TO YOUR TRAGEDY PAPER

Keep these key points in mind while writing your Tragedy Paper. (DO NOT lose this paper. I will not give you another one. Sharing these instructions with students who lost their sheet or missed my handing it out will result in the automatic dropping of two grade points.)

- Define a tragedy thoroughly and completely.
- Tell me when this very important literary discussion about tragedy began. And don't forget to tell me where in the world it started.
- Know the difference, if you decide there is one, between a tragic happening and a dramatic tragedy.
- Learn and express everything you can about Aristotle and how he pertains to tragedy.
- Discuss how Sophocles played a part. Or am I thinking of someone else? I hope you can help set me straight.
- Elaborate on the differences between Greek and Shakespearean tragedy— if there are any.
- Choose at least three plays by Mr. William Shakespeare and figure out why and how they belong in this research paper—then tell me about it. DO NOT ask me which ones to use. When this is all over, I will tell you how twelve Irving students got an automatic F for not taking this part seriously enough.
- Consider the importance, or the triviality, of the PLOT. What about the CHARACTERS?
- Make sure you understand and are able to tell me why the end of a tragedy is so important. Or is it?
- You be the judge (and please read up on this subject before you sit down on that bench): must a tragedy have an unhappy ending? Why or why not?
- Use at least four primary sources and five secondary sources.
- Know and use these key words and phrases (in no particular order, or should they be?): *reversal of fortune, pity and fear, error of judgment, fate, peripety, anagnorisis, hamartia, catharsis, mimesis, eleos, phobos, tragic flaw, order, chaos, recognition, conflict, status, inevitability, perception, hubris, monomania, commitment, unforeseeability, optimism,* and *irony.*
- Let me repeat one of those words: *irony.*
- And finally: *MAGNITUDE, MAGNITUDE, MAGNITUDE.*

ACKNOWLEDGMENTS

There are two people without whom this book would not exist. The first is my agent, Uwe Stender, who has literally walked with me through every step of this project. He is smart, loyal, and persistent—everything I could ever ask for in an agent (and a friend). I would like to thank Charlotte, Wendy, and Saskia on his behalf. The second is my senior English teacher at Hackley, Mr. Arthur Naething, for assigning me a Tragedy Paper when I was a senior, and for teaching me the most important lesson he could—that I love to write.

I want to thank my amazing editor at Knopf, Erin Clarke, for wanting to publish *The Tragedy Paper*, and for taking me through the long process with kindness, enthusiasm, and remarkable attention to detail. Thank you to my copy editor, Sue Cohan, and my proofreader, Lisa Leventer.

You both did a fantastically meticulous job with this book. Thank you also to Stephanie Moss, the jacket designer. I love the cover! I am so grateful to everyone at Random House.

I have often joked that my extremely generous friend Jennifer Weiner could make a second career out of supporting my writing. She is always willing to help, offer advice, and talk through a plot point or a character's motivation. She is also a lot of fun to hang out with. I want to thank my other wonderful friends: Simona Gross, Ivy Gilbert, Dawn Davenport, Charlie Phy, Doug Cooper, Nika Haase, Lisa Kozleski, Melissa Cooper, Meghan Burnett, Melissa Jensen, Angie Benson, Leah Kellar, and my pals who walked the halls of Hackley with me.

To my mentors, teachers, and editors: Dianne Drummey Marino at NBC News; LynNell Hancock and the late Dick Blood at Columbia Journalism School; and Tom Watson, Buddy Stein, and the late Ceil Stein at *The Riverdale Press*—I got here because of all of you.

The author S. E. Hinton changed the course of my life with *The Outsiders* and *That Was Then, This Is Now.* Reading her books made me want to be a writer. I wish I could thank her in person.

To Patty Rich and Terry LaBan—thanks for your confidence and love. To my in-laws, Joyce and Myron LaBan— I knew you took my writing seriously when you bought me a laptop ten years ago. You have continued to believe in me ever since, and that means more than I can say.

I wish my late father, Arthur Trostler, could be here to read this book. He is always with me, and his motto "Keep your eye on the ball" rings in my head constantly. To my mother, Barbara Trostler, who has continuously given me everything she has—I will never be able to thank you enough.

I couldn't have done any of this without my loving husband, Craig LaBan, who keeps up my strength by feeding me really well, and who has always buoyed my dream of being a novelist. (He also makes the best cappuccino I have ever had.)

And to my children, Alice and Arthur, thank you for jumping up and down when I told you I (finally) sold a novel. This one's for you. May your lives always be full of good books and great stories. I know everyone says this, but in this case it is true: you are the best kids in the world.

A CONVERSATION WITH ELIZABETH LABAN

***THE TRAGEDY PAPER* IS YOUR FIRST YOUNG ADULT NOVEL. HOW DID YOU COME UP WITH THE IDEA TO WRITE IT?**

I have wanted to write a book since I was in fourth grade. My friend Marshall Cooper would come over and we would try to come up with stories to fit a character we had named Chopped Suey. In my mind he was a cool, urban kid detective. We never got past designing the cover! But from that time on, I was always writing stories in my head. The idea for *The Tragedy Paper* came in different stages. I liked the concept of writing a classic love triangle. I was also struck by the notion of using an intense school assignment to help the story unfold. When I was a senior in high school, I was assigned a long-term project we called the Tragedy Paper, similar to and yet slightly different from the one the students at Irving write. My task was to define a tragedy, and then decide if it could exist in modern literature. Several years ago, I actually found my paper. Reading through it again so many years later made me want to write my own tragedy. Those words that become ingrained in Duncan's mind never really stopped swirling around in my mind, either. *Magnitude, reversal of fortune, hubris*—I have always loved those words. And then suddenly Duncan was walking under that archway. . . .

PLEASE TELL US WHY YOU DECIDED TO TELL THE STORY USING A DUAL NARRATIVE.

My agent suggested I read Johann Wolfgang von Goethe's *The Sorrows of Young Werther* when I was beginning to write my book. In it, Werther writes to a friend about his life and troubles. I loved that structure and had Goethe's story in my mind the whole time I was writing *The Tragedy Paper*. As a nod to the famous novel, there is a mention of linden trees—the type of tree Werther is buried under after he kills himself—when Tim and Vanessa take their fateful sleigh ride. I knew I wanted Tim to tell his story in his own words, but I also knew he had to be telling it to someone for a reason. I liked the idea that Duncan was just a normal kid who became connected to Tim by chance. They knew each other, but they also didn't know each other at all. The more I wrote, the more I liked Duncan and wanted him to have his own story, too.

DID YOU ALWAYS ENVISION TIM AS AN ALBINO OR DID THAT COME LATER IN THE WRITING PROCESS?

I pretty quickly decided Tim was an albino, and once I did it stuck for me. I knew Tim had to be an outsider, and not just because he was new to the Irving School. I wanted him to deal with an affliction that was with him all the time, but not something that made it hard to live his everyday life. As I did research about the things albinos have to sometimes deal with, making Tim an albino gave me a way to amplify the insecurities that are present in most teenagers, and offered so many possibilities for the choices he makes in the book.

THE PRIVATE SCHOOL SETTING PLAYS A BIG ROLE IN THE BOOK. WHAT INSPIRED YOU TO SET THE BOOK AT THE IRVING SCHOOL?

For my last two years of high school, my parents sent me to an amazing private school called Hackley in Tarrytown, New York. It sounds really corny, but I think my two years there changed my life. They weren't perfect years—I had a few run-ins with mean kids and I was really lonely when I first got there—but overall it was the first time I felt like I was truly a part of a place and the culture of that place. It was also the first time I understood the idea of enjoying learning. I just got a mailing from Hackley and there was a quote from an alumnus saying he wished he could return as a student. If he could, he promised he would read everything that was assigned to him and he would pay better attention in class. Couldn't he please go back in time? I realized after reading his words that writing this book and creating the world of the Irving School was doing just that for me. It let me go back to that wonderful place and hang out for a while.

THE ENDING DOESN'T TIE EVERYTHING UP IN A NEAT BOW. WHY DID YOU DECIDE TO LEAVE IT OPEN-ENDED?

I never wanted the ending to be so concrete that there was absolutely no hope. I always wanted there to be the possibility that anything could happen. There is no question that everyone involved is changed forever. I didn't think the stage had to be strewn with bodies. When I was a senior in high school, I tried to answer the question of whether classic tragedy could exist in contemporary literature. And if it does, can it be slightly different from William Shakespeare's vision of it? What do you think?

YOU SPENT SOME TIME TEACHING AT A COMMUNITY COLLEGE. DID YOU RESEMBLE MR. SIMON IN ANY WAY?

Not at all! I loved teaching, just as Mr. Simon does. But many of my students were adults, so the dynamic was very different from that between Mr. Simon and the students at the Irving School. Mr. Simon, who in many ways was based on my own senior English teacher, Mr. Arthur Naething (he really did dismiss us daily with "Go forth and spread beauty and light"), is so good at being accessible to the kids on one level and yet terrifying them on another. I never had the nerve to scare my students. I was just happy that they came to class and seemed interested in what I was saying.

LOWER SCHOOL

SCIENCE BUILDING

MR. SIMON'S
CLASSROOM

LIBRARY

SENIOR
DORMS

QUAD

HEADMASTER'S
HOUSE

ADMINISTRATIVE CENTER

DINING HALL